Dallas Schulze's engrossing saga,
A FAMILY CIRCLE, continues! You loved
A Very Convenient Marriage, were enraptured by
Another Man's Wife and were riveted by
Addie and the Renegade. Now Silhouette Books brings
you an utterly compelling read—*Tessa's Child*.

DALLAS SCHULZE

is loved the world over as one of romance's premier writers. She is the author of over thirty romance novels, both contemporary and historical, and is the recipient of many awards, including an award for the bestselling Silhouette Intimate Moments title of 1994 from B. Dalton's bookstores.

Dallas is a sucker for a happy ending, and hopes her readers have as much fun with her books as she does. She loves to hear from her readers, and you can write to her at P.O. Box 241, Verdugo City, CA 91046.

Dallas is fast at work on her latest books, *Home to Eden*, to be published by MIRA Books in the fall of 1997, and her next installment in THE FAMILY CIRCLE saga, to be published in 1998 in Silhouette Intimate Moments.

DALLAS SCHULZE

TESSA'S CHILD

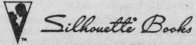

Published by Silhouette Books
America's Publisher of Contemporary Romance

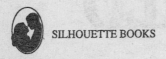 SILHOUETTE BOOKS

TESSA'S CHILD

Copyright © 1997 by Dallas Schulze

ISBN 0-373-48339-2

All rights reserved. Except for use in any review, the reproduction
or utilization of this work in whole or in part in any form by any
electronic, mechanical or other means, now known or hereafter
invented, including xerography, photocopying and recording, or in
any information storage or retrieval system, is forbidden without
the written permission of the editorial office, Silhouette Books,
300 East 42nd Street, New York, NY 10017 U.S.A.

All characters in this book have no existence outside the imagination of
the author and have no relation whatsoever to anyone bearing the same
name or names. They are not even distantly inspired by any individual
known or unknown to the author, and all incidents are pure invention.

This edition published by arrangement with Harlequin Books S.A.

® and TM are trademarks of Harlequin Books S.A., used under
license. Trademarks indicated with ® are registered in the United States
Patent and Trademark Office, the Canadian Trade Marks Office and in
other countries.

Printed in U.S.A.

Prologue

Keefe Walker cupped one hand around a match and set the flame to the end of his cigarette. Smoke stung the back of his throat, a reminder that he'd been smoking more than he usually did. A pack normally lasted him a couple of days, but he was halfway through his second since morning. Nothing like a wedding to make a man crave a nicotine fix, he thought.

Nothing like a wedding to remind a man of how alone he was.

He pushed the thought aside. Drawing deeply on the cigarette, he turned away from the house and the wedding reception taking place inside to look out over his sister-in-law's gardens. Kelsey cultivated nearly half an acre of vegetables, selling the produce to restaurants in the Santa Barbara area. The beds of vegetables, neatly separated by bark-covered pathways, stretched out from the rambling farmhouse in a patch-work of early-spring greens, punctuated here and there with brilliant splashes of color. Keefe remem-bered his brother Gage telling him that Kelsey was now supplying edible flowers to some of her custom-ers. So, while the warm golds and oranges were un-doubtedly there because of commercial enterprise rather than aesthetic inspiration, the end result was undeniably lovely.

A burst of laughter drifted through the French doors behind him, and Keefe's mouth curved in a smile. Cole certainly fit the image of a happy bride-groom. When he and Addie exchanged their vows, Cole had looked at her as if the sun rose and set in her eyes. A few months ago, if he was asked to de-scribe the kind of woman his youngest brother was most likely to marry, Addie Smith wouldn't have shown up on the list. Quietly pretty academic types had never been up Cole's alley. But looking at the two of them together, no one could doubt that they were very much in love. He was willing to bet that they were going to beat the odds and make their mar-riage last.

Which was more than he'd managed to do. And that was the real problem with weddings, he thought as he took one last drag on his cigarette. They made him think of his own marriage, set him to thinking about what had gone wrong, wondering if he could have changed things. Keefe's mouth twisted in a bit-ter half smile as he stubbed the cigarette out against the top of the low brick wall. There was no bigger waste of time than playing ''What if?'' He drew his cigarette pack from the inside breast pocket of his suit jacket and tapped another cigarette loose.

The past was past, he reminded himself as he struck a match against the rough side of a brick and lifted the flame to the end of his cigarette. There was no going back to change things, and wondering what might have been was a waste of time.

"Mind a little company?"

Keefe started, his head jerking toward the speaker. He'd been so absorbed in his thoughts that he didn't hear her approach. Tall and elegant, her straight posture belying her seventy-odd years of age, Molly Thorpe moved toward him across the brick patio.

"I don't mind a bit," he said, his expression easing into a welcoming smile. He straightened away from the low brick wall he'd been half leaning against.

"Don't get up for me," she said, waving one slender hand, the knuckles slightly swollen with arthritis. "Makes me feel like I'm an old woman. And just because that's what I am, it doesn't mean I like to be reminded."

"I don't think the word *old* will ever apply to you, Molly."

"If you're offering me flattery in hopes that I won't tell your mother you're out here smoking, you're wasting your time," Molly said as she sank down onto a redwood deck chair. There was a twinkle in her blue eyes as she looked up at him. "Your mother knows exactly what you're up to. On her behalf, I'll remind you that it's a filthy habit and bound to kill you."

"Did you come out here to lecture me about my

health?'' Keefe asked, eyeing her through a thin veil of smoke. Actually, he hadn't even been consciously aware that he'd lit another cigarette until she mentioned it. It was a good thing Cole was the last of his brothers to get married. Any more weddings in the family and he was likely to become a chain smoker.

"Certainly not. I figure a man of forty ought to be allowed to live his life without interference from his family and friends.''

"Thirty-seven,'' Keefe corrected her. Forty was creeping up fast enough as it was.

"Thirty-seven,'' Molly said, nodding her head. "That's certainly old enough to choose your own poison.''

"Thanks. I guess.'' Keefe stubbed the cigarette out against the top of the brick wall before turning a rueful smile in her direction. "There aren't many people who could make me feel like an antique and about twelve years old in the space of thirty seconds. That's a unique skill, Molly.''

"Thank you.'' She bent her head in regal acceptance of the compliment, her solemn expression at odds with the laughter in her eyes.

She was still a lovely woman. Age had both blurred the edges of her beauty and yet refined it in some mysterious way, drawing the skin over her high cheekbones and revealing the determined angles of her jaw. She must have been hell on wheels when she was a young woman, Keefe thought. She was a force to be reckoned with even now.

He'd known Molly for over a decade. She'd hired him to work on her horse ranch, the Rocking M, near

Solvang when he was in his early twenties. He'd worked there for over a year, and then quit to pursue his dreams of rodeo buckles. When he left, she'd told him he was a damned fool but added that, if he didn't break his neck, he was welcome back whenever he needed a job.

He'd worked for her off and on for the next five years, until the year he turned twenty-eight. Her greatniece had come to spend the summer with her that year, and he'd taken one look at Dana Wyndham and fallen head over heels in love. They'd been married less than a month after they met. Four years later, they'd been divorced. His relationship with Molly had proved more enduring than his marriage.

"Your brother seems very happy." Molly's comment drew Keefe out of his contemplation of the past.

"He is," he said, smiling.

"His little girl seems fond of her new stepmother."

"Mary's crazy about Addie, and the feeling is mutual." Keefe's smile grew soft at the mention of his niece. "Cole and Addie were going to wait to get married, because they wanted to give Mary time to adjust to the idea, but she finally asked them what was taking them so long."

"Children frequently have a great deal more common sense than the adults around them," Molly commented.

"I can't argue with you on that one."

Keefe slid his hands into the pockets of his charcoal-gray slacks and leaned back against the wall. Late-afternoon sunshine warmed his shoulders and slanted across the brick patio. He and his brothers had

put the patio in less than a month ago, but the mellow
patina of the used brick made it look as if it had been
there forever. The herringbone pattern had been a
nightmare to lay, but Gage had insisted that, if he
could engineer a suspension bridge, even the most
elaborate brickwork should be within his grasp. Halfway through the project, it had become obvious that
bridges and patios had little in common. The pattern
had become hopelessly tangled. Gage had endured his
brothers' ruthless teasing in stoic silence, scowling at
the bricks as if suspecting them of being possessed
by some malevolent force. It was Sam who'd saved
the day, hacking bricks in half with a ruthlessness that
had made Gage moan faintly in pain. The pattern had
been successfully continued, with only a slight devi-
ation in the middle—an artistic touch, Sam had de-
clared.

"You've been blessed when it comes to family,"
Molly said, as if reading his thoughts.

"I have been," Keefe agreed simply.

She shifted her position on the redwood chair, the
sunlight catching in her silver hair. "There's been
quite a few weddings in your family this last year or
two," she commented.

"Three of them." He pulled one hand out of his
pocket and started to reach for his cigarettes, changing
his mind when he caught Molly's interested expression. He ran his fingers through his hair instead, but
he doubted he'd fooled her. Not much got by Molly
Thorpe's sharp blue eyes.

"Must make you think," she said.

"About what?" With deliberate obtuseness, Keefe raised one dark brow.

Molly arched a brow in return, her expression reminding him that she knew him better than he might like. "Do not make the mistake of thinking that I'm getting senile, Keefe."

"I know better than that, Molly," he said with a reluctant laugh. "To answer your question, seeing my brothers get married does make me think, but it *doesn't* make me think about getting married again. For some of us, once is enough."

She frowned. "I thought you were too smart to let your experience with Dana make you bitter."

Keefe shook his head. "I'm not bitter." He took his cigarettes from his pocket and lit one, ignoring the faint disapproval in her eyes. "I'm just a bit more cautious than I was in my younger days, that's all."

"It's more than caution, if you've made up your mind that you're never going to marry again."

"I'd never say never." He gave her a lopsided grin. "That would be tempting fate. And I'm not foolish enough to do that."

Molly looked doubtful as she pushed herself to her feet. "Fate has a way of making fools of us all at one time or another, most especially when we think we're fooling it."

"Not fooling it," Keefe corrected her as he stubbed out his half-smoked cigarette. He stepped forward to slip his hand under her elbow as she turned toward the house. "I think of it as staying out of sight."

"No one can avoid their fate, Keefe." Molly's tone held both affection and warning. "I doubt fate has any intention of letting you spend the rest of your life alone.''

"We'll see," he said.

"So we will."

Tessa Evangeline Wyndham Mallory glanced down into the suitcase she'd just filled. It didn't seem possible that she'd spent four years of her life in this house and yet could leave it now with nothing but the contents of this one suitcase and know that she wasn't leaving anything of importance behind. It wasn't much to show for four years.

Of course, she was taking a great deal more with her than what was in the suitcase. Not just memories, but also a painfully tangible reminder of her marriage.

Her soft mouth tightened, her blue eyes turning to ice. Damn Bobby, anyway. Why couldn't he have managed to get himself killed a little sooner? But there was no point in thinking about what might have been, Tessa reminded herself. She could only deal with what was. She flipped the suitcase lid shut and jerked the zipper closed, the sound harsh as a scream in the quiet room.

She glanced around the luxuriously decorated bedroom one last time. There had been a time when she took a great deal of pleasure in the decor. She'd chosen the warm peach-and-ivory-striped wallpaper and soft blue-gray carpeting herself, haunted antique stores looking for just the right pieces of furniture. The end result was neither feminine nor masculine, but a careful blending of the two.

Too bad she hadn't been able to see into the future,

she thought now, taking no pleasure in the soft warmth of the room. If she'd known what her life was going to be like, she might have chosen more appropriate colors—like black and prison gray.

No. She wasn't going to think that way.

Tessa closed her eyes and drew in a deep breath. She wasn't going to let the past four years color the rest of her life with bitterness. The past was past. She couldn't change it. But she could move forward and try to make the future better.

When she opened her eyes again, they held a look of resolution that would have surprised some people who thought they knew her well. Moving to the dressing table, she tugged the heavy diamond engagement ring and thick gold wedding band off her finger. She weighed them in the palm of her hand, and for just a moment she allowed herself to feel regret for the dreams they'd once represented, for the happiness she'd thought she'd found. But the dreams had died a long time ago, and the happiness had proven no more substantial than a soap bubble. Turning her hand over, she let the rings fall. They clattered as they hit the wooden surface, sounding strangely like the rattle of a key turning in the lock of a prison door.

Tessa flexed her fingers, feeling the lightness of her hand. For the first time in weeks, her mouth curved in a genuine smile. Freedom. She'd forgotten what it felt like. Not that she was completely free, she thought as she caught a glimpse of her reflection in the mirror. But she was closer to it than she had been a few weeks ago. Her smile faded, and her delicate jaw tightened with determination.

For the past four years, she'd paid the price of her own foolish blindness, but fate had seen fit to give her a second chance. She was free—almost. She wasn't going to waste that gift in bitterness. Turning away from the mirror, Tessa lifted the suitcase from the floor. She closed the door behind her without looking back.

Chapter 1

"You expecting a visitor?" Jace Reno asked.

Keefe looked up from the posthole he was digging. He studied the cloud of dust making its way up the long dirt road that led to the Flying Ace's ranch house. "I'm not expecting anyone. Doesn't look big enough for a truck," he said. That eliminated most of the locals. This was ranching country, and trucks outnumbered cars by a fairly wide margin. He squinted a little to try and make out something of the vehicle beneath the dust cloud and then shrugged. "They're probably lost."

"Probably," Jace agreed. Since it would be another minute or two before the car reached them, both men returned their attention to the job at hand. "You planning on digging that hole all the way to China, or just halfway?"

"I don't want to have to do it again next year,"

Keefe said, jabbing the posthole digger into the narrow hole, the muscles in his arms flexing as he lifted out a bite of dirt.

"You dig it much deeper and the posts are going to sink so deep that we'll end up with the only two-foot-high corral fence in the neighborhood. Could have saved ourselves a lot of trouble by just drawing a line in the dirt and telling the horses not to cross it."

Keefe glared at his friend from under the brim of his dusty gray Stetson. "Tell me again why I took you on as a partner."

"My wit and charm?" Jace suggested, grinning.

"If that was the case, I made a lousy bargain," Keefe said dryly. "You want to set that pole in place, or are you planning on leaving it there to see if it will take root?"

"An oak tree might look real nice right about here." Jace lifted the post and began easing it down into the hole.

"It might, but getting an oak tree out of a cedar post would be a pretty neat trick." Keefe knelt to guide the base of the post. "Hold it straight and I'll start filling in around it."

He began scooping dirt into the hole, tamping it down around the post. Behind him, he heard the car pull to a stop in front of the house.

"A Mercedes," Jace commented. "If you've got to get lost, you might as well do it in style."

"Probably makes it easier," Keefe said without looking up. He heard a car door slam, and the crunch of footsteps on the dirt and gravel that passed for a front yard.

"Excuse me. I'm looking for Keefe Walker." The voice was soft, faintly husky, definitely female and oddly familiar.

Keefe felt something clench tight and hard in the pit of his stomach, a quick flare of recognition, followed by disbelief. It couldn't be... He rose and turned toward the visitor. But the woman approaching across the yard was not the ghost from his past he'd half expected to see. She was pretty, rather than stunningly beautiful. Her eyes held more gray than blue, and her hair was dark gold rather than moonlight-pale.

She was also heavily pregnant.

"Something you forgot to tell me about, buddy?" Jace murmured.

"Keefe?" She smiled uncertainly as she moved closer.

Keefe blinked, banishing old memories. Whoever this woman was, she wasn't his ex-wife.

"I know I should have called first," she said, looking even more uncertain. She linked her hands together in front of her, her fingers twisting in a childlike gesture of nervousness that contrasted oddly with the very unchildlike bulge of her stomach. The gesture evoked a new set of memories—a young girl, her hair in pigtails, her thin shoulders squared, her small chin set with determination—and the nervous movements of her hands betraying her bravado.

"Tessa?" The name was half question. Recovering from his surprise, Keefe crossed the distance between them in two long strides. He caught her hands in his. "Tessa."

"Have I changed that much?" she asked, her mouth curving in a smile that didn't quite chase the uneasiness from her eyes.

"It's been at least five years," he said, grinning down at her. "You were a little girl last time I saw you."

"I was eighteen. Not exactly a toddler," she said dryly.

"Not exactly an old woman, either."

"No, but I certainly thought I was filled with the wisdom of the ages," she said, her tone wistful, as if she envied her younger self that confidence.

"Who doesn't think that when they're eighteen?"

"True." Tessa shook her head a little, as if shaking away a memory. She changed the subject. "I hope you don't mind me just showing up like this. I know I should have called first, but I was kind of in the neighborhood."

"It's a pretty big neighborhood," Jace said as he walked up to them.

Keefe felt Tessa's hands tense in his at Jace's approach. Her eyes widened, and something that almost looked like fear flickered through them. He dismissed the thought immediately. In the years he'd known Jace Reno, he'd seen him inspire many emotions in women—lust, frustration, anger, an occasional urge to commit murder—but not fear. But then Tessa was pulling her hands away from his, turning toward Jace with a smile and nothing but friendly curiosity in her expression, and Keefe decided that his imagination had to be working overtime. Too many hours in the sun, he thought as he made the introductions.

"Tessa, this is Jace Reno, my partner on the Flying Ace. Jace, this is Tessa Wyndham— Is it still Wyndham?" he asked, glancing questioningly at her. "I heard you got married a while back."

"Yes, I did." Tessa's smile seemed to congeal, her eyes going empty for a moment, but the expression was gone so quickly that Keefe wasn't sure it had been there at all. "Wyndham is fine," she said, as she took Jace's hand.

"Wyndham?" Jace repeated, glancing at Keefe.

"Dana's sister," Keefe said, answering the question in his friend's eyes.

"Which makes me an ex-in-law," Tessa said brightly.

Too brightly, Keefe found himself thinking. There was something just a little...off in Tessa's smile, in her manner. She was trying too hard, making too much of an effort to seem at ease. Maybe she was uncertain of her welcome. His divorce from her sister had not been the most acrimonious on record, but it hadn't been a "friendly" divorce, either. Except for Molly Thorpe, the last time he saw any of Dana's family had been the day he walked out of the courtroom. But, whatever his feelings for his ex-wife and her parents, he'd always been fond of her little sister.

"You're not an 'ex' anything," he said easily. "Friends aren't part of a divorce settlement."

"Thanks." Tessa's smile seemed more genuine this time, held less forced brightness. But there were still shadows in her eyes, shadows that hadn't been there five years ago.

"I can finish setting the fence post," Jace said into the silence. "Why don't you pretend you have good manners and offer Tessa a drink and a place to sit down."

"Thank you, Ms. Manners," Keefe said dryly.

"Hey, I'm just trying to maintain a facade of civilization in the midst of the howling wilderness." His expression of martyrdom drew a genuine, if fleeting, smile from Tessa.

"It must be an uphill battle," she said sympathetically.

"It is." He shook his head, pulling his mouth down into a solemn expression that was at odds with the laughter in his blue eyes. "If it wasn't for me, we'd soon revert to savagery."

"Who was it suggested that we could save water by only washing our plates once a week?" Keefe asked pointedly.

"Just doing my part for water conservation," Jace insisted, looking hurt.

"You're full of nobility," Tessa said.

"He's full of something, all right," Keefe said dryly. "Come on up to the house, Tessa, and I'll see what we've got to drink."

They didn't speak as they started toward the house, and Keefe found himself thinking back to the summer he'd gotten to know Tessa. Right after he and Dana were married, they'd gone to live on her parents' horse ranch in Kentucky. The world of Thoroughbreds and racing was a long way from the rodeos and quarter horses where Keefe had worked, but Dana had persuaded him to try working for her father.

"If Daddy likes you, he might leave the ranch to us someday," she'd said, her sapphire-blue eyes sparkling with excitement.

Keefe hadn't been particularly anxious to spend twenty years or more working for his father-in-law on the chance that he'd someday inherit a Kentucky racing stable he didn't particularly want, but he'd been head over heels in love with his bride. Besides, two days after the wedding, he'd taken a ride on a bronc with the inviting nickname of Bone Buster. In the eight-second battle between man and animal, the horse had lived up to his name, coming out on top—literally—and breaking Keefe's leg in two places. Since Kentucky was as good a place as any to recuperate, he'd let Dana persuade him to accept the job her father was offering.

Keefe and his new in-laws had been a poor match. He'd thought Dana's father was a pompous ass and her mother was a featherbrain. They'd resented the fact that their beloved oldest daughter had married a rodeo cowboy who had neither money nor prospects. Their attitude had been condescending and their arrogance had been such that they never realized that Keefe was every bit as contemptuous of them as they were of him.

It had not been an easy two months.

It hadn't taken Keefe long to find out that the one place his in-laws never spent any time was in the stables. Owning a Thoroughbred ranch suited their image and afforded them with appropriate social opportunities but neither of the Wyndhams had any particular fondness for horses or riding. Keefe had appreciated the fact that their lack of interest provided him with a suitable retreat.

Though he couldn't ride, he'd enjoyed working with the horses, and Tessa had often joined him there. At fourteen, she'd been a pale, thin child with eyes older than her years and a quick smile enhanced by the chrome gleam of braces.

It had soon been apparent that, like him, she didn't fit into the Wyndham household. She'd been a surprise baby—an unwelcome surprise, she'd told him in a matter-of-fact tone that precluded sympathy or protest. If she was pretty and charming like her older sister, her parents might have been able to find a place for her in their lives. But she'd been a thin, contemplative child with none of her sister's sparkle, and Tessa's quiet prettiness had been completely overshadowed by Dana's golden beauty.

He and Tessa had spent a lot of time together that summer, and he remembered that she had, even at fourteen, been comfortable with silences. But the silence between them now was not that of easy companionship. Tension radiated from her. He wondered what had brought her here.

Tessa could feel Keefe glancing at her and knew he had to be wondering why she was here. She'd been crazy to come, crazy to think she could turn to him. She didn't have any right to ask for his help. She'd make a little polite conversation, drink a glass of water, then get in her car and go on her way. He'd probably think she was nuts to have traveled all this way just to say hello, but there was nothing she could do about that.

She became aware that he was adjusting his long stride to her much shorter steps and felt her stomach tighten with sudden tension. Bobby had been a big man, too, and it had been a source of constant irritation to him that she couldn't match his pace. When they were first married, she'd tried to point out that since her legs weren't as long as his, he couldn't expect her to walk as fast. But Bobby hadn't been interested in explanations, only in results. That was a catchphrase he'd picked up from his politician father and liked to apply to any situation where things weren't going his way. Tessa had soon learned that it was easier to give him what he wanted than to try and reason with him. She'd done her best to adjust her stride to his, feeling like a toddler forced to half run to keep up with the adults around her.

Now, realizing that she was slowing Keefe down, she reacted automatically, trying to move more quickly, her throat clogging with a familiar anxiety at the thought of angering the large man walking next to her. *Don't make him mad. Don't make him mad.* The words repeated in her mind, her own personal mantra. *Hurry, hurry, hurry. Don't make him mad.*

"Oh!" The exclamation escaped her as a stone rolled beneath her foot. She would have fallen, but Keefe's hand shot out, catching her upper arm and pulling her toward him so that, instead of hitting the ground, she landed against the solid width of his chest.

"I'm sorry." The words tumbled out breathlessly. She brought her hands up to push against his chest, her heart pounding. *He was so big.* "I didn't mean to be so clumsy. I'm sorry."

"Hey, you don't owe me an apology." Keefe took hold of her upper arms and set her on her feet, releasing her as soon as he saw that she was steady.

"I'm so clumsy," Tessa muttered. She didn't look at him, afraid of what she might see in his eyes, even more afraid of what he might read in hers.

"You aren't clumsy," he said. "But you might try slowing down a little. I was getting out of breath trying to keep up with you."

The humor in his voice brought Tessa's gaze to his face. He didn't look impatient or irritated. He was smiling at her, his dark eyes warm and friendly. She felt the knot in her chest loosen a little. This was Keefe. How could she have forgotten the way he could smile with just his eyes? The way he'd always been able to make her feel as if the world wasn't such a bad place after all?

"I thought I might be slowing you down," she said.

"And I thought you were racing me to the house. At the pace you were moving, I was starting to think I was going to have to break into a sprint just to keep up."

The idea was so ridiculous that Tessa's tense expression relaxed into a smile. "Sorry."

"Just keep in mind that, at my age, I'm not as fast as I used to be," he told her as they started walking again.

"You're not exactly an old man," Tessa protested.

"I'll be forty in a couple of years. As young as you are, that must seem pretty old."

Tessa didn't answer. Just smiled and shook her head. Inside she was trying to remember the last time she'd felt young.

"I thought bachelors were supposed to be slobs," Tessa commented, glancing around the tidy kitchen.

"I am a slob." Keefe got two glasses out of the refrigerator and set them on the wooden counter. "Lemonade okay? It's from a mix, but it's not half bad."

"Lemonade is fine. This doesn't look like the kitchen of a slob." Tessa pulled a chair out from the big oak table that sat under a window at one end of the room.

"For the first couple of years after I moved in, the place looked like a nuclear-waste dumping site. It got to the point where I was afraid to open the refrigerator unless I was armed, because some of the things growing in it were starting to develop teeth."

Tessa smiled as he set the glass of lemonade in front of her. "So what happened to change you into Mr. Clean?"

"Fear for my life," Keefe said as he sank down into a chair across the table from her. "I figured if one of the creatures in the fridge didn't get me, ptomaine would. And there was always the possibility that I'd open a closet one day and be crushed in the resulting avalanche. I doubt if I'll win any awards from *House Beautiful* but at least the place is no longer in danger of being designated a toxic waste site.''

"It's very nice," Tessa said.

"Thanks."

An uneasy silence followed, or at least it seemed uneasy to Tessa. She tried to think of something casual to say, something light and unimportant to keep the conversational ball rolling, but all she could think of was how tired she was. Exhaustion had crept into her very bones, weighing her down, draining her spirit.

"When is the baby due?" Keefe asked, and she was grateful to have the silence broken.

"Three months." Tessa heard the flatness of her response and forced herself to smile. "I can't wait," she said, trying to look happy, the way an expectant mother should look.

He smiled, but there was something watchful in his eyes, and Tessa looked away. She was going to have to be careful. Keefe was not someone who was easily fooled.

Silence fell between them again. Tessa turned her lemonade glass between her hands and tried to think of something to say. She should never have come here. She had no claims on Keefe. Whatever ties of family there might have been between them, they'd been severed when he and Dana split up. And even if she did have some family claim to him, she, of all people, knew how little that meant. She should say something pleasant about how nice it had been to see him again and leave. But she was so tired. So very, very tired.

"You want to tell me why you're here?" Keefe asked, his tone so gentle that Tessa felt something tremble inside her. She released her breath on a sigh and lifted her eyes to his face.

"I guess you didn't really buy the story about me being in the neighborhood, huh?"

"Like Jace said, it's a pretty big neighborhood. The High Sierras aren't exactly on the way to anywhere else, unless you're going hiking. All things considered, that doesn't seem likely," he said, nodding to her belly.

"No, I guess it doesn't." She took a sip of lemonade and let the tart, sweet taste of it dissolve in her mouth while she tried to find the words to explain her presence. "I guess I'm looking for sanctuary."

"Sanctuary?" Keefe's dark brows rose. "What are you running from?"

Tessa gave a short, humorless laugh. "My life." She rubbed her fingertips over her forehead, trying to soothe the ache building between her eyes. "I need someplace to stay where no one will think to look for me. Just for a little while."

She paused, trying to gather the words of explanation she'd rehearsed on the long drive from Santa Barbara to his ranch. She'd had hours to perfect her story—not a lie but something considerably less than the whole truth.

"All right."

It took Tessa a moment to register what he'd said. She'd been staring at the table, but now her head came up, her blue eyes wide with shock. It occurred to Keefe that it was the first totally honest reaction he'd seen since she arrived.

"All right?" she repeated in a tone of stunned disbelief. "What do you mean?"

"I mean you can stay here. There's a spare bedroom. It's not fancy, but it's reasonably comfortable. We'll have to share the bathroom, though."

"That's okay. It's only for a little while."

"You can stay as long as you need to," he said easily. "Jace lives in the ranch foreman's house, but we usually eat meals together. There's not a whole lot by way of entertainment, though. TV reception is pretty shaky and, as you probably noticed, we're a ways from the nearest town."

"I'm not looking for entertainment," she said, feeling almost dizzy with relief. It just couldn't be this easy. Nothing was ever this easy. "Don't you want to know why I need a place to hide out?"

"Anybody likely to come looking for you carrying a gun?"

"A gun?" Tessa stared at him a moment and then shook her head. "No one wants to kill me, if that's what you mean."

"Good."

"Would you...would you let me stay if I'd said someone wanted to kill me?"

"Yes, but it would have been a real pain to have to start carrying a gun every time I left the house."

He smiled when he spoke but there was something in his eyes that made Tessa believe that, if it was necessary, that was exactly what he'd do. She had to be dreaming, she decided. That was the only possible explanation for his easy acceptance of her, for his willingness to take her in without questions.

"Come on." Keefe pushed his chair back from the table and stood up. "I'll show you to your room, and then I can bring your stuff in from the car."

"Don't you want to know why?" she asked again.

He set his glass in the sink and turned to look at her. "Do you want to tell me why?"

No, she didn't want to tell him. She didn't want to tell him anything, especially since she wouldn't—*couldn't*—tell him the whole truth. But perhaps part of the truth was better than none at all. Maybe if she told him a little of the truth, she wouldn't feel quite as guilty about the rest of it.

"You deserve an explanation," she said at last.

"I don't need one but if it will make you feel better, go ahead."

Tessa hesitated. The careful web of half-truths she'd fabricated suddenly seemed tissue-thin. Perhaps it would have been better not to tell him anything at all than to tell him only a portion. But she could hardly change her mind now.

"You know I was married," she began carefully.

"Was?"

"Yes. My...my husband...Bobby... He passed away, almost two months ago."

Keefe felt as if he'd been kicked in the solar plexus. She was a widow? In his mind, she was still a girl, hardly old enough to be a wife. Yet here she was, six months pregnant and telling him she'd lost her husband. His first instinct was to go to her, to hold her, but there was an odd reserve about her—an invisible barrier that kept him at a small distance.

"I'm...sorry, Tessa."

"Thank you." She dragged one finger through the condensation on the side of her glass. "It was... terrible," she said, keeping her eyes on the aimless motion of her finger.

"An understatement," Keefe muttered. He pulled his cigarettes out of his shirt pocket and tapped one free. He was about to light it when his glance fell on the heavy bulge of her stomach. "Sorry." He put the cigarette back and dropped the pack on the counter. "What happened to your husband?"

"It was an accident," Tessa said. She'd repeated the statement so often that she almost believed it. She continued quickly, wanting to avoid any questions about what kind of accident it had been. "Are you familiar with Senator Robert Mallory?"

"I know the name, but not much more than that."

Tessa barely restrained a sigh of relief. She'd hardly dared to hope that he wouldn't have heard the news reports and rumors that followed Bobby's death. "Bobby—my husband—was Senator Mallory's son. Since his death, there have been reporters camped outside the house practically day and night. I just need to get out from under the glare of the spotlight."

She glanced up at him and then quickly looked away from the questions in his eyes. "Senator Mallory is being talked about as a candidate in the next presidential race. I guess that's why the press is focusing so closely on his son's death. You know what reporters are like."

"I don't have much personal experience with them."

"Lucky you." Her mouth tilted in a quick, humorless little smile. "They can be...difficult."

"So I've heard," he said. Keefe studied her face for a moment. He'd have been willing to bet his best horse that she was lying to him. Or, at the very least, telling him only part of the truth. Sometime in the past five years, she'd learned to lie, but she hadn't learned to do it very well. He pushed away from the counter. "Well, I doubt anyone is likely to trace you here. Even if they did, Jace and I can run them off."

"You're sure?" Tessa looked at him uncertainly.

"About running off a reporter or two?" Keefe asked, deliberately misunderstanding. "I think we can manage that. Might even be fun."

"I mean, are you sure about me staying here? I know, since you and Dana split up, we're not exactly family anymore."

"Yeah, but we're still friends," he said, and in his smile Tessa read the kind of easy welcome she could have expected from no one else she knew. She closed her eyes for an instant, forcing back the quick rush of tears. Funny, how she'd known that, even after five years, she could count on him.

"Thanks," she whispered.

"Don't thank me yet. The accommodations aren't exactly luxury class."

When she moved to stand up, he was suddenly next to her, setting his hand under her elbow to help her up. The casual touch was there and gone so quickly that she didn't have time to react. Exhaustion was

rolling over her in a thick, dark wave, but somewhere
in the back of her mind, Tessa was surprised to realize
that she didn't mind Keefe touching her, helping her.
It was something she'd have to think about later,
when she didn't feel so completely exhausted.

She followed him into the hallway, half registering
what he was telling her about the layout of the house.
He stopped long enough to get a clean set of sheets
out of the linen closet before pushing open another
door.

The bedroom was as plainly furnished as the rest
of the house. A double bed with a nightstand beside
it and a chest of drawers were the only furnishings.
The walls were off-white, as were the simple curtains
that covered the windows and the chenille bedspread
on the bed. The only color came from an old-
fashioned rug, braided in shades of blue and white,
that lay on the wooden floor next to the bed.

"It's not fancy, but it's comfortable enough. I don't
get much company up here—one of my brothers now
and again is about it."

"It looks wonderful," Tessa said with absolute sincerity. At the moment, a hovel would have looked
wonderful, as long as it contained a bed. But, aside
from a light coating of dust, the room was clean and
tidy. She couldn't remember when she'd last seen
anything that looked so wonderful, unless, perhaps, it
was the solid strength of Keefe's large body when
she'd first arrived.

"You look beat," he said as he dropped the sheets
on top of the dresser. "I'll make the bed, and then
you can lie down for a while."

"No, let me." Tessa moved forward. "I don't expect you to wait on me."

"It's no trouble." He pulled the bedspread toward the foot of the bed.

"No, really." She caught the other side of the spread. "I'd feel better if you'd let me do it myself."

Keefe looked across the bed at her, his hesitation plain. After a moment, he released the spread and straightened. "If you're sure," he said doubtfully.

"I'm sure." She reached into the pocket of the soft rose-colored shirt she wore with her dark gray maternity pants and pulled out her key ring. "If you could bring my suitcase in from the car, I'd really appreciate it."

"Sure." Keefe took the keys from her.

The minute he left the room, Tessa sank down on the bed. Her fingers knotted in the soft chenille bedspread, she looked around the room, dazed with relief. She was safe. For the first time in months—years— she was completely safe. The feeling was so foreign that she felt disoriented. Safe, she repeated to herself. For a precious space of time, she could let Keefe hold the rest of the world at bay.

She let the exhaustion wash over her.

When Keefe entered the room a few minutes later, he wasn't really surprised to find Tessa curled up on the edge of the bed, sound asleep. It was obvious that she'd reached the end of her strength. He set her suitcase down just inside the door and crossed to the bed. The heels of his boots clicked on the wooden floor, but the sound didn't penetrate her deep sleep. She didn't even twitch when he eased her toward the cen-

ter of the unmade bed and covered her with the bedspread.

He straightened and then stood looking down at her
for a moment, his expression brooding. After listening
to her careful explanation of why she'd come to him,
he had far more questions than answers. He wasn't
sure she'd actually lied to him, but he knew she
hadn't told him the whole story. How long would it
be until she trusted him enough to tell him what she
was really hiding from?

Chapter 2

It was the scent of food that woke Tessa. Someone was cooking something that smelled rich and brown and delicious, and her stomach rumbled demandingly even before her eyes were open. The room was dark and unfamiliar, but she didn't feel any sense of disorientation. She knew exactly where she was. She was on the Flying Ace, Keefe's ranch in California, a continent away from her old life. There was a deep sense of comfort in the thought.

The illuminated dial of the alarm clock on the nightstand told her that she'd slept for more than three hours, but there was none of the grogginess that she associated with sleeping heavily during the day. Even so, she'd spent too many sleepless nights lately to feel totally rested. She briefly considered closing her eyes and going back to sleep. But the empty, gnawing feeling in her stomach reminded her that she hadn't eaten anything since the Egg McMuffin she had for breakfast a good ten hours before. And not only was she hungry, she was in urgent need of a bathroom. Just one of the many joys of pregnancy, she thought as she rolled awkwardly from the bed.

When she left the bathroom ten minutes later, she was feeling almost human again. She'd splashed cold water on her face and run a brush through her shoulder-length hair. The nap that had served to refresh her had had a less beneficial impact on her clothes, and she considered—briefly—changing into something else. But anything she pulled out of her suitcase was going to be at least as creased as what she had on, and the scent of whatever Keefe was cooking was making her stomach growl. At the moment, eating was more important than her appearance. Besides, it was just Keefe, and he wasn't going to notice—or care—what she looked like.

It wasn't until she heard the low rumble of masculine voices that Tessa remembered that it wasn't "just Keefe." She stopped abruptly. The partner. She'd forgotten all about him. Keefe had introduced them when she first arrived. What was his name? Surely she couldn't have forgotten it in this short space of time, not after four years of being a politician's daughter-in-law. Remembering names was the most elemental of political skills. Her mind remained blank and she felt her throat clog with a familiar panic.

How could she have been so careless? He'd be so angry. He'd tell her she was an idiot, and she couldn't argue, couldn't defend herself. She was *stupid. Stupid.*

"Tessa?"

She'd half turned away, intending to go back to the safety of her room rather than risk revealing her mistake, but at the sound of Keefe's voice, she turned toward him, her eyes wide, her face devoid of color. For a moment, she saw another man standing in front of her—someone not quite as tall, his shoulders less broad, his handsome features twisted in an expression of contempt.

"Are you okay?"

"I'm...fine," she lied. She blinked, clearing her vision of the odd double image. This was Keefe, she reminded herself. Keefe, who'd given her shelter without asking questions, who'd never shown her anything but patience and kindness.

"Dinner's about ready. Could I interest you in some beef stew?"

Tessa started to say that she wasn't really hungry, but she couldn't force the lie out.

"Actually, I'm starving," she admitted.

"You'll have to be, to eat the cooking around here," Keefe said with a grin. "I've been known to burn boiling water, and Jace isn't much better."

"Whatever you're cooking smells wonderful," she said. She felt almost dizzy with relief. *Jace.* His name was Jace.

"Of course it's wonderful," Jace said, catching her comment as she and Keefe entered the kitchen. "It's Reno's bodacious beef stew."

"Bodacious?" Keefe arched one dark brown in question.

"An old family recipe, dating back to my great-great-grandmother's day," Jace said. He was standing at the stove, stirring something in a big cast-iron pot. "She traveled west on the Oregon Trail, and this stew was a mainstay on the journey."

"No doubt she was the first one to call it 'bodacious,'" Keefe said. An oak table sat at one end of the big kitchen. He led Tessa to it and pulled out a chair for her. "I can just hear her now, asking the other members of the wagon train to have a bowl of *bodacious* stew."

"Each generation has added to the recipe," Jace said. "The name is my personal contribution."

"It's dumb," Keefe said flatly. He took silverware out of a drawer and brought it to the table.

"It's creative," Jace corrected him. "A special name for a special dish."

"It's a dumb name. Besides, the most 'special' thing about your stew is when you don't burn it." Keefe glanced at Tessa as he distributed the silverware around the table. The smile in his eyes reassured her that the conversation really was as nonsensical as it seemed. The little knot of tension that had been building in the pit of her stomach eased away. Humor had played such a small part in her life during the past few years that she'd almost forgotten what it was.

"Tessa likes the name. Don't you?"

Tessa started a little, her gaze jerking toward Jace. He was looking at her, his expression holding a laughing demand. His eyes were blue, a startlingly vivid shade that would have made a summer sky look pale in comparison. "You think it's a good name, don't you?"

"Well, it does seem a little...well..." She hesitated, her nose wrinkling as she considered the question. "Actually, it makes me think of surfers and tofu and alfalfa sprouts," she admitted in a rush.

Keefe's laugh held a wicked edge of triumph. "So much for images of wagon trains," he said, glancing at his partner. "Unless your great-great-grandmother *surfed* her way across the prairie."

Jace shot him a sour look. "It's clear I'm surrounded by people with no appreciation for creative genius. Pearls before swine," he muttered as he lifted the heavy pan of stew and carried it to the table.

Tessa wondered if her chuckle sounded as rusty to her companions as it did to her.

Keefe contemplated the trail of smoke that drifted upward from the end of his cigarette. It caught the light that spilled onto the porch from the windows behind him, twisting and turning in ghostly wreaths as it drifted upward and dissipated in the cool night air.

He wouldn't be able to smoke in the house as long as Tessa was staying with him, he thought. Probably just as well. He'd been smoking more than he should—especially since Cole's wedding, almost a month ago. Maybe having to go outside every time he wanted a smoke would provide him with some incentive to cut back.

Maybe he'd even quit altogether. He studied the

orange glow of the cigarette's tip and considered the possibility. He'd done it before. Dana had hated cigarette smoke, so he'd quit the day they were married. He'd lit his next cigarette the day he got his final divorce papers. He still wasn't sure why. Maybe out of some misguided desire to show that his ex-wife's likes and dislikes no longer mattered in his life. His mouth twisted in a rueful half smile. Talk about cutting off your nose to spite someone else's face.

Well, maybe it was time to quit again. Having a pregnant woman in the house was as good a reason as any. When he thought about it, it seemed funny that he'd quit eight years ago because of Dana, and now here he was thinking about quitting again because of her little sister.

Dana's little sister. Keefe stared into the darkness, his expression thoughtful. It was difficult to associate the painfully brittle woman who'd appeared on his doorstep this afternoon with the quiet little girl he'd known. Five years was a long time, but not long enough to account for the changes he saw in Tessa.

At dinner, she'd been almost painfully cheerful. She'd smiled frequently, but the expression had almost never moved past a quick, meaningless curve of her mouth. Her eyes had remained still and—

He frowned, the cigarette burning, forgotten, as he considered just what it was he'd seen in her eyes. Nothing. There was simply nothing in her eyes. It was as if she'd learned to show the world a bright smile while the real Tessa hid somewhere inside, behind the carefully blank wall of her eyes.

Once or twice, real emotion had broken through

that wall and her smile had been genuine, reminding him of the girl he'd known. But those moments had been fleeting. The only other time he saw real emotion had been toward the end of the meal, when Jace asked her about the baby.

"Are you expecting a girl or a boy?" he asked with friendly interest.

There was a pause before Tessa answered him, and something in the quality of her silence made Keefe look at her. Her smile was gone, and there was a moment when he thought he saw something bleak and cold in her eyes, but it was gone so quickly that he couldn't be sure it wasn't his imagination. And then her mouth curved in a bright, meaningless smile. She glanced at Jace, but Keefe didn't think she'd really seen him.

"I don't know. I decided I'd rather be surprised." The bright enthusiasm in her voice was as false as her smile.

"I'm all for surprises," Jace said. *His eyes met Keefe's across the table, full of questions his partner couldn't begin to answer.*

Thinking about it now, Keefe wondered if maybe he was making too much of Tessa's behavior. She had been widowed recently. If she seemed not herself, that alone was reason enough. When his older brother's first wife died of cancer, Sam had changed. He'd been quieter, less inclined to smile, and there had been a kind of emptiness in his eyes that didn't go away completely until he met and married Nikki Beauvisage. Everyone coped with pain in their own way. Maybe Tessa's too-cheerful facade was her way of dealing with her grief.

Keefe took one last drag on his cigarette before stubbing it out against the porch railing. Grief might offer a reasonable explanation for Tessa's odd behavior, but he didn't believe it was the right explanation—or at least he didn't believe it was the only one. There was just something about her that didn't ring true. He was willing to bet that she was hiding something, running from something more than a pack of persistent reporters. He straightened away from the post he'd been leaning against and turned back into the house. It was a waste of time to speculate on what was really going on. Tessa would tell him the truth when she was ready. And if she never told him, he could live with that, too.

The phone rang as he stepped through the kitchen door. Keefe glanced down the hall as he walked into the living room to answer it. Tessa's door was closed, and he could see no light beneath it. She'd gone back to her room right after dinner, pleading exhaustion. It was one of the few things she'd said today that he believed without reservations. A good night's sleep would put some color back in her cheeks and erase the smudgy circles of exhaustion under her eyes, but he doubted it would be enough to solve her other problems. Whatever was eating at her, it wasn't something that sleep would cure.

He picked up the phone in the middle of the third ring. "Hello?"

"Keefe?"

"Hello, Molly." It wasn't until he heard her voice

that he realized he'd been more than half expecting this call. On some subconscious level, he'd realized that there had to be a connection between Tessa's arrival and his friendship with her great-aunt. "She got here safely."

"Already?" It was typical of Molly Thorpe that she didn't waste time questioning how he knew what she was calling about. "She must have driven straight through. I told her not to. I told her to stop halfway and spend the night."

"She didn't."

"Obviously not," she said, sounding mildly annoyed. "I was calling to tell you to expect her tomorrow."

"I appreciate the thought," Keefe said dryly.

"Well, as long as she got there safely, there's no harm done."

"She's pretty beat but, other than that, she's okay."

"Good." There was a brief pause, which Keefe made no attempt to fill. She cleared her throat. "I suppose I should have called sooner." Another woman might have sounded apologetic, but Molly managed to make the words almost a challenge.

"Doesn't matter." Keefe perched on the arm of the huge old leather armchair that sat next to the table that held the phone.

"You must have been surprised to see her."

"A bit." He thought of the moment when he'd heard Tessa's voice and thought she was Dana. Surprised? *Relieved* might be a better word for what he'd felt when he saw Tessa.

There was another pause, and he knew Molly was waiting for him to elaborate. He said nothing. He was very fond of Molly, but she could be more than a bit arrogant. A little unsatisfied curiosity would do her no harm.

"Aren't you going to ask why I sent my great-niece to you?" she asked finally.

"I figured you'd tell me if you wanted to."

"And if I don't want to?" Her tone made the question a challenge.

"Then I guess I'll just have to spend my life racked with curiosity," he said, sounding more sleepy than racked.

There was another silence, the phone line all but humming with her frustration. "Next time I see your mother, I'm going to have to offer her my condolences. You must have been a great trial to her."

"I did my best," Keefe said modestly. "But I can't take all the credit. My brothers did their part." He grinned at her quick bark of laughter.

"I'll offer her condolences times four, then," she promised.

"You do that."

"Tessa tell you anything about what's going on?" Molly asked, getting back to the subject at hand.

"Just that she needs a place to stay until the media finds something to interest them besides her husband's death."

"That's what she told me," Molly said. She hesitated, and Keefe could picture her fine brows drawing together in a frown. "Do you believe her?"

The question surprised him, and he took his time

in answering it. From where he sat, he could look through the living room doorway and catch an angled glimpse of the hallway that led to the bedrooms. He thought about what Tessa had told him. When he spoke, his tone was slow and considering, "I think it's the truth, as far as it goes."

"But it's not all of the truth." Molly's words fell halfway between statement and question.

"Maybe not," he conceded reluctantly. He felt uncomfortable discussing Tessa's veracity—or lack thereof—with someone else, even with Molly. Perhaps she sensed as much, or maybe she felt as uncomfortable with the idea as he did, because she didn't pursue the subject.

"Whatever is going on, she said she needed a place to stay where no one would think to look for her. I figured your ranch pretty much fit the bill."

"It should," Keefe agreed. He hadn't seen any of his ex-wife's family in five years, since nearly a year before the divorce became final. It wasn't likely that anyone would look for Tessa here.

Tessa had been the only one of the Wyndhams he regretted losing contact with, but it had seemed awkward to try and keep in touch with his former wife's younger sister. Since Tessa didn't try to contact him, he'd assumed she felt the same. Now he was sorry he'd let her slip out of his life so easily. Maybe, if he'd kept in touch with her, he'd have some idea of what was going on.

"I told her my ranch was the first place any self-respecting reporter would come if they were looking for her," Molly said, interrupting his thoughts. "I'm her only family, apart from her parents. And that nit-wit niece of mine and the fathead she married are off in Europe somewhere, not that they'd be any good to anybody even if they were on the right continent.''

Keefe's mouth quirked at her acid-tongued summation of Tessa's parents. Unfortunately, she wasn't exaggerating. His former in-laws weren't particularly intelligent, nor were they in the habit of concerning themselves with much beyond their own comfort.

''What about Dana?'' he asked.

''She's in Europe with her parents.''

And Tessa wouldn't be likely to turn to Dana for help anyway, Keefe thought. The sisters had never been close. Dana's indifference to her younger sister had puzzled Keefe, who came from a tight-knit family. But it hadn't taken him long to realize that a lack of close ties wasn't the only way the Wyndhams differed from the Walkers.

''Tessa's welcome to stay here as long as she wants,'' he told Molly.

''I told her you'd feel that way,'' Molly said, sounding satisfied at having been proven right. ''A fellow came by today, asking about her.''

Keefe's fingers tightened around the receiver. ''A reporter?''

''Could have been.''

''But you don't think so?'' he asked, picking up on the doubt in her voice.

''I don't know. He didn't say, and when I asked him outright what he wanted with my great-niece, he sidestepped the question very neatly.''

''What did you tell him?''

"I told him Tessa had been to see me but she wasn't here now and it was none of his damned business where she'd gone. I also told him that, if I found out he'd been harassing my great-niece, I'd call in favors from Sacramento and he'd find himself so tangled up in government red tape that his life would become a living hell. He immediately remembered that he had business elsewhere," she finished modestly.

"I can almost feel sorry for the guy." Keefe grinned as he pictured her routing her visitor. Molly and her late husband had been heavily involved in state politics for over thirty years. Half the state legislature owed her favors. If her visitor really was a reporter, there was a good chance he knew that hers was no idle threat. "I'm sure he got the message."

"I think so. I have no patience with people who make their living by digging into the lives of private citizens. However, if someone is really determined to find Tessa, they may manage to track her down, even at your place."

"I'll take care of her," Keefe promised.

Molly was quiet for a moment, and then she exhaled softly, as if with relief. "Yes, I know you will. That's why I sent her to you."

When Keefe hung up the phone a moment later, his expression was thoughtful. It was all very well to say he'd keep Tessa safe, but it would be nice to know just what it was he was supposed to be keeping her safe from.

"Next time that section of fence goes down, I think we should hire someone to stand guard and just shoot

any cow that tries to cross the property line.'' Jace
groaned as he swung down out of the saddle.

"Be a little hard on the cow, don't you think?''
Keefe asked. He looped the reins around the top rail
of the corral fence.

"Days like this make me think the only good cow
is a dead cow,'' Jace said darkly. He loosened the
cinch strap and gave his horse a companionable slap
on the neck.

"Maybe, but a dead cow is harder to sell than a
live one,'' Keefe pointed out. He arched his back,
stretching the kinks out of his spine. They'd spent the
morning repairing fence. It was hot, dusty, muscle-
straining work.

"I don't see why anyone should object to buying
already-dead cows,'' Jace argued. "We could call
them prekilled and market them as a time-saving innovation.''

"Prekilled?'' Keefe grinned. "Like preowned
cars?''

"Something along those lines. Seems to me there
could be an untapped market for them.''

"Could be, but I doubt it.'' Keefe took off his hat
and ran his fingers through his thick, dark hair.

"You need to expand your thinking,'' Jace said.
"Look at the guy who invented the Pet Rock.''

"*You* look at him. All I want to look at right now
is a cold beer and some food. I could eat a grizzly.''

"Now *there's* an innovation. Grizzly ranching! We
could become the world's first bear ranchers,'' Jace
said, looking struck.

"There's even less of a market for bear meat than there is for prekilled cows," Keefe told him.

"You never know until you try."

"Trust me, the world isn't ready for bear ranching."

Their horses taken care of, they started up to the house. Keefe wondered how Tessa had spent her morning.

"How's your houseguest?" Jace asked, his thoughts following the same lines. It was the first time he'd mentioned Tessa.

"She was asleep when I left this morning."

"Probably the best thing for her. She looked like she'd hit the end of her rope."

Keefe's silence was agreement. If he had to guess, he'd have said Tessa had been running on nothing but nerves for a long time. Jace was right—the best thing for her was plenty of rest.

Tessa stepped back from the window. She didn't want to be caught peering through the curtains like a junior-grade spy. She looked around the kitchen, searching for something she'd forgotten, anything out of place. It was always best to double- and triple-check things, rather than risk a mistake.

Mistakes are caused by carelessness. Stupid people are careless. Are you stupid, Tessa? Stupid, stupid, stupid.

With an effort, she choked off the internal recording, blocking out the hateful echo.

"I'm not stupid," she whispered fiercely. "I'm not."

If she was stupid, she couldn't have learned to be so careful, so very careful. Everything was right. She'd made sure of it. Everything was perfect. But that reassurance didn't stop her heart from pounding like a drum against her breastbone when she heard the sound of booted feet on the porch floorboards. The door was thrust open, and she set one hand against the back of a chair to supplement the somewhat shaky support of her knees.

Keefe and Jace stepped through the door, and the big kitchen seemed to shrink. They didn't immediately see her standing beside the table, and that gave Tessa a moment to observe them. Both were big men, though Keefe was a little taller and broader through the shoulders. Both were dark. Keefe's hair was a brown so dark that it could almost be called black, and his eyes were the color of bittersweet chocolate. Jace's hair was dark, also, but it was a rich, burnished shade of brown, holding hints of red, and his eyes were the purest, deepest blue Tessa had ever seen.

Despite their similarities in coloring and size, no one would ever have mistaken them for brothers. Keefe was all steady strength. There was a feeling of solidity about him—a sense that he would be a rock to cling to in any storm. There was strength in Jace's features, but there was something more mercurial about him, a gleam of mischief in his eyes. They were both strikingly attractive men, Tessa thought, and then was vaguely surprised that she'd even noticed such a thing.

Jace saw her first and smiled. "Hello."

"Hello." Tessa almost winced at the thin sound of

her own voice. *Speak up, for God's sake! You're not in a library. Why do you always whisper?* She cleared her throat and widened her smile a fraction.

"Hi." Keefe's dark eyes went over her in a quick, searching look that missed nothing. "How did you sleep?"

"Very well," Tessa said. It was the truth. It had been a long time since she slept so deeply and dreamlessly. "I overslept, though."

"Overslept for what?" Keefe asked as he turned on the water in the sink and reached for the soap. "Did you have an appointment this morning?"

"I was going to make breakfast."

"For us?" Jace's brows rose in surprise.

"Yes. It seemed the least I could do."

"You don't have to earn your keep." Keefe pulled a blue-and-white plaid towel off the rack and dried his hands.

"I'd like to do something. You've been so kind, letting me stay here—both of you." She was careful to include Jace in her gratitude. "I can help around the house—do the cooking and cleaning, things like that."

"I don't expect you to be my housekeeper," Keefe said. There was an edge of temper in his voice that made Tessa's stomach knot.

"I just...I'd feel better if I could help." Her fingers twisted together in front of her rounded stomach. "I took cooking lessons, and I'm a pretty good cook. Even Bobby said so," she added, unaware of how much her words revealed. "I'd... If you wouldn't

mind...I'd like to... But if you'd rather I didn't..."
She let the words trail off.

*When was she going to learn? Don't argue. Never
argue. It would just make him mad, and she didn't
want to make him mad.*

"Are you kidding? We'd love to have someone
else do the cooking," Jace said, filling the silence
before it became noticeable. "Like Keefe said last
night, neither one of us is much good in the kitchen.
I certainly wouldn't mind eating some decent food
for a change."

Tessa's gaze was focused on the floor, so she
missed seeing the quick warning look Jace gave
Keefe. But Keefe saw it. Saw, also, the oddly taut
expression on Tessa's face. He didn't like the idea of
her cooking for them, but it was obvious that it meant
a great deal to her.

"If you really want to cook a meal or two, I have
no objection," he said. "As long as you don't feel
like you have to do it."

"I'd like to." Tessa's smile was fleeting, but at
least she no longer looked as if she expected him to
bite. She gestured to the table. "I made lunch for
you."

There was something so anxious in her expression
that Keefe looked away to conceal the anger in his
eyes. What the hell had happened to her in the last
five years?

"It looks great," he said automatically. It wasn't
until he was sitting down that he really saw what
she'd done. It *did* look nice. She'd set the table with
the same thick white china plates that he and Jace

always used, but the silverware was neatly arranged at each place setting. In the center of the table she'd set a canning jar full of wildflowers and early roses from the bushes that grew alongside the house—remnants of some former owners' attempt to beautify their surroundings. The shrubs had survived hard winters, dry summers and total neglect, and always seemed to have a handful of flowers hidden among their tangled vines.

"I couldn't find any napkins," she said, reaching out to twitch a fork into more precise alignment with a knife. "I hope paper towels are okay."

"It's what we always use," Jace assured her. But they'd never taken the time to fold them into neat little wedges and arrange them beside the plates.

"Oh, good." She seemed relieved, as if she'd thought that the lack of proper linens might give offense. "I'll get the food. I wasn't sure what you'd want to drink."

"Beer," Keefe answered for both of them. "I'll get them."

"No. Just stay there. I'll get them."

He started to argue, but caught Jace's look and settled back into his chair. It went against the grain to sit still while a woman waited on him—particularly a woman who was six months pregnant. But it was obvious that any interference upset Tessa. Maybe after she'd been here a day or two, she'd relax a bit.

"There was some leftover roast beef, so I made sandwiches and soup," Tessa said as she pulled open the refrigerator door.

Keefe's stomach rumbled in anticipation. After

fighting that damned fence all morning, he was hungry enough to eat an entire cow. Thick slices of beef between slabs of bread sounded like pure heaven. And whatever the soup was, it smelled good. Maybe it wouldn't be such a bad thing to let her do the cooking, as long as she enjoyed it.

"I couldn't find exactly the right ingredients for the soup, but I think it turned out fairly well." She set a plate of sandwiches in the center of the table before going back to the stove. A moment later, she carried two bowls of soup back to the table and put one in the center of each of their plates. "I'll get your beer."

Keefe looked at the bowl of soup. A crusty slice of bread floated in the center of a pool of dark, rich broth. French onion soup. He'd had it in restaurants a time or two. If he remembered correctly, it was good but not particularly filling. Jace's boot nudged his ankle. When he glanced up, Jace rolled his eyes in the direction of the sandwiches. Keefe stared at them. Thin slices of bread, with the crusts removed, enclosed slices of beef so thin they appeared to have been shaved from the roast. Each sandwich had been cut into four neat little triangles.

"I made some potato salad," Tessa said as she brought a bowl to the table. "I got the recipe from one of my cooking teachers. She liked to use baby Yukon Gold potatoes, but I thought it would be okay with the boiling potatoes you had in the vegetable bin. The Yukon Gold are a prettier color, though."

"These look just fine," Keefe assured her truthfully. What didn't look so good was the amount of potato salad. Hungry as he was, he could eat the whole bowl himself, polish off the sandwiches and have room left over for dessert.

"There." Tessa set a glass of beer in front of him. A glass? Keefe tried to remember the last time he'd had beer in a glass. "Did I forget anything?"

More food. He looked at her hopeful expression and forced a smile. "I can't think of anything."

"How do you think she got that meat sliced so thin?" Jace asked. They were back in the saddle, heading out to finish the fencing job.

"I don't know." Keefe tugged his hat down against the early-afternoon sun and slouched lower in the saddle, his body adjusting automatically to the rhythm of the horse's gait.

"I don't think I've ever seen meat sliced that thin," Jace continued. "Must have taken a lot of work to get it like that."

"Must have." Keefe didn't want to think about how thin the meat had been sliced, because it reminded him of how empty his stomach still was.

"And that soup. I bet that took a lot of work, too, but there wasn't anything but a slice of bread and a few onions in it." Jace's tone was wondering.

Keefe grunted. He didn't know how much work the soup had been, but he did know that it hadn't been particularly filling. Jace fell silent and Keefe tried to think of something besides food.

"What the hell is a Yukon Gold potato?" Jace asked suddenly.

"Probably some kind of gourmet potato."

"She said they were a prettier color. What color do you figure they are?"

"Yellow, maybe, if the name is a clue." Keefe shrugged. His stomach sent up a polite inquiry about the remainder of lunch, and he tried to ignore it. He'd tried to eat slow, in hopes that it might fool his stomach into thinking it was being filled, but it hadn't worked.

"She looked so anxious."

"Yeah."

"I couldn't bring myself to say anything."

"Me neither."

"What do you think she's going to make for dinner?"

"I don't know." Keefe's voice was heavy with dread.

"Everything tasted good."

"Sure did."

They rode in silence a while longer, and then Jace spoke again, his tone wistful. "What do you think she did with the bread crusts?"

Chapter 3

When Keefe was married to Dana, he'd been riding the rodeo circuit and they'd lived out of trailers and motels—only one of many things she'd hated about the life-style. She hadn't minded being on the road, but she'd hated traveling cheap.

After the divorce, he'd spent a few months riding horses no one else would ride, drinking too much, smoking too much and generally doing a good imitation of a man hell-bent on self-destruction. He might have succeeded, too, if he hadn't gotten into a poker game in Montana. He'd been just drunk enough to bet everything he owned on the chance that he could draw to an inside straight. He'd won a run-down ranch in the High Sierras.

When he looked back on it, he figured drawing that card might have saved his life. The ranch had given him something to focus on besides the mess he'd made of his life. He'd taken what was left of his rodeo winnings and moved to the ranch. In the three years since, he'd worked like a dog to put the ranch back into shape. In his mind, the ''ranch'' consisted of the land, the stock and the outbuildings. The house was merely a place to eat and sleep and do paperwork. He did what was necessary to make it reasonably comfortable and then gave it no more thought.

And then Tessa had come to stay. He'd forgotten what it was like to have a woman around the house. He couldn't put his finger on what had changed, but everything seemed different. It might have been the way the delicate floral scent of her shampoo lingered in the bathroom after she showered, or the soft sound of her footsteps in the hall. He couldn't describe it, but he knew it was there—some indefinable, unmistakable change in the very air he breathed—something that spoke of woman.

The whole house seemed different. If he'd ever thought about it, he would have dismissed the old cliché about a house needing ''a woman's touch.'' But he couldn't deny that, under Tessa's touch, the old house had seemed to shake itself awake. He'd lived there for three years without making much of an impact. In less than a week, Tessa had made the place look lived-in. The changes were subtle. She certainly hadn't rearranged the furniture or hung new curtains, but the thin layer of dust that had coated every surface was gone, there were flowers on the table and the windows were thrown open, letting in fresh air and sunshine.

Pleasant as the changes were—and he liked them

more than he cared to acknowledge—he didn't want her to feel as if she had to work to earn her keep.

"You're a guest—a *welcome* guest," he told her three days after her arrival. "I don't expect you to cook or clean to earn your keep."

"I don't mind." Tessa continued kneading the mound of bread dough that sat on the flour-dusted table.

"*I* mind." Keefe slapped his hat lightly against the side of his leg and frowned at her. He'd come up to the house in the middle of the afternoon to make a phone call and found her elbow-deep in bread dough. "You don't have to work for room and board, Tessa."

"It probably sounds stupid, but I actually like cooking and cleaning."

"Unbelievable, maybe, but not stupid," Keefe muttered, his eyes drawn to the rhythmic motion of her hands as she worked. Her fingers curled gracefully as she dug the heel of each hand into the dough. It seemed to push back, resisting her movements even as it yielded to them. There was something earthy in the motion, a sensuality that caught him off guard. It took a conscious act of will to look away.

"I really like making bread." Tessa glanced at him, her mouth curved in a soft smile—a real smile, he saw. Not one of the bright, false smiles that had come so frequently—and meaninglessly—when she first arrived.

She looked better, he thought, studying her profile. Not exactly right. Certainly not like the girl he remembered. There were still shadows in her eyes, and when she thought no one was watching, there was a haunted quality to her expression, a deep emptiness that made him want to hold her and promise to take care of whatever was wrong. But she looked better now than she had three days ago. There was color in her face, and the dark circles that had been under her eyes were almost gone. She smiled less often, but they were real smiles, not those bright, meaningless displays that put up walls between her and the rest of the world. He still didn't know what had brought her to him, but it was obvious that she needed more time to heal. He was glad to give her that.

"There's something about kneading bread that's soothing," Tessa continued. "I had an electric mixer back...where I used to live, but I didn't like to use it for bread. I like to feel the dough change under my hands. It starts out sticky and fighting your every move, but as you work it changes, starts to come alive. It's like creating life, I suppose," she finished, her smile taking on a self-conscious edge.

Keefe had been staring at her hands, almost hypnotized by their movements. But, at her last comment, his eyes shifted to her stomach for an instant before lifting to her face. He smiled. "You seem to be getting quite a bit of experience in that lately."

He could see the exact moment that she realized he was referring to her pregnancy. Her mouth tightened subtly, and the skin seemed to draw taut over her cheekbones. He couldn't see her eyes, but he knew they were empty, hollow.

"I guess I am," she said, her tone devoid of expression, the curve of her mouth perfunctory. There was an uncomfortable little silence, and then Tessa flashed him one of those bright, meaningless smiles that he was coming to hate. "I hope you're not going to insist that I do nothing around the house but sit on my hands all day. That would get tedious pretty quickly."

"You're welcome to do whatever you want," he said slowly. He turned his hat between his fingers, his eyes on her profile. He wished he knew what was going on behind those walls she put up. Even more, he'd like to know what it was that had taught her to build those walls in the first place. "As long as you don't do anything major. I don't want you to hurt yourself."

"I'll be careful," she assured him with another of those smiles that didn't reach her eyes.

"I'll see you at lunch, then," he said. Frustration tugged at him as he left the house. He couldn't shake the feeling that there was something more he should say, something more he should do. But he couldn't help her if he didn't know what was wrong, and it was obvious that she had no intention of confiding in him—not now, maybe not ever.

Tessa had been staying on the Flying Ace a little more than a week when she added the laundry to her list of chores. When Keefe protested, she said that she had to wash her own clothes—washing his wasn't that much more work. He gave in, guiltily aware that he wasn't entirely sorry to rid himself of a job he cordially detested. But when he saw the results of her efforts, it was clear that his moment of weakness was not to go unpunished.

Jace pushed his hat back with his thumb, narrowing his eyes against the brilliance of the morning sun. His clear blue eyes moved over Keefe, widening a little when he got to the sharp creases that marched down each leg of his jeans with military precision.

"You going to a party?" he asked.

"Shut up." Keefe glared at him.

"Must be a party somewhere," Jace continued, ignoring the menace in his partner's expression. "Either that or you figure the cows will appreciate your fashion sense."

"One more word and I'm going to feed you your teeth." Keefe swung up into the saddle.

"I don't know what you're getting so upset about." Jace set his heel against his horse's side, sending the big bay after Keefe's mount. "I think you look real nice," he said, but his earnest tone was at odds with the gleam in his eyes.

"You're walking a real thin line," Keefe warned as they rode out of the ranch yard. "I can think of any number of places on this ranch where I could dispose of a body."

Jace looked hurt. "Here I am trying to pay you a compliment, and all I get for my trouble is threats against my life. I think you just might set a new trend in ranch wear." He frowned thoughtfully at the mountains that loomed ahead of them, his tone becoming philosophical. "When you think about it, there's no excuse for cowboys to go around looking like something the cat dragged in. A man ought to take pride in his appearance.''

"Glad you feel that way," Keefe said, his tone so cordial that Jace felt a quick rush of alarm. "When I left the house, Tessa was just starting in on *your* laundry."

"Oh, no." Jace's expression was horrified.

"Oh, yes." Keefe's grin was pure malice.

"We'll be laughingstocks," Jace said gloomily.

"Nobody's going to see us but the cows."

"They'll never take us seriously."

"The cows?" Keefe's brows rose.

"A cowboy wearing jeans with a crease?" Jace shuddered. "What kind of authority figure is that?"

"You figure the cows are going to notice?"

"They'll ignore us," Jace predicted in a tone of doom. "Pretty soon, they'll start muttering about mutiny. Next thing you know, we'll have a riot on our hands."

Keefe's shout of laughter startled a Stellar's jay out of a nearby tree. The bird took off, a flash of sapphire and black against the pale blue of the morning sky, his squawk expressing his annoyance.

"I figure we should be safe enough as long as we don't let them get hold of weapons," he said, still grinning.

"Probably." Jace shook his head. "There's got to be a way to stop her."

"I don't know what it is." Keefe's smile faded as he considered his houseguest. "I was going to tell her that I didn't want my jeans ironed, but…" A helpless shrug completed the sentence.

"Yeah, I know. She looked at you." Jace understood completely.

"Yeah."

They rode in silence for a moment, each contemplating the impossibility of saying anything even marginally critical to Tessa. Neither of them was willing to risk doing anything that might bring back the haunting emptiness that had marked her expression when she arrived. Military creases in their jeans were a small price to pay to keep that look out of her eyes.

"What did she make for lunch?" Jace asked after a while.

"Ham sandwiches."

"No crusts?"

"No crusts."

"What do you think she does with all those crusts?" The question had been nagging at Jace for over a week.

"Maybe she used them in that stuffing she made last night." Keefe said. He shook his head. "Littlest damned chickens I've ever seen."

"They were game hens."

"I've seen sparrows bigger than that."

"Tasted good."

"Tasted great. But half of one of those pigeons wasn't enough to feed a two-year-old." He frowned as he thought about the beautifully presented meal Tessa had served the night before. Half a game hen, a spoonful of delicately flavored stuffing and two different vegetables, carefully arranged on each plate. "What do you suppose she did with the fourth half?"

"She's probably going to make soup out of it,"

Jace suggested. They contemplated that possibility in gloomy silence.

"What did you bring for lunch?" Keefe asked.

"Cold fried chicken, potato salad and some of those apple turnovers from Gleason's."

Keefe's mouth watered in anticipation. When Tessa took over the cooking, it had become immediately apparent that they had a problem. She was an excellent cook, each dish perfectly seasoned and elegantly presented. If they'd been holding down desk jobs rather than running a ranch, there would have been nothing to complain about. As it was, at the end of the first full day of Tessa's reign in the kitchen, Keefe had met with Jace in the foreman's cottage after she went to bed. While they devoured potato chips and dip—the only thing edible Jace had to hand—they'd worked out their strategy.

The next day, when Jace went into town to fill Tessa's grocery list, he'd also bought enough food to stock the kitchen in the tiny foreman's house, enabling them to supplement Tessa's beautifully cooked meals with more rough-and-ready fare. Jace packed their lunch in his saddlebags in the morning, and in the evening Keefe waited until Tessa went to bed and then made his way across the ranch yard to Jace's kitchen to finish filling the hollow in his stomach.

It wasn't the most convenient arrangement, but it was better than trying to explain to Tessa that she was about to starve them to death.

Tessa ran the scrub brush over the floor in brisk little circles. It was obvious that cleaning floors had not been high on Keefe's list of priorities. She was willing to bet that it had been months since the floor was mopped, and probably years since it was thoroughly scrubbed. She'd thought the floor was actually covered in prison-gray linoleum until she discovered a rather pleasant ivory-and-slate-blue pattern underneath the dirt.

At least the floor wasn't covered in layers of old wax, she thought as she dipped the brush in the bucket of soapy water beside her. She didn't have to worry about stripping years of wax away. Not that she could have done that, anyway. An afternoon spent breathing ammonia fumes wasn't on any list of recommended prenatal activities. She wouldn't do anything that would be bad for the baby. That was one thing she'd promised herself when she found out she was pregnant. She would follow every instruction she was given and do everything she could to ensure the baby's health.

And she'd kept her promise, she thought. She'd taken her vitamins. She'd consumed so much milk, it was practically coming out her ears. She'd exercised moderately and tried to eat right. Of course, the doctor had also told her to avoid stress. She'd nearly laughed out loud when he told her that. But even she hadn't guessed just how much stress she'd be called on to endure.

If only there had been some way to know that Bobby was going to die, she might have made other choices.

Tessa shook her head as if physically pushing the thoughts aside. She wasn't going to look back. That was another promise she'd made herself when Bobby died. The past was past, and she wasn't going to waste any of the present on regrets. She was going to move on and make something of her life.

You? Make something of your life? You're even stupider than I thought. The sneering voice was so real that Tessa froze, her fingers clenching around the scrub brush. She was half-afraid to look over her shoulder for fear she'd see him there, his handsome features twisted in contempt, his eyes mocking. *You're not smart enough to make something of your life. You're too stupid, Tessa. Stupid. Stupid. Stupid.*

"No," she whispered. "I'm not stupid."

Are you arguing with me? The low voice held a silky threat that made the hair on the back of her neck stand up.

Imagination, she thought desperately. It was just her imagination replaying unwelcome images on a mental screen. He was gone, and she didn't have to be afraid of him ever again.

"What the hell are you doing!"

The male roar of anger was punctuated by the slam of the screen door. Caught in the nightmare of memory, Tessa felt her heart stop. The thud of boots on the half-washed floor brought her around to face that voice. Made clumsy by the heavy bulk of her stomach, she sat down heavily on the damp floor. The tall male figure striding toward her sent her sliding down a long, dark tunnel into the past.

"Have you gone completely crazy?" Keefe demanded angrily. Three long strides took him across the damp floor. "Dammit all, Tessa! I told you not to do anything heavy. Get up off the damn floor."

He bent over her, one hand outstretched to help her up. Trapped in past nightmares, Tessa saw the tall figure looming over her and saw his hand come out. Her reaction was instinctive.

"Don't!" She cringed back against the cupboard, hunching her shoulders, one hand curling protectively across her belly, the other coming up to shield her head from the expected blow.

Keefe froze. Even his heart seemed to stop beating for a moment. He stared down at Tessa, crouched on the floor in a classic defensive posture, her small body curled up as tightly as possible, considering the bulk of her stomach. He breathed in slowly, the air rasping in his throat.

"My God," he whispered hoarsely. "You thought I was going to *hit* you?"

The stunned disbelief in his tone penetrated the black wall of fear that enclosed her. Keefe. It was Keefe. She slowly lowered her arm, but she didn't look at him. She was too afraid of what he might see in her eyes. Her mind raced frantically. She had to explain, had to tell him... She didn't know what, but if she didn't say something, he might guess the truth, might guess the secret she'd kept so carefully.

"Tessa, I wouldn't..." Feeling as if he'd aged ten years in the past ten seconds, Keefe straightened slowly. He stared at the hand he'd reached out to her, as if he might find an explanation for what had just happened written on its palm. But there was nothing to see but a faint unsteadiness. He let it drop to his side. "I've never hit a woman in my life," he said finally, his voice hoarse and strained.

His dazed tone brought Tessa's head up. He looked as if he'd just taken a hard blow to the solar plexus. The skin across his cheekbones was drawn tight, sharp lines bracketed his mouth and his eyes.... Tessa's breath caught. For the first time in a long time, she was aware of someone else's pain, someone else's anguish.

"I would never hurt you, Tessa."

"I know," she whispered.

"You cringed." He lifted one hand and thrust unsteady fingers through his dark hair. "You cringed as if you thought I was going to— You were *afraid*. Of me."

"No." She couldn't let him think that. "It wasn't you. It was... I was thinking, remembering, and I thought...for just a second, I thought you were someone else."

"Who?" he asked immediately.

"It doesn't matter."

"Doesn't matter?" Keefe crouched in front of her, bringing his eyes more on a level with hers. She noticed that he was careful not to reach out to her, not to get too close. His care caused a sharp little pain in her chest. "You were scared to death, Tessa. You thought I was going to *hit* you. And then you tell me that you thought I was someone else and that it doesn't matter? Like hell it doesn't!"

There was anger in his voice, but it wasn't directed at her. Emotionally battered as she was, she could still recognize that. He wasn't angry *at* her. He was angry

for her, angry at whoever had frightened her. Tessa
stared at him as the difference seeped slowly into her
consciousness. It had been so long since anyone took
her side in anything, and in her entire life she couldn't
remember anyone caring enough to be angry on her
behalf. Gratitude welled up inside her. But she'd kept
this particular secret for four long years.

"It's over," she said, looking away from him.

"It's not over if it can still make you react like
that," he said flatly. She shivered, and his voice gen-
tled. "Sometimes talking can help, Tessa."

"No." She shook her head. Her voice was tight
and thin with suppressed emotion. "Talking doesn't
change anything. I promised myself that I wouldn't
look back. It's over. He's dead and it's over."

"Your husband?" Keefe's tone was gentle, but
there was determination there, a quiet warning that he
wasn't going to be easily dissuaded. He reached out
to take her hand, in a slow, careful movement. "Is
that who you thought I was?"

Tessa looked at her hand in his. Her fingers appeared slender and fragile lying against the width of
his palm. There was strength in his hand. Bobby had
been strong, too. As she remembered that strength,
her hand trembled in Keefe's hold, but she didn't
draw away. This was Keefe, and she could never be
afraid of him.

"Tessa?"

Slowly, almost reluctantly, she lifted her eyes to
his—and felt some long-held wall inside her start to
crumble. The feeling of vulnerability was frightening.
She turned her head away and tried to withdraw her

hand from his, but his fingers held hers with gentle implacability.

"Tessa? Did your husband abuse you?"

"No!" The denial was immediate. Her eyes jerked back to his face and she shook her head. "He didn't. He just...sometimes he... But it was my fault," she insisted. "It was always my fault. It was only when I was stupid that he... It was my fault."

Keefe had never known he was capable of such powerful anger. It was a white-hot wave sweeping over him, making him feel as if the top of his head might lift off with the force of it. He drew in a slow breath, struggling to control his rage. Anger wasn't what Tessa needed right now.

"Your fault?" he questioned softly. "He *hit* you and you think it was your fault."

Tessa looked away. "Sometimes I did stupid things and he'd...he'd get upset. I didn't mean to, but I did."

The ticking of the wall clock was clearly audible in the silence that followed. When Keefe broke it, his voice was low, each word distinct.

"That is the biggest load of crap I've ever heard in my life."

Tessa felt the wall tremble again, shaken by his calm assurance. "You don't understand," she whispered. "I was—"

"You didn't do anything." Keefe's fingers tightened over hers. "Look at me, Tessa."

The sheer force of his will brought Tessa's eyes to his face. She felt herself start to come apart inside, as if all the tension that had been holding her together for so long were suddenly dissolving and draining away, leaving her as fragile and vulnerable as a newborn kitten.

"You could never do anything to justify him hitting you. Never."

"But I—"

"Never. It wasn't your fault, Tessa. Not ever."

"But—"

"There are no buts. It wasn't your fault."

Tessa felt the protective wall dissolve forever beneath the impact of the quiet words. During the first two years of her marriage, she'd shed a sea of tears, but after that she'd stopped crying. She'd felt as if she'd given all the tears she had to give, as if something had dried up inside and she'd never cry again. But Keefe's quiet assurance that she hadn't done anything to deserve Bobby's treatment of her brought long-buried emotions shivering to painful life.

She pulled her hand from his and pressed it against her mouth as tears stung her eyes. "I'm sorry." Her whisper was choked. Her face crumpled, and tears began to roll down her cheeks. "I'm sorry."

"It's okay." Keefe gathered her into his arms and stood up, lifting her up off the damp floor as easily as if she were a child. Cradling her against his chest, he carried her from the kitchen.

His experience with a woman's tears was limited to his ex-wife. Dana had cried easily, stormy bouts of sobbing that, in the early days of their marriage, made him feel like the lowest villain on the face of the planet and generally resulted in her getting whatever it was she wanted. Over the years, his concern had become more rote and he'd been less willing to give in to her wishes. By the time their marriage ended, he'd felt nothing but a great weariness when she cried.

In contrast to her sister's dramatic displays, Tessa cried almost silently. Her small body trembled in his arms as slow, painful tears seeped out from under her lashes. He knew, on some deep, visceral level that was beyond questioning, that she'd learned to cry quietly because it was safer not to draw any attention to herself. The thought made his gut knot with anger. His arms tightened around her, as if to shield her from past hurts.

Keefe carried her into the living room and sat down with her on the sofa. The worn springs groaned under their combined weight. He didn't say anything, didn't try to top her tears. He simply held her and let her cry.

"At first, it only happened when he was drinking."

Tessa didn't look at Keefe as she spoke. She wasn't sure she'd ever be able to look at him again. He'd held her while she cried, and when her tears finally stopped, he'd gotten a box of tissues from the bathroom and, pulling a handful loose, proceeded to mop her face as if she were four years old. She'd been too tired, too drained by her emotional storm, to object. Leaning back against the worn fabric of the sofa, she'd let him take care of her.

He hadn't asked her anything, hadn't demanded to know how she'd let herself become a victim of Bobby's abuse. He'd just dried her face and then looked at her, his dark eyes unfathomable. And she found herself talking, offering explanations he hadn't demanded, trying to make him understand something she didn't even begin to understand herself.

"Bobby didn't drink unless he was upset about something, and I thought that, if I were a good enough wife, if I made him happy, then he wouldn't drink and he wouldn't...wouldn't hit me anymore."

Her attention on the tissue she was shredding into fine confetti, Tessa missed seeing the sudden tightness in Keefe's jaw, the rage that flickered in his eyes. If Bobby Mallory hadn't already been dead, no power on earth could have stopped him from tracking the bastard down and tearing his lungs out through his nose.

But his anger wasn't what Tessa needed now. He forced it back, making his voice level and calm.

"He had a problem you couldn't solve, Tessa." Keefe reached out and set his hand over hers, stopping her mutilation of the tissue. "No one can make someone else happy. That's something you have to do for yourself."

The look she gave him was doubtful. "Maybe." She shook her head a little as she looked away. "I don't know. I thought, if I could just be the perfect wife, I could make my marriage work."

"It takes two to make a marriage work. One person can't do it all on their own."

"Is that what happened to you and Dana?" she asked, glancing at him sideways. "Only one of you was willing to work on the marriage?"

Keefe's hand tightened over hers for a moment,

and then he pulled it away, sitting back on the sofa. He was surprised by how much the reminder of his failed marriage still stung. He'd thought he'd gotten past all that a long time ago. Catching Tessa's questioning look, he lifted one shoulder in a half shrug.

"Dana and I couldn't make our marriage work because neither of us was willing to give enough."

Privately Tessa thought that it was unlikely anyone would ever be able to give enough to satisfy her beautiful older sister. Dana had been raised to expect the rest of the world to fall at her feet, and it came close enough to keep her expectations high. But Keefe's marriage to her sister was none of her business.

"Well, I was willing to give enough for two," she said with a sigh. "But it was never enough."

"Why didn't you leave him?" Keefe asked quietly.

"I don't know." Tessa let her head fall back against the worn green upholstery. "At first, I kept thinking he'd quit drinking and everything would be okay. And then, later, I was afraid of him, afraid of what he'd do to me if I tried to leave." She turned her head and looked at him, her eyes much older than her years. "It wasn't because he loved me. I realized that a long time ago. It was because he liked having control of me, liked having control of something, even if it was only a wife he despised." She sighed and looked away, missing the rage that flickered in Keefe's dark eyes.

"His father—Senator Mallory—is a very powerful man. I don't mean politically. I mean personally. I don't think Bobby ever felt like he had any control over his life. So he married me and I...I let him control me."

Keefe responded instantly to the shame in her voice, reaching out to cup her chin in his hand and turn her face back to his. "It wasn't your fault, Tessa."

"Wasn't it?" Her wry smile nearly broke his heart. "I made the choice to stay with him."

"You were frightened."

"I was embarrassed," she corrected him.

"Embarrassed?" Keefe repeated, his brows going up in disbelief. "Embarrassed about what?"

"I didn't want other people to know what was happening, didn't want them to know what a sham my marriage was, what a mess I'd made of my life." She read the blank incomprehension in his eyes and smiled self-deprecatingly. "I guess it sounds pretty dumb. It *was* dumb. But I felt as if all I had was the facade, and if that was gone, I wouldn't have anything."

Keefe tried and failed to understand her reasoning. "What about your family? Didn't they know something was wrong?"

Tessa's laugh held little humor. "Have you forgotten who we're talking about? My parents were delighted when I married Bobby. He was rich, handsome and, even better, from a good family. I was never as pretty as Dana or as popular, but I married bet—" She broke off, her eyes widening, when she realized what she'd almost said.

"You married better than she did?" Keefe finished for her. One corner of his mouth curled in a rueful smile. "Don't worry about hurting my feelings. Your parents never made any secret of what they thought of me."

"They were wrong," Tessa said fiercely. "Dana was lucky to have you."

"Yeah? Well, there seem to be some differing opinions about that," he said lightly. He shifted the subject away from his marriage. "So you didn't feel you could go to your parents. What about Dana? I know the two of you weren't close, but under the circumstances…"

"I just couldn't." Tessa couldn't even begin to explain all the reasons she couldn't have told her sister about Bobby's abuse.

"Okay. What about Molly?" Keefe asked. "She would have helped you. I suspect she eats senators for breakfast."

Tessa's smile was shaky but genuine. "I wouldn't be surprised if Aunt Molly could single-handedly take on the entire Senate and have them on their knees by lunch." Her smile faded, and she shook her head. "There were times when I thought of going to her, asking her to help me. But she's so strong."

"And this is a bad thing?" Keefe asked.

"No. No, it's a good thing. But just thinking about her made me feel stupid and helpless—exactly the things Bobby said I was." Her fingers shook as she finished shredding the tissue into tiny pieces. Her voice dropped to a whisper. "I was so ashamed. I didn't want her to know the truth."

Keefe looked away from her, grabbing for his self-control. He wanted to shout that it wasn't her fault, that she was the victim in what had happened. He wanted to put his fist through a wall. But what he wanted most of all was to have Bobby Mallory standing in front of him, alive and well just long enough to give him the pleasure of beating him half to death.

He felt frustrated by Tessa's conviction that she'd somehow been to blame for her husband's abusive behavior. And he felt hopelessly ill-equipped to deal with the situation. She'd spent four years in an abusive marriage. She should probably have professional help, counseling. But all she had was him.

"It doesn't matter anymore why you didn't ask for help," he said, choosing his words with care. He looked at her, his dark eyes serious. "You're here now. And you're safe. You and your baby."

"Thank you." Tessa's eyes filled with tears of gratitude. He'd opened his home to her, taken her into his life as easily as if she had a right to be there. She wondered if he'd be as openly welcoming if she told him the whole truth.

Chapter 4

Tessa hadn't realized how much she needed to talk to someone about the nightmare that had been her marriage. *It wasn't your fault.* Four simple words that she'd desperately needed to hear. There was a part of her that had fiercely denied the blame Bobby heaped on her, a part that had insisted that she wasn't stupid, that she wasn't to blame for everything that went wrong in his life. That small core of belief had been all but suffocated by years of abuse. Hearing Keefe tell her that she wasn't to blame for what happened had lifted a burden of guilt from her.

She'd promised herself that she wouldn't spend time looking back, wouldn't waste a minute of her future in bitterness over the past. But it wasn't possible to close the past four years of her life behind a locked door and simply forget about it. She'd needed to look at what had happened, needed to really *see* it before she could finally start to let go of the pain.

Keefe had helped her do that.

Tessa leaned her forearms on top of a stall door and let her eyes roam over the pretty chestnut mare inside. It had been barely a week since she told Keefe about her marriage, but she felt as if in those few days she'd finally begun the process of moving forward with her life.

She shifted position and her belly bumped against the side of the stall, reminding her that there was one undeniable, unbreakable tie with the past. She frowned. It was just like Bobby to have found a way to control her life even from the grave.

"That's Lady. She generally manages to live up to her name."

Tessa had been occupied with her thoughts and hadn't realized she was no longer alone until Jace spoke from behind her. Startled by the sound of a male voice so unexpectedly close, she swung around to face him.

"Hey," Jace stretched out his hand. She recognized that the gesture was intended to reassure, but too late to stop her instinctive move to step back and put some distance between them.

The big barn was suddenly very quiet, as if even the animals were holding their breath. Jace let his hand drop.

"Sorry. I didn't mean to startle you." He smiled, but there was something watchful in his blue eyes.

"I'm the one who should apologize." Her laugh

sounded brittle, even to her own ears. "Stupid of me to react that way. I don't know why I did. I'm sorry."

"Don't apologize," Jace said easily. "I'm used to having women fall back in stunned disbelief when they see me. It's the price I pay for being so incredibly good-looking."

Tessa laughed, just as he'd intended, but privately she thought it wasn't much of an exaggeration. From the solid angle of his jaw to the sharp slant of his nose and the heavy wave of dark hair that fell onto his forehead, Jace Reno was classically handsome. But the vivid electric blue of his eyes, surrounded by thick black lashes, took him from merely handsome to something approaching pure masculine beauty. The fact that he seemed oblivious to his looks only added to his appeal.

"So, you and Lady were getting acquainted," he said as he came forward. He wasn't quite as tall as Keefe, or as broad-shouldered, but he still loomed over Tessa's five-foot-nothing, and she had to make a conscious effort not to edge away from him, to put some distance between herself and the danger represented by his size and masculinity.

"I don't think Lady was terribly interested in getting to know me," Tessa admitted, and was pleased by how casual she sounded—how normal. "She seems supremely disinterested in my presence."

"She's just being coy," Jace said. At the sound of his voice, the mare lifted her nose from the feed box and turned her head toward him. "She doesn't want to look easy, do you, girl?" The mare's ears swiveled forward, and she snorted, as if in confirmation.

"But I know her weakness," Jace said as he reached into the pocket of his faded blue work shirt. He pulled out a sugar cube and offered it to the mare. "She's got quite a sweet tooth."

Lady stepped across the stall and took the offered treat, crunching it between her strong teeth with delicate greed. Forgetting her uneasiness, Tessa moved closer, smiling at the mare's obvious enjoyment.

"Here. You feed her the next one." Tessa glanced from the sugar cube Jace was offering to his face. There was something in his eyes that made her wonder if he wasn't using the sugar to coax her closer, much the way he'd done with the mare. Her mouth softened into a rueful smile, and she reached out to take the sugar from him.

Lady snuffled the cube from her hand, and Tessa reached out to rub her forehead as the mare crunched the treat.

"I told you she could be bought," Jace said, leaning his hip against the side of the stall. "Just don't tell Keefe. He has this idea that sugar is bad for their teeth."

Tessa grinned at the furtive look he shot over his shoulder, as if he expected to find Keefe looming up behind him. "How ridiculous. He should know better."

"That's what I think." Jace gave her an approving look. "Nothing that tastes as good as sugar could possibly be bad for you."

"Just as long as you brush after every meal and floss at least once a day." She gave the mare a stern glance. "You do floss, don't you, Lady?"

As if on cue, the mare snorted and shook her head. Tessa and Jace both laughed, but Lady ignored them, more interested in getting her ears scratched than in whatever had amused her human companions.

"You're good with the horses," Jace commented. "I've seen you down here this last week. They like you."

"I like them, too." Tessa said. She heard the wistfulness in her voice and slanted a quick, self-conscious smile in Jace's direction. "I practically lived in the stables when I was a girl. I had all kinds of fantasies about being a horse trainer, or maybe a breeder. Silly stuff."

"Sounds reasonable enough to me," Jace contradicted. "What happened?"

"I...married someone who didn't like horses. He didn't even like me to ride. I kept it up for a little while after we were married, but it was such a hassle to drive to my parents' house every time I wanted to ride." *And Bobby had been furious when he found out I was still riding after he'd expressed his opinion of it.* Though the big barn was pleasantly warm, the memory of his anger was enough to make Tessa shiver. "It was easier to give it up," she finished, pushing the memories away.

"He was probably afraid of horses," Jace said.

"Who? Bobby?" Tessa shook her head. "He wasn't afraid of them. He just didn't like them."

"What's not to like? They're friendly. They'll give you a ride for the price of a bucket of oats." Jace gestured to the chestnut mare, as if to illustrate her finer points. "They're ecologically sound—no ozone depletion here. In my experience, a lot of people who say they don't like horses just don't want to admit that they're afraid of them.''

Tessa started to shake her head again and then hesitated. The idea that Bobby had been afraid of horses—afraid of anything, really—seemed ridiculous. In her mind, he was such a looming, threatening figure that she just couldn't imagine him being afraid of something as comparatively harmless as a horse. And yet...

There'd been a time, before they were married, when he came to her parents' house to pick her up. He'd been early, and she'd been in the stables, working one of the horses. When Bobby walked up to the corral, she'd ridden the big gelding up to the fence to greet him. Bobby had stepped back from the railing rather quickly, looking less than happy. She'd never been able to coax him any closer than that to a horse, even in the months when they were dating and he was still pretending that he wanted to make her happy.

Tessa glanced up and caught Jace's questioning look. She shrugged. ''I don't know. Maybe Bobby *was* afraid of horses. I never thought of him as being afraid of anything, except maybe his father.''

''Does his father look like a horse?''

''What?''

''Well, if his father looks like a horse, then maybe your husband was afraid of horses because they reminded him of his father.''

Tessa stared at him blankly for a moment and then burst out laughing. All she could think of was how much Robert Mallory would hate the idea of being compared to a horse—and yet his long, aquiline features might be considered vaguely equine.

Jace smiled, pleased with himself. He had the feeling that there hadn't been enough laughter in Tessa's life lately. It was good to hear her laugh and to see the shadows gone from her eyes, even temporarily. She was usually so quiet and serious that he sometimes forgot how young she really was, but for a moment she didn't look a day more than twenty-three.

"I don't think my father-in-law would appreciate the idea that he resembled a horse," she said when her laughter had subsided.

"I don't know why. I've known some very handsome horses."

"Come to think of it, so have I."

An easy silence fell between them. Jace leaned against the side of the stall and watched Tessa without seeming to watch her. She looked better than she had when she first arrived. The fine lines of tension that had bracketed her mouth were gone, as were the dark circles that had looked like smudgy fingerprints against her pale skin. She'd gained a little weight, which he thought was remarkable, considering the way she cooked. She smiled more often, and they were genuine smiles, not those bright, empty expressions that had no meaning.

But she was too young for the shadows that lurked in the back of her eyes, too young for the quick fear he'd seen in her face earlier. He would have given a great deal to get his hands on whoever had put that fear there. If his guess was right, the responsible party was currently facing a much higher authority. But there might be something else he could do to help Tessa.

"I could teach you self-defense." Jace said it so casually that it took Tessa a moment to realize what he'd said.

"Me?" She turned her head to look at him, her eyes wide with surprise.

"Sure. It wouldn't take long to learn a few basic techniques. A long time ago, in a land far away, I actually taught self-defense."

"*You* did?"

"Guilty." He moved away from the stall and sank into a half crouch, his elbows bent, his hands curved in front of him at chest level.

It was a pose she'd seen many times on television, usually assumed by some mystical-looking guy wearing a cotton robe and no shoes. Jace was standing in the aisle of a dusty barn, wearing jeans and cowboy boots. He should have looked ridiculous. But there was nothing ridiculous about the easy grace of his movements—dangerous grace, Tessa thought, looking at him. He was smiling, but she had the sudden sense that if he stopped smiling he might be rather frightening.

"Behold, the terror of the seamy element of downtown Dubuque."

"Dubuque?" Tessa gaped at him. "You're kidding."

"You think Dubuque doesn't have a seamy side?" Jace straightened and then slid back into what she'd come to think of as a classic cowboy slouch. One corner of his upper lip curled in a superior sneer. "Don't be naive. Evil lurks everywhere."

"In Dubuque?" she repeated.

"Okay, maybe not actual evil," he admitted sullenly. "Maybe more of a cranky element. But they were really scared of me."

"Cranky element?" Tessa giggled helplessly. "Did you subdue them single-handedly?"

He sighed heavily. "It was a tough job, but somebody had to do it."

"I hope the citizens of Dubuque were suitably grateful."

"A job well done is its own reward," he informed her in a superior tone.

"Of course it is." Tessa tried to remember the last time she'd had such a nonsensical conversation. It had been years. Maybe during that first summer after Keefe and Dana were married. Keefe had a similar flair for the ridiculous. She'd laughed more that summer than she had before or since.

"So, now that you know you're dealing with an expert, would you like some lessons in self-defense?"

Tessa's smile wavered. She shrugged. "I don't know that I have much use for self-defense."

"You never know. It's more than just the physical knowledge you gain. Knowing how to protect yourself can really boost your self-confidence."

"Is it so obvious that mine needs boosting?" Tessa asked ruefully.

"I didn't say that." Jace's smile took away any possible sting. "But it never hurts to know a few good moves."

"You're probably right." The idea of being able to defend herself held real appeal. She hadn't thought of it before this minute, but she suddenly realized that she didn't ever want to feel small and helpless again. But it wasn't quite that simple. "I'm not exactly in any condition to be throwing people over my shoulder at the moment," she said, brushing her fingers self-consciously over the solid bulge of her belly.

"Maybe not this minute," Jace agreed. "But we could start after the baby's born."

"That's two and a half months from now," she said. "I have no intention of imposing on you and Keefe for that long."

"Who says you're imposing? We both like the company. Besides, we like your cooking." It wasn't a lie, Jace thought. She was a terrific cook. She just didn't cook *enough*. "You wouldn't condemn us to endless pots of my stew and Keefe's charred steaks, would you?"

Tessa smiled a little and shook her head. The truth was, she didn't have anywhere to go if she left. She supposed a stronger woman would strike out into the world, make her own way and not use a mere pregnancy as an excuse for imposing on her ex-brother-in-law. But then, a stronger woman wouldn't have spent four years in an abusive marriage, either. She touched the top of her belly and then let her hand fall to her side, her breath escaping her in a soft sigh as she half turned away from Jace. "A lot can happen in a couple of months," she murmured, speaking half to herself.

"It must be hard to separate what you feel about

the baby from what you feel about the father,'' Jace said softly.

Tessa stiffened. "I don't know what you mean."

"Don't you?"

Almost unwillingly, Tessa looked at him. There was knowledge in his eyes—knowledge, and a compassion that undermined her already fragile defenses.

"Keefe—"

"Didn't say a word," Jace said, answering the question before she could ask it. "And I haven't asked him anything."

"Then how could you know?" she whispered.

"A long time ago, there was someone I cared for very much. You remind me of her a little."

"What happened to her?"

He looked past her, seeing things visible only to him. "She didn't get out in time," he said slowly. He blinked and seemed to almost physically shake off the memory. "You did."

"Circumstances threw me out," she corrected him. "As for the baby…" She sighed softly and set one hand against her stomach. It was the first time Jace had ever seen her touch her stomach the way pregnant women seemed to do so often, as if in silent communication with the life they carried. "I've never lost sight of the fact that whatever Bobby was, whatever he did, none of it was the baby's fault."

"It wasn't yours, either," he countered softly, and Tessa felt her eyes fill with quick tears.

For four years, she'd been held to blame for everything, whether it was the dry cleaner putting too much starch in Bobby's shirts or the caterer failing to provide enough glassware for a dinner party. Now, in the space of barely a week, she'd been told by two different people that she wasn't to blame for the abuse she'd endured.

"I wish I was sure of that," she said.

Jace heard the pain in her voice. He reached out and drew her into his arms. Tessa stiffened for an instant and then relaxed against him, allowing herself to draw on the comfort he was offering.

"The hurt will go away," he said. "You just have to give it time."

He bent to brush a kiss over her forehead. As he straightened, he caught a flicker of movement out the corner of his eye. He turned his head and saw Keefe standing a few feet away. The light was at his back, but Jace had no trouble reading the disapproval in his friend's expression.

Keefe leaned over to set down the bucket he was carrying. The soft thud as it hit the ground was enough to alert Tessa to his presence. She stiffened, and Jace let his arms fall away from her as she stepped back.

"Hello, Keefe." She tugged at the hem of the loose shirt she wore and then reached up to smooth back a tendril of wheat-colored hair that had worked its way free of the pins she'd used to pull it back. She was embarrassed that Keefe had caught her practically crying in Jace's arms. He was probably going to think that she made a habit of sobbing on every male shoulder that presented itself.

"Are you all right, Tessa?"

"I'm fine," she said, and then winced at the false brightness of her tone. "I...think I'll go start lunch."

She threw a quick smile in Jace's direction and left the barn as quickly as she could manage, considering that the bulk of her stomach precluded actually running.

Jace waited for Keefe to break the silence that fell after Tessa's departure.

"I don't want to see Tessa get hurt," Keefe said at last.

"Neither do I."

"She's vulnerable right now."

"Are you warning me not to seduce her?" Jace asked with a kind of irritated amusement.

Keefe scowled. That was exactly what he'd been trying to do, but said out loud, it sounded a little ridiculous. "Not exactly," he muttered.

"Because we're friends, I'm not going to ask you to explain 'exactly' what you did mean," Jace said. "But I'd like to point out that, while I may have done my share of catting around, I don't think I ever tried to seduce a woman who was six months pregnant and just starting to recover from an abusive marriage."

"She *told* you about her marriage?" Keefe asked in disbelief. He'd damn near had to pry the truth out of Tessa.

"She didn't deny it when I guessed as much," Jace said. "And it wasn't all that hard to guess. And I'll tell you something else." He jabbed a finger in the direction Tessa had gone. "That girl is running from something more than a bunch of pushy reporters. I don't know what it is, but she's scared to death of something."

Keefe didn't argue. The same thought had occurred to him. He didn't want to think that Tessa had lied to him, but he had the feeling that she hadn't told him the whole truth.

"Maybe," he admitted. "But whatever she's running from, I'd appreciate it if you'd watch your step while she's here. Like I said, she's vulnerable right now. A kid like her could misinterpret things, get the wrong impression."

There was a moment's silence. When Jace spoke, his tone was conversational. "If I didn't know that you're just trying to look out for Tessa, I think I'd probably do my damnedest to feed you a few of your teeth right about now. As it is, I'll consider the source. But let me point out—again—that I'm not in the habit of seducing vulnerable young women." He held up one hand to stop Keefe from interrupting. "And Tessa is hardly a kid. She's a widow, about to become a mother. Even without all that, twenty-three isn't exactly a babe in arms. She's a grown woman, and despite what's she's been through, she doesn't need you to play big brother. Neither do I." He brushed past Keefe and walked out of the barn with long, angry strides.

Keefe stood where he was for a moment. The big barn seemed to echo with silence. Using the side of his thumb, he pushed his hat back on his head and stared into the middle distance, contemplating his own capacity for stupidity. He knew Jace well enough to know he didn't need to be warned about Tessa's vulnerability. Jace Reno was about as likely to hurt her as he was to flap his arms and take off flying. It was just that, when he walked into the barn and saw Jace holding Tessa, he'd thought— What the hell *had* he thought?

He reached for his cigarettes. As he set a match to the tip of one, he glanced up and saw Lady watching him, her big eyes seeming to hold a reproach.

"I know I said I'd quit," he muttered defensively as he inhaled smoke. "I'm down to less than half a pack a day, okay?"

She snorted and shook her head in apparent disapproval before turning to go back to her interrupted lunch.

"I must be out of mind," Keefe said out loud. "First I insult my best friend, then I start making excuses to a horse."

He shook his head and watched the slow tendrils of smoke rise from the tip of his cigarette, drifting upward to disappear in a shaft of sunlight that spilled in through a dirty window.

Chapter 5

Keefe caught the phone on the second ring, stretching out one long arm to snag the receiver from the hook while continuing to turn the bacon sizzling in the skillet. On the other side of the stove, Jace was whisking milk into a bowl of pancake mix. Half a dozen eggs sat waiting on the counter, ready to break into the pan of bacon fat as soon as the bacon came out. Breakfast was the one meal Tessa didn't insist on cooking for them, and they made the most of it.

"Yeah?"

"You sound wide awake. I suppose you've been up for a couple of hours," a disgusted voice muttered in his ear.

Keefe grinned. His oldest brother, Sam, was not a morning person. "Barely an hour." He glanced at the clock, raising one brow in surprise. "What drags you out of bed so early? Or are you just getting off work?'' Sam was a police detective, and his hours could be erratic.

''I figured this was the only time of day I could be relatively sure of catching you in the house.''

''Is there a problem?'' Keefe caught Jace's questioning glance, the concern in his eyes. Their brief confrontation over Tessa the day before had blown over and been forgotten.

''No. Last I heard, everyone is okay,'' Sam said, correctly interpreting his brother's question. The Walkers were a tight-knit family. As far as they were concerned, if one member of the family had a problem, they all had a problem.

''So what's up?'' Keefe shook his head at Jace to indicate that there was no immediate emergency.

Jace nodded and reached out to take the fork. ''I got this.''

Keefe nodded and backed away from the stove.

''You got anything going on I should know about?'' Sam asked on the other end of the line.

''What do you mean?''

''Somebody's been making inquiries, asking about us.''

''*Us?* About the Walkers in general, or me in particular?'' Keefe immediately thought of the reporters Tessa had said were bothering her. He'd had his doubts about the truth of that. Maybe he'd done her an injustice.

''According to my sources, someone's been asking around about all of us. Some pretty sophisticated computer inquiries. This computer crap is all a mystery to me but apparently they really know their stuff.

I already talked to Gage and Cole, but neither of them has a clue."

"I might know what it's about," Keefe said slowly. "Tessa Wyndham showed up a couple of weeks ago."

"Wyndham? As in Dana?" Sam's voice rose, the last of the morning sluggishness vanishing in surprise.

"Her sister."

"She showed up at the Flying Ace? Why?"

Keefe repeated Tessa's explanation as succinctly as possible, ending with "I guess she figured that, since Dana and I didn't exactly remain friends, this was the last place anyone would look for her."

"I sure as hell wouldn't expect to find any of your ex-in-laws seeking refuge with you."

"Tessa was different," Keefe said, answering the annoyance in Sam's tone, more than his comment. "She's a nice kid."

"Kid? How old is she?"

"Twenty-three."

"Not exactly a little girl," Sam commented, unknowingly echoing Jace's words.

"She's young enough to seem like a kid to me."

"Yeah, thirty-seven makes you practically old enough to be her grandfather."

"Well, I'm damn near old enough to be her father," Keefe snapped.

Sam's snort of laughter was echoed from behind him, and he turned on one heel to glare at Jace's back. "Don't forget who you're talking to," his brother said. "You weren't fathering any children at fourteen."

"I didn't say I was." Keefe couldn't figure out how he'd ended up having this discussion. "All I said was that I was nearly old enough—"

"Yeah, I heard you the first time." Sam interrupted with the casual rudeness possible of an older brother. "I'm older than you are, and I don't feel anywhere near old enough to be the father of a twenty-three-year-old."

Neither did he, Keefe thought. But this wasn't just any twenty-three-year-old they were talking about. This was Tessa and, for some reason, it felt important to make sure that everyone understood that his relationship with her was strictly familial.

"Speaking of fatherhood, when are you and Nikki going to make me an uncle again?" he asked, deciding a change of subject was in order. He knew his brother and sister-in-law had been trying to get pregnant for the past few months.

"Not in the next few months." It was said casually enough, but something in Sam's tone set off warning bells.

"Problem?"

The silence on the other end of the line spoke volumes. "Not exactly," Sam said finally. "Nikki's worried that something might be wrong. She's talking about going in for tests."

"Seems a little soon for that, doesn't it?"

"That's what I said, but she's hell-bent on finding out why she isn't pregnant."

Keefe could hear the worry in his brother's voice, and he sought to offer reassurance. "Maybe, once she's had the tests and realizes there's nothing wrong, then she'll be able to relax.''

"Maybe, but from what I can gather, it can take years to pin down an infertility problem—*if* there is one. I don't want Nikki going through one test after another, each one more invasive than the last. Having kids isn't that important to me.''

"But maybe it is to her," Keefe said quietly.

"Yeah." Sam sighed. "It is to her."

They spoke for a moment longer, and Sam promised to let Keefe know if he found out anything more about whoever was making inquiries about the Walkers. Keefe hung up the phone and turned to find Jace scooping the last of the fried eggs out of the bacon fat.

"Everything okay?" he asked as he set a plate on the table.

"Yeah." Keefe pulled out a chair and sat down. "Sam wanted to let me know that someone's been making some computer inquiries about the family."

"Tessa's reporters?" Jace glanced across the table, his expression questioning.

"Could be. Seems odd that they'd be looking at the Walkers, though. Tracking me down might be a long shot, but it makes some sense. But Tessa never even met the rest of my family." He stabbed a pancake with his fork and dropped it on his plate.

"Who else has a reason to be looking you guys up?" Jace slathered butter on his own pancakes.

"Nobody I know of." Keefe shrugged. "We aren't that hard to find."

"Gotta be somebody looking for Tessa, then."

"Seems likely."

"You going to mention this to her?" Jace asked as he sprinkled a generous quantity of Tabasco sauce on his eggs.

"I don't think so. It may not have anything to do with her. Even if it is a reporter, she already knows they're looking for her. Why worry her? If they track her down, we'll deal with them."

"*If* it's a reporter," Jace commented. It was a reminder of the doubts they both had on that score.

"We'll deal with whoever it is," Keefe said flatly. Whoever—whatever—Tessa was hiding from, they were going to have to come through him to get to her.

The truth will make you free.

For the first time in Tessa's life, she felt as if she understood the meaning of those words. She'd spent four years thinking that nothing could be more terrible than for someone to find out the truth. That fear had been a part of the reason she never tried to escape her marriage to Bobby. Yet, now that it was out in the open, she felt as if a huge burden had been lifted from her. Perhaps it shouldn't have made as much difference as it did. It wasn't as if her marriage had suddenly become a topic of casual conversation, but there was a tremendous relief in just knowing that she didn't have to pretend anymore.

"Come on, now. You're not really afraid of this saddle. You're just acting skittish to show you've got a sensitive nature, aren't you?" The young horse rolled one eye at the saddle Jace was holding and demonstrated her sensitive nature yet again by shying away when he moved closer. "Come on, now. Show some courage. You don't want everyone to think you're a coward, do you?"

"I don't think she's worried about what we think," Tessa commented as Jace's voice drifted across the corral to where she and Keefe stood watching him try to coax the mare into letting him put a saddle on her back for the first time.

"I doubt it, but Jace claims that appealing to an animal's pride is the best way to get them to do what you want."

"Does it work?"

Keefe shrugged. "I don't know, but I do know Jace is about the best I've ever seen when it comes to talking a balky horse into letting him on its back. Only person I've ever seen that's as good or better is Kel Bryan, a friend of mine who runs a place in Wyoming. Kel works a little different, but they've both got a way with horses that's close to magic."

Tessa leaned her arms on the top rail of the fence as she watched Jace coax the skittish mare to accept the saddle. It was late in the afternoon, the sun was warm on her back, dinner was simmering on the stove, she had nothing she had to do, nowhere she had to be. For the first time in years, her life was hers to do with as she pleased—almost hers, she corrected herself, as her belly bumped against the fence. But today, not even that reminder could spoil her contented mood.

"Did Jace grow up on a ranch?" she asked Keefe.

"Not that I know of." He set one booted foot on the bottom rail and leaned his elbows on the top. Tipping his hat back on his forehead, he reached for his cigarettes, then glanced at Tessa and slid them back in his pocket.

"I don't mind if you smoke," she said, catching the movement out the corner of her eye.

"I'm trying to quit, anyway. It's a lousy habit, and I've heard rumors it's bad for your health."

"No kidding? I've heard the same rumors." She looked at him, her eyes laughing while her mouth remained serious. "Do you think there's any truth in them?"

"Probably not, but I figure there's no sense in taking a chance."

His lazy grin stirred emotions that Tessa had thought long dead. The years melted away and, for a moment, she was a girl again and deep in the throes of her first—and only—infatuation. The rest of the family might think Dana had married beneath her, but as far as Tessa was concerned, Keefe was as nearly perfect as it was possible for a person to be—a great deal more nearly perfect than her spoiled older sister deserved.

"Do you remember that first summer after you and Dana got married?" she asked.

"What about it?" Keefe's gaze shifted back across the corral to where Jace was still talking, soft and low, to the young horse.

"Did you know that I had the most tremendous crush on you that summer?"

"What?" He jerked his attention back to her.

"You must have guessed," Tessa said, laughing a little at his startled expression. "I practically lived in the stables that summer. Even my parents commented on it, and they rarely noticed my existence."

"I thought you were horse-crazy."

"I was. But I was even more crazy about you."

"You were just a kid," he protested. "I was twenty-eight."

"I was fourteen—just the right age for a mad infatuation. You were tall, dark and handsome and, best of all, you didn't care that I was skinny and plain and wore braces."

"You weren't plain," he protested.

"Pigtails, braces, freckles, skinned knees and a bra size that read in the negatives?" Tessa shook her head as she listed the physical failings that had made her early teenage years miserable. "I was a disaster. But you didn't seem to notice any of it. That might have been enough to throw me into a state of mild infatuation, even if you hadn't been so gorgeous."

"Gorgeous?" he repeated, sounding appalled. Much to Tessa's amusement, color crept up over his cheekbones.

"Gorgeous," she repeated firmly, taking a mischievous pleasure in his obvious embarrassment.

"I think you needed glasses more than you needed braces," he muttered. He reached up to tug his hat down so that the brim shadowed his face.

Tessa's laugh drew a reluctant smile from him. For a minute, she looked very much like the girl he'd met that summer. Despite what she thought, she'd been far from plain. She'd been too thin and solemn to be truly pretty but, even then, there'd been a sweet, almost fey charm about her. He remembered thinking that, when she was older, it would be a lucky man who captured her affection. Remembering that now, he felt a renewed anger that things had turned out the way they had. Tessa deserved so much more than what she'd gotten.

"Well, I think I've got her just where I want her." Jace's comment interrupted Keefe's thoughts as he approached across the corral.

"I must have missed something. I thought the point was to get the saddle *on* the horse, not for you to carry it around," Keefe said.

"It's all a matter of strategy," Jace said as he swung the saddle up onto the top rail of the fence. "Now she knows she doesn't have to be afraid of the saddle."

"Looks to me like she's doing a victory dance," Keefe said, nodding toward the mare, who was trotting along the back fence, tossing her head.

"Strategy," Jace repeated, ignoring Tessa's laugh. He slid between the fence rails and straightened, his eyes going over Keefe's shoulder. "Are we expecting company?"

"Not that I know of." Keefe and Tessa both turned to look at the cloud of dust making its way toward the ranch. "Jim Sinclair said he'd stop by sometime this week to take a look at that gelding of his, see how the training is going."

"It would go better if that horse wasn't the dumbest animal I've ever seen," Jace said. "I'm afraid to leave him out in the rain for fear he'll turn his head up to the sky and drown, like a damned turkey."

"I think that's an old wives' tale," Keefe said as Tessa giggled. "I don't think turkeys are really that stupid."

"No? Well, that horse is." Jace frowned at the dust cloud. "Come to think of it, Jim Sinclair ain't much brighter."

"He doesn't have to be bright. All he has to do is pay us for training his horses."

"True. Let's hope he doesn't get caught in a rainstorm before he can write us a check."

Keefe's chuckle was drowned out by the crunching sound of tires on gravel as a car drew to a stop in front of the house. It was a new car, a white, four-door sedan of undistinguished make and model. Dust settled slowly on and around it after it came to a stop.

"Not Jim Sinclair," Jace commented.

"Doesn't look like it," Keefe said as the doors opened.

The couple who got out of the car were as out of place in the dirt ranch yard as a Waterford vase in a mud hut. Both were in their mid-to-late fifties. The man was tall and lean, with silvery gray hair that gleamed in the sunlight. He wore a conservatively tailored charcoal-colored suit and a pair of shoes that had probably cost more than most people's mortgage payments. The woman was nearly as tall. Her hair was a colorless shade that could have been either very light blonde or gray. She wore a tailored dress made of some nubbly fabric in a shade of red that made Keefe think of cranberries. A black-and-gray scarf was tied around her neck in an elegant bow and she wore black pumps.

The whole outfit—both of them—would have looked right at home in an office or maybe in a fancy restaurant, but plopped down in the middle of the Flying Ace, they looked more than a bit out of place.

"Got to be lost," Jace said, taking in their elegant clothing and general air of wealth.

"I figure." Keefe started toward the newcomers, but Tessa grabbed his forearm, her fingernails digging through the fabric of his shirt and biting into his skin. Startled, he glanced down. She was looking at the older couple, her face tight and still, her eyes full of fear. She looked as if her worst nightmare had just come to life.

Whatever she was running from, it had just caught up with her.

Chapter 6

"You certainly did manage to bury yourself in the back of beyond, didn't you, Tessa?" It was the man who spoke, his tone pleasant, his expression almost amused. "It's a long drive from here to just about anywhere. I didn't expect it to take us this long to find you."

Tessa didn't move as he approached, but the color drained from her cheeks, leaving her as pale as she'd been when she first arrived, and Keefe had the sense that she was shrinking in on herself, trying to make herself smaller, less noticeable, as if she could somehow vanish from sight. He felt a quick rush of anger directed toward the stranger who had so easily stripped her of the fragile layer of confidence that he'd seen building over the past few weeks.

He took a half step forward, forcing Tessa to release her hold on his arm as he moved in front of her, stepping between her and the newcomers. At the same time, Jace moved forward so that the two men stood nearly shoulder-to-shoulder.

The older man stopped and looked from one to the other, his pale eyes taking in the unmistakably protective posture, the cool warning in two gazes—one brown, one blue. His dark brows rose slightly, but that was the only outward sign that he recognized the message.

"It's nice to see that Tessa has such good friends," he said, his affable smile unwavering. "Which one of you is Keefe Walker?"

"I am," Keefe said, unsmiling.

"I'm pleased to meet you, Keefe. I'm Robert Mallory. Senator Mallory." He put a slight but unmistakable emphasis on the title.

Keefe hesitated an instant before taking the man's hand. *Senator* Mallory? This must be the father-in-law Tessa had told him about, the one she'd said was a powerful man, both politically and personally.

"And you must be Jace Reno," Senator Mallory said, extending his hand to Jace.

Keefe raised one brow. No doubt Mallory intended the casual use of Jace's name to impress, and it succeeded, at least to the extent that it demonstrated how much he knew. He thought of his conversation with Sam three days ago. His brother had said that someone was making inquiries about the entire Walker family. Keefe had no doubt that he was looking at the driving force behind those inquiries. Tessa's former father-in-law had the power to start a search like the one Sam had described. But that didn't explain why he'd wanted to find Tessa or why she should be so terrified of being found by him.

"This is my wife, Anne," Mallory said, completing the round of polite introductions.

"Mrs. Mallory." Good manners dictated acknowledgment of the woman, although, from the look of cool disdain on her patrician features, he doubted she appreciated his consideration.

"I do hope you intend to acknowledge us, Tessa," Robert Mallory said, his falsely pleasant tone laced with a condescension that set Keefe's teeth on edge. "We've come quite a long distance to see you. I hope you don't plan to hide behind Mr. Walker all the time we're here."

"Of course not." Tessa's voice was colorless.

Keefe glanced at her as she moved to stand beside him, and saw that her expression matched the voice. This was how she'd looked those first few days after she came to the ranch, as if she'd put up a wall somewhere inside herself and the real Tessa was crouched behind that wall, hiding—leaving nothing but a shell for the rest of the world to see. His hostility toward the man in front of him increased.

"You're looking well, Tessa. You've been taking care of yourself, I hope." Something in Mallory's tone made Keefe think that there was more to the inquiry than polite concern. Of course, she *was* carrying his grandchild, which gave him something of a vested interest in her well-being, but Keefe had a gut feeling that there was more to it than that.

"I'm fine, thank you," Tessa said in that same colorless little voice.

"I'm glad to hear it. Perhaps there's somewhere we could talk?" He phrased it as a request, but his tone made it a command.

"Do you want to talk to him, Tessa?" It was Jace who spoke, his blue eyes ice-cold. He stood with his legs slightly spread, his hands held loosely at his sides, a subtle threat in the stance. If Tessa didn't want to talk to her former in-laws, he was obviously willing to escort them from the property.

Tessa would have given a great deal to be able to take him up on the unspoken offer. The last thing she wanted to do was talk to Bobby's parents. She didn't want to talk to them or even to see them ever again. She'd run three thousand miles to avoid them, but deep inside, she'd always known that she couldn't run far enough or fast enough to get beyond Robert Mallory's reach.

"I'll...talk to them," she said quietly. *He can't hurt me,* she reminded herself. *He has no hold over me. He can't make me do anything.*

"We can talk up at the house," Keefe said.

"This is a private conversation, Mr. Walker," Senator Mallory said, his tone pleasant but firm. His mouth smiled, but his eyes were cool and watchful.

"Tessa?" Keefe spoke to her, but his gaze remained unwavering on the other man.

"You don't have anything to say that Keefe and Jace can't hear," she said.

"I'm sure you don't mean that." Anne Mallory spoke for the first time, her well-modulated voice revealing the influence of the expensive finishing schools she'd attended. "This is family business, Tessa. We don't need outsiders."

"Keefe and Jace aren't outsiders." Arguing with her mother-in-law took courage. In her four years of marriage, she'd learned the hard way that it was safer to acquiesce. But her fear of dealing with Bobby's parents was enough to overcome years of conditioning.

"Don't be ridiculous—"

"We're staying." Keefe's flat statement ended the discussion and brought a pinched tightness to Anne Mallory's mouth. Her husband was no happier with the arrangement than she, but years in politics had taught him to accept defeat graciously.

"In that case, perhaps we could move this indoors?"

Keefe wondered what the penalty was for punching a United States senator. Was there some law on the books that made that a worse crime than simply decking an ordinary citizen? Mallory's smile tempted him to find out.

No one spoke as they walked up to the house. Keefe and Tessa led the way, his hand resting on the small of her back. He glanced down at her, but could read nothing from her expression. Whatever she was thinking or feeling, she was keeping it hidden—something she'd probably learned to do during her marriage, he thought, and felt angry all over again at what she'd endured.

Five people crowded the living room. Or maybe it was taut emotions that made the room seem filled to overflowing. Anne Mallory sat down on the sofa, her feet, in their expensive black pumps, set side by side with military precision, her hands lightly clasped in her lap. Her husband took a position near the fireplace, well-shod feet slightly apart, suit jacket pushed back to allow him to slide his hands into the pockets of his slacks.

Tessa sank down in the big leather chair. She was grateful for its support, even more grateful that Keefe stood next to her, one hand resting on the back of her chair. Jace took a position a little behind his partner.

Like armies facing each other across a battlefield, she thought.

"I generally offer guests some refreshments," Anne Mallory said, looking at Tessa.

Tessa responded immediately to that familiar tone of quiet reproach. She'd heard it often during the past four years. Bobby had repeatedly told her that she was stupid. His mother never had to say the words out loud. She was able to convey her disappointment in her daughter-in-law with nothing more than her tone of voice.

"I'm sorry," Tessa said automatically. She started to rise, but Keefe set one hand on her shoulder, stopping the motion.

"This obviously isn't a social call. Let's not pretend otherwise," he said flatly.

Anne's mouth tightened, but Robert's smile remained unwavering. Keefe was starting to hate that smile.

"I admire a man who knows how to cut to the chase, Mr. Walker. It's a rare quality in my line of work."

"So, why are you here?" Jace asked.

"You could say we've come to finish a conversation we'd begun with Tessa shortly before she left home so precipitately."

"The conversation was finished before I left," Tessa said. Inside, she was trembling and scared, but her voice was steady. She was proud of that. It was proof that she'd changed in the weeks since she packed her bags and ran away in the middle of the night.

"I don't believe we had finished it."

His avuncular tone made Tessa's stomach knot. How many times had she heard him use that same tone with Bobby? How many times had that soft, concerned voice delivered words sharp enough to draw blood and then left her to bear the brunt of her husband's rage at his inability to stand up to his own father?

That's all over now. She drew a shallow breath and forced down the familiar wave of fear. She didn't have to be afraid anymore.

"I gave you my answer."

"But not your *final* answer, I hope."

"Does somebody want to fill us in on what the question was?" Jace asked.

Tessa met her father-in-law's eyes. Beneath the surface expression of false concern she could see contempt. He didn't think she'd answer Jace's question. He thought she was too frightened of him. A few weeks ago, he would have been right. She'd been afraid of her husband, but she'd always known that the real power in the family lay in her father-in-law's grasp. Bobby had known it, too, and it was that knowledge, more than anything else, that had made him what he was, that had fueled his rage.

But Bobby was dead, and she was no longer alone. She had friends, people who cared about her. The knowledge helped ease the knot in her stomach. Tessa lifted her chin and met Robert Mallory's eyes directly.

"They want the baby," she said, in answer to Jace's question. "They want to take it and raise it as their own." She had the satisfaction of seeing a flicker of surprise in her father-in-law's eyes.

"Your baby?" Jace asked.

"Our grandchild," Anne Mallory said, before Tessa could respond. "All that's left to us of our son."

"Tessa's child," Keefe pointed out. "I think a mother's claim has priority."

"Not if she doesn't want it," Anne's tone made the words an accusation. She looked at Tessa with something approaching hatred. "And she doesn't want it. She hates this baby as much as she hated my son."

"I don't hate this baby," Tessa said, the words coming with difficulty. Her feelings toward the life she carried were too complex to be so easily categorized.

"You hated my son," Anne said, her elegant features made ugly by hatred.

"If she hated your son, she had reason." Keefe set his hand on Tessa's shoulder, and she drew strength from that light touch. "Men who abuse their wives rarely inspire much affection."

There was an instant of dead silence. Anne sucked in an audible breath, her expression shocked. Her husband's features tightened and, for just a moment, Tessa saw the real man, rather than the political facade he took such care to show the world. The glimpse sent a chill down her spine. It was gone immediately. His frown was sorrowful, rather than angry.

"I'm disappointed in you, Tessa," he said, his tone heavy with regret. "I never thought you'd tell that ridiculous story outside the family."

"You knew?" Keefe sounded disbelieving. His hand tightened on Tessa's shoulder. "You knew what was going on and you didn't do anything to stop him?"

Robert shook his head. "I don't know what Tessa has told you, Mr Walker, but—"

"Not nearly as much as she could have," Keefe told him, interrupting ruthlessly. "I know enough to know that your son was a miserable bastard who made himself feel like a man by beating his wife. And if you knew what he was doing and didn't do anything to stop it, you're no better than he was."

"How dare you—"

"Anne!" Her husband's sharp tone cut through Anne Mallory's furious protest. She fell instantly silent, but her hands were clenched in her lap, and her face was flushed with anger.

Robert looked at Keefe. "A small piece of advice, Mr. Walker—don't make judgments until you know all the facts. I appreciate your loyalty to Tessa, but you might want to consider the fact that you haven't seen her in quite some time. Not since your divorce from her sister, I believe. People change in that time."

"If you're suggesting that Tessa is lying about what your son did to her, you can save your breath." Keefe couldn't ever remember feeling such a soul-deep rage.

"I don't think it's fair to say that she's lying," Robert said carefully. "I think Tessa actually believes what she's saying. Her doctor says we shouldn't blame her for these little 'stories' she tells."

"What doctor?" Keefe demanded.

"Why, her psychiatrist, of course." Robert looked surprised. "Didn't she tell you about Dr. Mendham? She's been seeing him for the last three years."

"No!" Tessa gasped out the denial. She twisted around in her chair, looking up at Keefe with panic in her eyes. "It's not true, Keefe. I haven't been see-ing him. I swear it!"

"It's all right." He sank down on the arm of the chair. Putting his arm around Tessa's shoulder, he drew her against his side. She was trembling like a leaf in a high wind. He looked across the room at the senator and felt a moment of real regret that murder was not a viable option.

"There's no reason to lie about it, Tessa," Mallory said. "There's no shame in being treated for an ill-ness."

"I'm not ill," she whispered. She pressed her fore-head against Keefe's side, the fingers of one hand curling into the faded blue chambray of his shirt.

"Dr. Mendham runs a very fine clinic near our

home," Mallory said, ignoring Tessa and addressing his words to Keefe. "Not long after Bobby and Tessa were married, we realized that she had a...problem with the truth. Dr. Mendham has been treating her ever since."

"Are you saying she's a pathological liar?" Jace asked incredulously.

"I'm not sure of the exact clinical term for Tessa's illness." Mallory shook his head, his expression one of deep regret. "She'd made a great deal of progress, but then, after Bobby's death, she seemed to get worse. No doubt the stress was just too much for her rather fragile mental state."

"He's lying," Tessa whispered, pressing closer to Keefe. "I'm not crazy."

"No one has ever used the word crazy, Tessa. We've told you again and again that no one blames you for your illness. We just want to see you get better. That's why Dr. Mendham has been treating you and keeping such careful records of your visits to him," he added in a gentle tone that sent chills down Keefe's spine.

He couldn't have made the threat any more clear if he'd laid it out in plain English. Whoever this Dr. Mendham was, he was willing to produce records that said he'd been treating Tessa for the past three years. Keefe tightened his arm around her, trying to offer wordless reassurance.

"So, your argument is that Tessa isn't mentally stable enough to have care of a baby, and that's how you plan to force her to give the child to you."

"We don't want to have to *force* her to do anything,'' Mallory said. "We were hoping that Tessa would see that this is the best thing for all concerned, particularly for the baby.''

"No.'' Tessa straightened in the chair, turning to face her father-in-law. "No. I won't give this baby to you.''

"You can't possibly think that you could win a court battle,'' Anne said, speaking for the first time in several minutes. "Robert is a *senator.*''

"Senator or no, I think the courts lean pretty heavily toward the mother in a case like this,'' Jace said.

"Not when she's mentally unstable. What's more natural than for us to want to raise our grandchild? After losing our only son in a tragic accident, we—''

Jace's inelegant snort cut her off in midsentence. "Tragic accident? That's not the usual term for a drug overdose. Cocaine, wasn't it?'' He caught Keefe's surprised look and shrugged. "I read the papers.''

"That's a terrible lie. Bobby didn't use drugs.'' Anne's voice was shrill, and her eyes were wild. Keefe realized that, whatever else was false—and almost everything about the Mallorys was false—her grief was real. He supposed that a better man might feel more compassion for her pain, but all he could think of was that she'd known what was happening to Tessa and done nothing to stop it.

"The papers seem to think otherwise,'' Jace said. He shrugged again. "Of course, a lot of it is probably speculation, but I'd guess the rumors haven't done much to raise your stock in the party's eyes, Senator. A presidential candidate with a drug addict for a son isn't exactly a dream come true. A grieving father shouldering the responsibility for his grandchild—that looks considerably better, doesn't it?''

Not a trace of emotion showed in Mallory's eyes. ''The reasons really don't matter, Mr. Reno. What matters is that my wife and I can provide a much better environment in which to raise a child. If necessary, I can provide proof that Tessa is unstable. I would prefer not to do so, of course, but we *will* get custody of our grandchild.''

The cold threat in his tone seemed to lower the temperature of the room by several degrees. Keefe's arm was still around Tessa's shoulders, and he felt a sharp tremor move through her. That little movement solidified his determination to do whatever he had to do to protect her and the baby she carried.

''There's only one problem with this scenario,'' he said, his tone easy.

''What's that, Mr. Walker?'' Mallory's tone held an impatient edge.

Keefe tightened his grip on Tessa's shoulder. She was stiff as a board, and he knew she was holding herself together with sheer willpower. The knowledge put an edge in his voice. ''This baby you're so hell-bent on taking away from its mother?''

''Our grandchild,'' Ann Mallory reminded him, as if that were all the excuse they needed to ride roughshod over Tessa's rights.

''No, it's not,'' Keefe said.

''Not what?'' Mallory asked.

''Not your grandchild.'' Keefe's fingers tightened

on Tessa's shoulder and then relaxed. "The child Tessa is carrying is mine."

Tessa had never before understood what people meant when they said they'd had an out-of-body experience, but the phrase suddenly made perfect sense to her. For a moment, she seemed to see the whole scene from outside herself, as if she were looking at a photograph.

She could see herself, looking small in the big chair. She saw every scuff mark and worn spot on the aged brown leather with perfect clarity. Keefe sat next to her, one foot braced on the floor, his arm around her shoulder. His tanned, work-roughened hand contrasted sharply with the pale blue sand-washed silk of her loose shirt. In his faded jeans, boots and work shirt, he looked as if he'd stepped right out of a western movie. Jace stood on Keefe's left, similarly dressed, his hands held loosely at his sides, like a gunfighter waiting for the right moment to draw his weapon.

On the other side of the room from the three of them were the Mallorys—expensively dressed, perfectly coiffed, their expressions holding equal measures of disbelief and outrage.

That was when Tessa realized that this must all be a dream. Because only in a dream would it be possible to see her former in-laws expressing such honest emotion. In real life, neither of them ever allowed anything to ruffle the surface calm they wore like armor. But anything was possible in a dream, including seeing the Mallorys gape like trouts. Even hearing

Keefe claim her baby as his own made sense, if this was a dream.

"That's impossible," Robert Mallory snapped.

"What makes you think so?" Keefe asked.

"We *know* the baby is our son's."

"How do you know?"

"Tessa would never have dared to be unfaithful to Bobby," Anne Mallory said calmly, her usual control back in place.

"She wouldn't have *dared?*" Keefe repeated the phrase in a tone of soft menace. "Because she was afraid of him? Because he was a wife-beating son of a bitch, which you knew and refused to do anything about? Is that why Tessa wouldn't have dared?"

"There was no abuse. We've already made that clear." Mallory shot a warning glance at his wife, who lowered her eyes. "Tessa wouldn't have been unfaithful to our son because she knew it would be wrong. Isn't that right, Tessa?"

Tessa felt herself pinned by his pale gaze. His expression reminded her of the way Bobby would look at her just before he told her how she'd failed yet again, before he— She slammed a door on the memory. That was the past. This was the present, and it was neither dream nor nightmare. But she wasn't alone this time, facing a husband who would express his displeasure with his fists.

For the first time in her life, she had someone to stand with her, friends who believed in her. Keefe's lie would buy her time—time to decide how to combat her in-laws, time to find somewhere else to hide, if she had to. All she had to do was back him up.

"He's telling you the truth. It's not Bobby's baby," she said, astonished by the steadiness of her voice.

"You don't expect us to believe this ridiculous story?" Mallory asked, his genial facade slipping fractionally.

"I don't see that you have much choice," Keefe said calmly.

"Of course we have a choice. A paternity test would prove, beyond the shadow of a doubt, that this is my son's child."

"I don't need a paternity test. I know Keefe is the father," Tessa said.

"I'm sure I could arrange for a court order requiring you to submit the child for a paternity test," Mallory said.

"Now, that would make a nice headline," Jace commented, his tone casual. "'Senator forces son's widow to submit to paternity test.' It certainly does have a ring to it, doesn't it? Something like that would probably be just the thing to reignite interest in your son's death."

"It wouldn't reflect particularly well on Tessa," Mallory said tightly.

"But Tessa isn't hoping to be the next president of these United States," Jace pointed out almost gently.

Keefe shot his friend an appreciative look. He'd never realized what a good liar Jace was, though, considering what he knew of Jace, maybe he should have guessed.

"I don't have much experience with the press myself,'' Keefe drawled. ''But I'd be willing to bet that they could have a field day with a story like this.''

Mallory's expression told him that the senator was well aware of the damage a scandal like the one they were describing could do to his career. At the very least, it would end his chances of a presidential bid. Rage and frustration warred in his eyes, all traces of false affability disappearing in a rush of genuine emotion. He was trapped and beaten, at least for the moment, and he knew it.

''This isn't finished,'' he said tightly.

''I disagree.'' Keefe rose from his seat on the arm of Tessa's chair. ''I don't think there's anything left to say, except perhaps to make sure you understand that Tessa isn't alone anymore. She has friends now— family. If you cause her a problem, you'll have us to deal with.''

Mallory sneered. ''Very noble.''

''Just a statement of fact,'' Keefe said calmly. ''I think it's time you left. And perhaps I should warn you that, if you set foot on my property again, I'll call the law and have you hauled off for trespassing.''

''Now wouldn't that make a hell of a headline?'' Jace commented wickedly.

Mallory ignored him. He glanced at Tessa, and then his gaze locked on Keefe. ''This isn't over.''

Keefe didn't argue. Tessa had to be nearing the end of her rope, and there was no sense in prolonging the scene. ''Jace, do you mind seeing Senator and Mrs. Mallory off the property?''

''My pleasure.'' Jace stepped back to leave a clear path to the door. ''After you.''

Anne Mallory rose, her spine stiff as a poker, her expression icy enough to freeze a lava flow. She looked at Tessa with something approaching hatred in her eyes. "You didn't deserve my son," she said in a tone of contempt.

"I agree with you on that one," Keefe said, feeling Tessa flinch away from the venom in the older woman's voice. "She certainly deserved a great deal better than a man who was so weak he had to pound on her just to make himself feel strong."

Anne whitened and, for a moment, he almost regretted his harsh words. Whatever else he was, Bobby Mallory had been her son, and he was willing to believe that his death had genuinely grieved her. But then he remembered that this woman had known what was happening to Tessa and had done nothing to stop it, and his sympathy ebbed.

"Come, Anne." Mallory put a hand beneath his wife's elbow and urged her toward the door. "There's no point in saying anything more."

Jace's eyes met Keefe's as the couple walked past him. "I'll see them to the highway," he promised. He glanced at Tessa, who seemed to be huddled in the big chair. He looked as if he might say something to her, then changed his mind. Without another word, he turned and followed the Mallorys out of the house.

Tessa listened to the silence that followed the closing of the door. She should say something. Something that would show that she was calm and in control. But it was hard to sound in control when what she really wanted to do was collapse in a quivering, sobbing heap.

"Thank you," she said, her voice barely above a whisper.

"My pleasure. Getting rid of obnoxious senators is something of a specialty of mine."

His light tone brought Tessa's head up. He was smiling at her, and she felt the nervous knot in her stomach start to unwind. "You're very good at it," she said, smiling a little shakily.

"Thanks." Keefe's smile faded, and he sank down on the battered ottoman that sat in front of her chair. The position put their eyes on the same level. "You don't have to be afraid of them, Tessa. Even if it came to a court case, no judge would award custody to them. You don't have to be afraid of losing your baby."

Tessa looked away, focusing her gaze on the amateurish painting of a horse that hung on the wall next to the fireplace. The painting had come with the house, along with most of the furniture, Keefe had told her.

"The painting is crooked," she said.

Keefe followed her gaze. "So it is."

"Bobby knocked me across the room once for not straightening a picture properly." She said it almost casually. Keefe felt the hair on the back of his neck rise at the image her words evoked. The idea of someone hitting her because of a crooked picture—or for any other reason—made his stomach knot with anger. He looked back at her, and Tessa's eyes slowly shifted to his face. "I wasn't sorry when he died."

"No one could expect you to be sorry," he said, wondering where this conversation was headed.

"When the police came to tell me he was dead, I didn't feel anything at first. I didn't even feel anything when I had to identify his body. Shock, I guess." She smoothed her fingers over the knee of her stretch pants, her eyes on the aimless movement. "It wasn't until the next day that I really started to feel something, and then it was anger."

"Anger's a natural thing to feel when someone dies," Keefe said cautiously. He felt as if he were tiptoeing through an emotional mine field.

"I wasn't angry because he'd died. I was angry that he hadn't died sooner. I kept thinking that, if he'd died sooner, I'd have been truly free. But as it was, I was still trapped."

"Because of the baby," Keefe guessed.

"Because of the baby." She lifted her eyes to his face, and he felt his heart twist at the stark pain he saw there. "I don't want the baby," she admitted, rushing the words as if that were the only way she could get them out. "It was Bobby who wanted it. He thought it would make his father happy. If I...if there'd been a way to do it without Bobby finding out, I would have...I wouldn't have had this baby."

Keefe caught her hands in his, stilling their restless movements. He held her eyes with his. "Tessa, did he...did he rape you?"

"Oh, no!" Her denial was quick, but she continued before he had a chance to feel relieved. "I didn't want... But then, I never did, not after the first few times. I wasn't very good at...well, at 'it.'" She looked away, color running up under her pale skin. "Bobby said it was like having sex with a plastic blow-up doll—that I didn't *do* anything. But I could never figure out what I was supposed to do." Her shoulders lifted in a helpless little shrug. "After a while, I just stopped trying. He didn't... We didn't sleep together very much after the first few months. At first, I wondered if he...had other women, but I don't think he did. I don't think sex was particularly important to him. Once in a while, he'd come to my room. I didn't... But it was easier to just let him. The last time he... That's when I got pregnant." The choppy little sentences trailed off. She kept her gaze focused on their linked hands. "Then he died, but it was too late."

Keefe looked at her downbent head and wished, for the hundredth time, that he'd had the chance to meet Tessa's husband and beat him to a bloody pulp. As near as he could tell, the only decent thing the bastard had ever done was kill himself with drugs, and he hadn't even done that soon enough.

"What do you plan to do when the baby's born?" he asked her.

She shook her head, her fingers tense in his. "I don't know. I thought I might see about a private adoption. But I don't know. What if, after it's born, I can't give it up? I've made so many mistakes. I don't want to make another one."

"If you don't want the baby, why not give it to the Mallorys?" he asked.

"I couldn't do that." Tessa raised her head and looked at him as if surprised that he could ask such a question. "They made Bobby what he was. I know it sounds melodramatic, but I think they're truly evil people. I would never let them get their hands on a child. This baby is the one true innocent in this whole mess."

Keefe could have pointed out that she was as innocent of wrongdoing as the child she carried, but he doubted she'd hear him.

Keefe was on his way to bed when he saw light gleaming along the bottom edge of Tessa's door. He stopped and stared at that thin streak of gold. He'd been thinking ever since the scene with the Mallorys this afternoon. His common sense said that what he'd been thinking was crazy, but he couldn't shake the idea that had come to him.

Now, looking at the light under Tessa's door, he hesitated. He hadn't planned on talking to her tonight, but there was really no reason to put it off until morning. Tessa had barely spoken all through dinner, and the haunted look had been back in her eyes. Maybe hearing what he had in mind would ease her worry. Of course, maybe it would convince her that he was crazy, he thought ruefully. But, crazy or not, he was going to talk to her about it. He lifted his hand and knocked.

"Come in."

He pushed open the door. A table lamp cast a pale circle of light across the bed and created deep shadows around the edges of the room. Tessa was standing beside the window, staring out into the moonlit darkness. She was wearing a cheap ankle-length blue terry-cloth robe, belted awkwardly above the bulge of her stomach. Beneath it, he could glimpse a plain white cotton nightgown. Her hair was pulled back from her face and held by a gold-toned clip at the base of her neck. She looked young and vulnerable.

"Have you ever noticed the way the snow on the mountaintops catches the moonlight?" she asked without turning. "It looks like someone spilled frosting on them."

"A little bit." He glanced out the window but he had things on his mind besides the natural beauty of the mountain. "I've been thinking, Tessa, and I've got an idea that might solve your problems with the Mallorys and with what to do about the baby."

"I think that would take a miracle," she said softly.

The despair in her voice solidified his determination. It might not be a miracle, but he knew what he had in mind would work. All he had to do was convince her of that. Thrusting his hands in the pockets of his jeans, Keefe sought the best words to tell her what he was thinking. In the end, the best words—the only words—were the simplest.

"I think we should get married."

Chapter 7

"What?" Tessa turned from the window and stared at him, her eyes wide with shock.

"I think we should get married," he repeated.

The words didn't seem any more real the second time he said them than they had the first.

"Why?"

"When you think about it, it's the obvious solution to your problems."

"Obvious?"

"It makes perfect sense."

"It does?" She lifted one hand to her head, wondering if pregnancy caused auditory hallucinations.

"Here." Keefe crossed the room with quick strides and took her by the arm. "Sit down and I'll explain it to you."

"That would be nice," Tessa said, allowing him to lead her over to the bed. She sank down on its edge and waited for him to explain why getting married was so obvious and made such perfect sense.

Seeing her expectant gaze on him, Keefe cleared his throat and took a moment to organize his thoughts.

"If we get married, it will get your former in-laws off your back. They didn't believe for a minute that I'm the father of your baby, which means they're not just going to give up and leave you alone. You could leave, but if they found you here, they could probably find you anywhere you went. Anyway, you can't spend the next couple of months on the run."

Tessa couldn't argue with that. Her thoughts had been running along just those lines for the past few hours.

"If we get married, it makes my claim to the baby that much stronger. They might still be able to force a paternity test, but my bet is that they won't risk the negative publicity, and I think we convinced them that we would be sure the whole thing was public knowledge. The fact that you're married and can provide a traditional home for the baby is bound to weaken their case, even these days, when single parenting is so common."

He'd been pacing the room as he spoke, but he turned to look at her now. "Are you with me so far?"

"I'm with you, but... Oh, Keefe—" Tessa's voice cracked a little on his name "—I can't tell you how much it means to me that you'd be willing to do something like this for me, but I can't possibly let you."

"Why not?"

"Because I'm not a total user." Her laughter held

little humor. "I know it's hard to believe, considering the way I descended on you, but I do have some pride."

"What does pride have to do with it? You need help. I can provide it."

"It's not that simple. You'd be putting yourself at risk. I don't think you understand how powerful Senator Mallory is. You don't want him for an enemy."

Keefe cocked one brow, his mouth twisting in a half smile. "It's a little late to be worried about that, isn't it? I don't think he was feeling particularly warm and fuzzy toward me when he left here."

"No, he wasn't." Tessa looked distressed. "I hate it that I've dragged you into the middle of this. He can be a very dangerous man."

"If you ask me, his wife is more dangerous than he is. Good old Robert is always going to do what's best for his career. I'm not so sure about her. I'm not too sure she has both oars in the water."

"Anne was devastated by Bobby's death. At the funeral, I had the feeling that she wanted to throw herself into the grave with him." A chill slid down her spine at the memory of her mother-in-law's grief. She forced the memory aside and focused on the present. "The Mallorys may not be crazy about you at the moment, but it's nothing compared to how they'll feel if you get in their way again. They're absolutely determined to get custody of this baby."

"The best way to see that that doesn't happen is for us to get married," Keefe said firmly.

"It's a crazy idea," Tessa said. "Marriages of convenience only happen in books."

"You might be surprised," Keefe said, smiling a little as he thought of his older brother's marriage. Sam and Nikki had barely been able to stand the sight of each other when they said "I do." They'd married for practical reasons and ended up falling in love. Thinking of them was what had given him this idea in the first place. Not the falling-in-love part of it, of course. *That* certainly wasn't going to happen if he and Tessa got married.

"I wouldn't be surprised. I'd be astonished," Tessa said, interrupting his thoughts. "Marriage isn't something you jump into casually."

"This isn't casual." He ran his fingers through his dark hair, frowning a little as he tried to think of a way to make her see how practical the idea was. "If you strip it of the usual emotional complications, marriage is basically a contract, that's all. Marriage to me will provide you with an extra level of protection. The Walkers may not wield a lot of political leverage, but we're pretty hard to push around."

Tessa felt herself weakening. She had to be even more tired than she'd realized, because what he was suggesting was starting to make sense. Surely, if she was married to Keefe and he was willing to claim this baby as his, Bobby's parents would think twice about forcing her into a custody battle.

"I can't use you like that," she said, and wished she sounded more definite in her refusal. "And don't tell me you'd do this for any friend. Marriage goes way beyond offering hospitality. If marriage is a contract, then there has to be benefits to both people. This 'contract' is completely one-sided. Thank you for your incredibly generous offer, but I just can't accept."

Keefe looked at her, and Tessa thought she read an uncharacteristic indecision in his expression, but it was gone so quickly she thought she might have imagined it.

"Would it make you feel better if you thought I was getting something out of it?"

"What on earth could you possibly get out of marrying me?" Tessa asked blankly.

"You said you've been considering arranging a private adoption after the child is born," he said slowly.

"Y-yes." Tessa's agreement was tentative. She knew adoption was the most practical option, but she wasn't entirely sure she'd be able to go through with it. Her feelings for the child she carried were confused and ambivalent. That was why she hadn't contacted an adoption attorney yet.

"What if you didn't have to arrange an adoption? What if you could just leave the child with your husband?"

"My..." Tessa's voice trailed off, and she stared at him blankly for a moment. "You? You want to adopt my baby?"

"If we were married and I was listed on the birth certificate as the child's father, it wouldn't take an adoption. I could simply have custody of the child."

"But why would you—? You don't want a child!"

"Actually, I think I do." Keefe laughed a little, sounding as if he found the idea almost as astonishing as she did. "I've been thinking about it ever since you told me you wanted to give up the baby. And the more I thought about it, the more right it seemed.''

He was pacing again, his long strides eating up the distance between door and window and then back again. Energy vibrated from him, making Tessa feel almost dizzy. Or maybe it was his suggestion that had set her head spinning.

''It's not the kind of thing you can decide on the spur of the moment,'' she said.

''It's not spur-of-the-moment. I've always wanted children, but after Dana and I got divorced, I kind of gave up on the idea. I thought about adoption a couple of times, but it's still pretty tough for a single man to adopt. And I've been busy with the ranch and all. I'd pretty much decided that fatherhood wasn't in the cards for me.''

''You might remarry,'' Tessa pointed out.

''Anything's possible,'' he said, his tone making it clear that, on the possibility scale, he ranked remarriage somewhere between Sasquatches and little green men from Mars.

''Lots of people get divorced and then remarry. There's no reason you won't do the same.'' It distressed her to think of him giving up on marriage. She didn't like to think of him being alone.

''I'm not saying I'll never marry again.''

Keefe stopped by the window and looked out at the moonlit landscape. Tessa's concern was an echo of what he'd heard in Molly Thorpe's voice at Cole's wedding reception and the worry he sometimes saw in his mother's eyes. He knew they all thought that divorce had made him bitter about marriage, but they were wrong. He thought marriage was a damned fine arrangement when it worked. If he'd ever doubted that, he had only to look at his three brothers, see the difference marriage had made in their lives. He wasn't against marriage in general, and he wasn't bitter about his own marriage. But only a fool failed to learn from his mistakes. And his marriage to Dana Wyndham had been a mistake of epic proportions, one he wasn't anxious to repeat.

"I could get married again," he said, turning to look at Tessa. "Anything's possible." His mouth curved in a half smile. "But some things are highly unlikely."

Tessa looked down to hide the distress she felt. Dana must have hurt him badly. She wondered if he still loved her beautiful older sister.

"Even if it was likely that I'd marry again, that doesn't mean I couldn't adopt this baby," Keefe said, interrupting her thoughts. "I'd be a good father, Tessa."

"I know you would." Tessa pressed two fingers over the ache starting to build behind one temple. It was too much to absorb all at once. She was still reeling from the confrontation with her in-laws, and he was throwing a brand-new twist into the situation. "I just don't know, Keefe. It's… I just don't know," she said helplessly.

"You don't have to make a decision right now," he said. "Think about it as long as you want, but I know it could work."

He sounded so sure. Tessa realized that she wanted to believe him. It would be so easy to agree, so easy to let Keefe take care of everything. But she couldn't just take the easy way out. She had to try and decide what would be best for all of them—herself, Keefe, and the unborn child.

She set one hand against the heavy bulge of her stomach. She rarely let herself think of the child she carried in anything more than the most abstract of terms, yet, in an odd way, all her recent actions had been dictated by the desire to do what was best for the baby—the one complete innocent in the disaster her life had become.

"I don't know," she murmured, speaking more to herself than to him.

"Marrying me wouldn't obligate you to give up your baby," he said quietly, his eyes understanding. "You could take your time, be sure that was what you wanted."

"That's not fair to you," she protested.

"Let me worry about what's fair to me." He slid his hands into his pockets and gave her a smile that made her heart crack a little.

"Oh, Keefe—" Her voice broke on his name, and she felt tears sting the back of her eyes. She lifted her hands and let them fall helplessly. "I don't understand."

"What don't you understand?" He pulled his hands out of his pockets and closed the small distance between them, sinking down on his heels in front of her, putting their eyes nearly on a level.

"Why you're so nice to me." She looked at him with honest confusion, her eyes bright with tears she refused to shed. "No one has ever...cared enough to...to do things for me, and you...just... You can't just marry me to keep me safe, Keefe. You can't.''

"Seems like a pretty good reason to me," he said. He caught her restless hands in his. "Stop worrying about taking advantage of me, Tessa. And stop making me sound like Mother Teresa's nearest competition. This isn't such a big deal.''

"Marriage is a pretty big deal," she protested.

"It doesn't have to be. Tessa, I want to do this. I want to help you, take care of you and the baby.'' His tone was coaxing, and she felt herself weakening.

After Bobby died, she'd hadn't been able to imagine herself marrying again, but her imagination had stopped short of the kind of arrangement Keefe was suggesting. It was insane, of course. There was no reason to believe that marrying Keefe would protect her from her former in-laws. Even if it would, she had no right to drag him farther into her problems.

She dragged her eyes from his face and looked down at their joined hands. His palm was hard, callused by work, unmistakably masculine. In contrast, her fingers looked delicate, fragile. Helpless.

Tessa caught back a sigh. She'd been so determined to stand on her own, to never let herself depend on anyone again, to be strong. But maybe there was strength in knowing her own limitations. She couldn't fight the Mallorys by herself. She didn't have the strength. She needed Keefe, needed what he was offering. If she'd had only herself to worry about, it would have been different. But it wasn't her they wanted. It was the baby. She wasn't as sure as Keefe was that marrying him would stop Bobby's parents, but if there was a chance it would work, she had to take it. For the baby's sake.

"All right." Her agreement came so quietly that it took Keefe a moment to realize what she'd said.

"All right?" he repeated. "You'll marry me?"

"If you're sure that's what you want." Her eyes were full of doubt. "Are you sure?"

"I'm sure." Keefe grinned at her, his fingers tightening over hers. "You won't regret it," he said.

Tessa managed a weak smile. She wasn't worried about whether or not *she'd* regret it.

"Walker." Sam's voice was slurred with sleep.

"Did I wake you?"

"Keefe?" Sam was instantly alert. "What's wrong?"

"Nothing. I need to ask a favor." Keefe was well aware that this call could have waited until morning—*should* have waited until morning—but he hadn't been able to resist the urge to call Sam. Though he was close to all his brothers, he was closest to Sam.

Dead silence echoed from the other end of the line. "You called me at—" there was a pause while Sam looked at the clock "—midnight to ask a favor?"

"I need you to arrange a wedding."

"A wedding?" Sam sounded as if he were still half-asleep. "Whose wedding?"

Keefe laughed. He was feeling strangely euphoric for a man who was about to make drastic changes in his life. "*My* wedding. I'm getting married."

"You're doing what?" Sam's voice rose to something just under a bellow, all traces of sleepiness gone. Keefe heard his sister-in-law's voice in the background, and then Sam's response. "Go back to sleep. It's Keefe and he's drunk."

Keefe laughed again. He hadn't expected to find anything amusing about his decision to marry Tessa, but Sam's reaction struck him as funny. "I'm sober as a judge," he assured his older brother.

"I've known some pretty boozy judges," Sam said darkly. A police officer, he held no illusions about the sobriety of those who ran the legal system. "If you're not drunk, then you must be suffering from a head injury. Did you get thrown on your head?"

"Nope. I'm sober and sane."

"Who are you planning on marrying?"

"Tessa."

There was a moment of silence while Sam considered the name. "Tessa? Tessa who's staying with you? Tessa Wyndham? Dana's kid sister?"

"She's not exactly a kid," Keefe said, his good humor fading a little. Reminded of the fourteen-year gap in their ages, he felt uncomfortably like a cradle robber. But he'd only have to worry about that if this was going to be a real marriage. As things stood, the age difference didn't really matter. Still, the reminder made him feel vaguely defensive. "She's twenty-three."

"What does her age have to do with anything?"

"Nothing."

"Then why are we discussing it?" Sam demanded irritably.

"You brought it up."

"I did not." Sam's voice rose on the denial, and

Keefe heard Nikki say something, her tone concerned. "He's not drunk. He's stark, raving mad," Sam told his wife without bothering to cover the phone.

Keefe grinned. Maybe he was a little crazy. He knew Tessa thought so. But, crazy or not, he wanted this marriage. His smile faded as he considered just how much he wanted it, but he shoved the thought aside. His gut told him this was the right thing to do. He didn't want to look any deeper than that.

Tessa's first wedding had taken six months to plan. There had been three hundred guests in the church and nearly twice that many at the reception. Her gown had been made of ivory silk satin, trimmed with hundreds of seed pearls, each hand stitched in place. Cobweb-fine lace had trimmed the sleeves and neckline. More pearls had been scattered across the floor-length veil, and the gown's train had been longer than she was tall. Selected members of the press had been allowed to attend, and pictures of the bride and groom had been on the society pages of every major newspaper in the country.

Her second wedding bore little resemblance to the first. The arrangements were made in barely a week. The only guests were the groom's family and the bride's great-aunt. This time, her wedding dress was an off-the-rack maternity gown that Molly Thorpe purchased for her in Santa Barbara. It was simply cut and made of pale blue cotton sprinkled with white daisies. There was no church with vaulted ceilings and sunlight gleaming through exquisite stained-glass windows. Instead, the ceremony was held at Keefe's mother's home.

Tessa stood in the bedroom Rachel Walker had shown her to the night before. She was getting married in less than an hour. She remembered back to her first wedding. An hour before the ceremony, a makeup artist had been artfully darkening her brows, lengthening her lashes and adding fullness to her lips. When he was done and she looked in the mirror, she'd felt as if she were seeing another woman's face painted over her own, obliterating all traces of Tessa Wyndham.

Looking back, it seemed his work had been prophetic. The girl she'd been had vanished forever that day. The problem was that she wasn't sure just who she'd become in the four years since then. Looking at her reflection in the mirror over the dresser, Tessa wished she knew who the woman looking back at her really was.

Someone knocked on the door, and she turned, grateful for the interruption. But her gratitude was replaced by uneasiness when she saw who her visitor was.

"I thought you might like some help getting ready," Rachel Walker said as she entered the room and closed the door behind her.

"That would be nice," Tessa lied, wondering why Rachel had really come.

She'd met Keefe's mother for the first time the day before, when she and Keefe and Jace arrived at Rachel's home in Los Olivos, a small town not far from Santa Barbara. Rachel had been pleasant, accepting

Keefe's introduction with unruffled calm, as if finding out her son was marrying a woman who was seven months pregnant with another man's child was an everyday occurrence.

Tessa knew better than to believe that facade. Bobby's mother had been the soul of gracious acceptance when they were introduced. It had been months before Tessa realized how much Anne Mallory resented her. Maybe Rachel Walker preferred to take the gloves off right away, she thought. Maybe she'd come to put a stop to the wedding. Her fingers twisting unconsciously in the belt of her robe, Tessa waited for the older woman to start the conversational ball rolling.

"Perhaps I could help you put your hair up?" Rachel suggested. "If you plan to wear it up, that is."

"I hadn't given it any thought," Tessa admitted. She turned to look at her reflection, but the pale woman in the mirror made her uneasy, and she looked away. "I guess I should do something with it, shouldn't I?"

"It looks very nice down," Rachel said. "But, if you'd like to put it up, I could give you a hand."

"I... Thank you."

"Here. Why don't you sit down, and I'll see what I can do?"

Tessa sat down in the chair Rachel dragged over in front of the mirror.

"You have lovely hair," Rachel said as she began brushing it.

"Thank you."

Tessa knew she should think of some pleasant bit

of chitchat. If there was one thing she'd learned in the four years she was married to a politician's son, it was how to converse with total strangers. If she could exchange pleasantries with the president, she should certainly be able to say a few words to the woman who was about to become her mother-in-law. But her mind remained blank. All she could do was wonder what insanity had possessed her, that she'd agreed to this marriage.

"When is the baby due?" Rachel asked, breaking the silence before it became too obvious.

"Two months." Tessa's response was subdued. She knew Keefe had told his family the truth about why he was marrying her. His mother must surely hate her for the way she was using him, and Tessa couldn't blame her. She could never expect Rachel to understand how desperately she needed the shelter Keefe had offered.

"I always thought those last few weeks were the hardest." Rachel gathered Tessa's hair in one hand and began twisting it into a soft knot.

"Did you?" Tessa couldn't imagine how the last two months of her pregnancy could be any more difficult than the first seven had been.

"It was the waiting, I think," Rachel continued cheerfully. "Wondering if it was a boy or a girl, trying to decide on names. Too much anticipation, I guess."

"Probably." Tessa tried to sound as if she knew exactly how Rachel must have felt. It wasn't hard to understand. Most women probably felt the way Rachel did. Anticipation, excitement, hope—those were

normal emotions for a woman about to bring a new
life into the world. She wished she could feel that
way, wished she could feel something besides— She
couldn't even put what she did feel into words. It was
as if there were an empty space inside where all that
sweet anticipation and eagerness should have been.
She felt almost numb.

"Do you know if it's a boy or a girl?" Rachel
asked as she slid pins into place, deftly securing
Tessa's golden hair into a soft knot on top of her
head.

"No, I—" Tessa choked on the lie that she wanted
to be surprised. The truth was, she didn't want to
know if it was a boy or a girl, didn't want to know
anything that might make the child she carried seem
more real. "No, I don't know," she said in a flat little
voice.

Something made her lift her eyes, and her gaze met
Rachel's in the mirror. What she saw there shocked
her. There was compassion in Rachel's eyes. Compassion and concern and—most astonishing of all—
understanding. Tessa looked away quickly, her eyes
stinging. She didn't want to cry. She'd done enough
of that to last a lifetime.

"It's all right, you know," Rachel said softly.

"No, it's not." Tessa didn't pretend not to understand. "I should be stronger. It's not right to let
Keefe... I don't want to use him."

"Don't underestimate my son." Rachel smiled a
little as she teased a few locks of dark gold hair loose
from the knot and coaxed them to lie against Tessa's
nape. "Keefe is no one's fool."

"I never thought he was," Tessa said quickly. "I think he's kind and generous. Too kind and too generous."

Rachel's warm chuckle was unexpected enough to bring Tessa's gaze back to the mirror. The older woman's eyes sparkled with humor. She shook her head a little.

"Don't make him out to be a saint, either. He has his share of faults."

Tessa couldn't think of any, but it didn't seem polite to argue with Keefe's mother, so she said nothing. Rachel's smile deepened. She set her hands on Tessa's shoulders and squeezed gently.

"There. I think that looks nice."

Tessa allowed her attention to shift to her hair, relieved at the change of topic. She didn't feel as if she had the right to discuss Keefe with his mother. Her hair did look nice. Rachel had pinned it up in a soft knot, with a scattering of fine curls left loose around the sides. The style was both simple and attractive.

"It looks very pretty. Thank you." It was the first completely natural smile Rachel had seen. It lit Tessa's face, giving her an almost gamine beauty, and Rachel found herself wondering if Keefe was being totally honest with himself about the reasons for this marriage.

"Are you sure you know what you're doing?" Sam asked.

Keefe glanced in the mirror as he slid a tie under his shirt collar. Less than an hour before the wedding, and all three of his brothers were crowded into the small bedroom, offering to help him get ready for the wedding. He could have pointed out that he'd been dressing himself for quite a few years now, but he didn't bother. He knew they weren't here to make sure he buttoned his shirt straight.

"I'm getting married," he said, giving the most obvious answer to Sam's question.

"Yeah, but do you know what you're doing?" Gage asked dryly. Three years younger than Keefe, he shared his brother's dark coloring, but where Keefe's eyes were deep brown, Gage's were a clear, sharp blue.

"I know what I'm doing," Keefe said. He frowned at his reflection in the mirror as he fumbled with the tie. He wore one so seldom that he always had to relearn how to knot it.

"You're getting *married*," Sam said.

"That's what I just said." Keefe tugged loose a half-tied knot and started over again. "I know exactly what I'm doing. I'm marrying Tessa Wyndham."

In the mirror, he saw his brothers exchange a look among themselves. Caught between exasperation and amusement, he let the ends of the tie fall free and turned to face them.

"Look. I haven't lost my mind, and I'm not under the influence of illegal substances—or legal ones, for that matter. Tessa needs someone to look out for her for a little while. Marriage is the best way to do that. It's no big deal."

"Sure. No big deal." Cole nodded, as if that made perfect sense to him. His usually rumpled dark gold hair was neatly combed for a change. His tone was mocking, but there was real concern in his brown eyes. "Any friend of mine needs looking after, I'd certainly marry them."

"Don't you think your wife might object?" Gage asked dryly.

"Nah. Addie's real understanding."

"I've always wondered what it would be like to have been born an only child," Keefe commented, to no one in particular.

Gage grinned. "Think of all the fun you'd have missed if we hadn't been around to add excitement to your otherwise dull and uneventful life."

"You mean if you hadn't been around to make my life hell," Keefe said.

"Hey, what are brothers for?" Cole asked.

Keefe looked at Sam. "Tell me again why we let them live to grow up."

"It seemed like the right thing to do at the time," Sam said, looking as if he had his doubts now.

"It's too late to change your mind," Cole said.

"I suppose so," Keefe said wistfully. He turned back to the mirror and tackled his recalcitrant tie again.

"Speaking of changing your mind," Sam said. "You're really sure about this wedding thing?"

"I'm sure."

"Because it's not too late to call it off. Between the four of us, we ought to be able to keep Tessa's evil in-laws at a distance."

"*Ex*-evil in-laws," Keefe corrected him as he tucked the end of his tie through the knot and pulled it snug. He studied the end result in the mirror for a moment before reaching for his suit jacket. He looked at his brothers as he shrugged into the garment. "Look, you guys, I appreciate the concern. I know you all think I've lost my mind."

"Hell, *that's* been missing for years," Gage murmured.

"But I actually have thought this through," Keefe continued, ignoring the interruption. "This isn't as crazy as it looks."

"It couldn't be." That was Cole, adding his two cents' worth.

"It's not a big deal," Keefe insisted. "All it's cost me is a marriage license, a little time and a lot of harassment from the three of you. Now, if you'll all get out of my way, I've got a wedding to attend."

He knew he hadn't convinced them. Hell, he hadn't even convinced himself. No matter how many times he told himself that a marriage license was nothing but a piece of paper, a simple legal contract that could be interpreted in any way the participating parties wished, he couldn't shake the feeling that he was taking an irrevocable step.

But that was ridiculous. He, of all people, knew just how easy it was to break this particular contract.

"Dearly beloved, we are gathered together in the sight of God and these witnesses..."

Tessa had heard the words before, of course. In movies and on television. She'd attended other people's weddings and listened as ministers of a variety of denominations recited more or less the same service. A lifetime ago, she'd stood in front of an altar, trembling with nerves and filled with hope, as she gave herself into Bobby's keeping. There was nothing she hadn't heard before, yet it all sounded different this time.

For better or worse, for richer or poorer, in sickness and in health. The solemnity of the vows struck her in a way they never had before. *As long as you both shall live.* She was promising to spend the rest of her life with Keefe. Her hand trembled, and she felt his fingers tighten over hers, as if offering her silent reassurance. Almost reluctantly, Tessa lifted her eyes to his face. He was watching her, his dark eyes calm and steady, as he repeated his vows.

Standing here, in his mother's living room, which was filled to overflowing with his family, they were promising that this union would last forever, that they were going to grow old together, that they'd found everything they wanted in each other.

They were playing pretend. But what would it be like to stand here and listen to Keefe promise to love her forever and know that he meant it?

You may kiss the bride.

The words seemed without meaning until she saw Keefe's mouth tilt in a crooked smile as he bent his head to hers. Tessa drew in a quick, startled little breath and her free hand lifted to his chest—whether in protest or for support, she couldn't have said. His mouth settled over hers in a kiss that asked nothing but acceptance. The gentle warmth was as unfamiliar as it was irresistible. Tessa's lips softened beneath his, her body curving subtly toward his as her fingers curled around the lapel of his suit jacket.

The kiss lasted only a few seconds, but that was long enough for Tessa to feel the world shift beneath her feet. This was what it should have been like the first time, this sense of rightness, of belonging. She'd never felt that with Bobby, never felt her world settle into place just because he was next to her.

Keefe lifted his head slowly, ending the kiss as softly as it had begun. Tessa wished she could read the expression in his eyes, but she looked away, afraid of what he might read in hers. What if her eyes revealed her sudden, desperate wish that this was all real?

Chapter 8

"Okay. Enough of that." Sam's voice broke into the taut little silence that had fallen at the end of the ceremony. "As head of the family, I claim the right to kiss the bride first."

"Head of the family?" Gage repeated the phrase derisively. "What makes you head of the family?"

"If a superior intellect isn't reason enough, how about seniority?" Sam asked. Ignoring the less-than-impressed snorts from his brothers, he took Tessa by the shoulders and bent to kiss her cheek. "Welcome to the family, Tessa."

"Thank you," she murmured. She felt dazed by the realization of what she'd just done. Married. She was married to Keefe. It didn't seem possible.

"My turn," Cole said, elbowing his eldest brother aside. "Seniority or not, you don't get to hog the bride." His dark eyes smiling, he planted a kiss on her cheek. "Welcome to the Walker madhouse, Tessa."

"Out of the way, little brother." Gage smiled down at her. "Try not to judge us all by my brothers' uncouth behavior, Tessa. Some of us are quite civilized."

If she hadn't known otherwise, Tessa would have thought that the Walkers believed this was a real marriage. They welcomed her to the family as if she belonged, as if she were marrying Keefe for love rather than expediency. When she remembered the cool, formal congratulations that had followed her marriage to Bobby—a "love match"—she had to swallow an hysterical urge to laugh. There was something irresistibly ironic about the contrast between the two.

Keefe watched Tessa accept his family's good wishes with shy pleasure and thought back to his first wedding. He and Dana had gotten married in Vegas, in a chapel lit by multicolored neon candles. None of his family had been there—only Jace and Kel Bryan, another friend from the rodeo circuit. He'd worn a pair of almost-new jeans and a crisp western-style shirt, and he'd slapped polish over the worst of the scuffs on his boots. The bride had worn white—a midthigh-length knit dress that clung to every curve and exposed an astonishing length of tanned leg. A ceremony stripped of all the traditional trimmings had amused Dana. He remembered being vaguely grateful that they weren't being married by an Elvis imitator.

Funny that, this time around, when he wasn't marrying for love, the ceremony should seem so much more real. He'd found himself listening to the words as if he were hearing them for the first time. When he married Dana, he hadn't felt this need to protect her, to take care of her. But then, Dana hadn't needed anyone to protect her. She'd been well able to take care of herself.

Tessa was so totally unlike Dana that it was hard to believe that they were even related. Despite her cool blond beauty, Dana had radiated a fiery sexuality. A man had only to look at her and his thoughts veered toward cool sheets and hot sex.

Tessa was a completely different story. She was attractive, though her beauty was quieter, less obvious than her older sister's. But she had something more than physical beauty. There was an inner sweetness, a gentle warmth, that Dana had never had. Tessa cared—about other people, about what was right. Tessa was...special. She deserved a great deal more than the hand life had dealt her so far.

Keefe frowned a little as he considered the kiss that had come at the end of the ceremony. That kiss had felt more real than he liked to admit, even to himself. Her mouth had yielded to his so sweetly and she'd leaned into him so trustingly that, for a moment, he'd forgotten that this was all for show, forgotten that he was just doing this to protect her, and almost lost himself in the warm, womanly taste of her. There hadn't been anything avuncular about that kiss.

His frown deepening, Keefe reached for his cigarettes, then remembered where he was and let his hand drop. He'd almost given the habit up, but there were still moments when he craved a nicotine fix. The moment he realized he was attracted to his bride was one of them.

Molly Thorpe hugged her great-niece with a strength that belied her years. The delicate scent of White Shoulders perfume wafted Tessa back to childhood, when visits to her Aunt Molly's California ranch had been the highlight of every summer. She closed her eyes and, for just a moment, allowed herself to pretend that she was that little girl again, looking forward to weeks of California sunshine and horseback riding. Life had been so much simpler then.

"You've got yourself a good man," Molly said as she stepped back and looked at her great-niece. The rest of the wedding party was busy admiring Gage and Kelsey's infant daughter, the youngest member of the family, leaving Tessa and her aunt momentarily alone.

"He's not mine," Tessa reminded her. "You know that. This isn't a real marriage."

"Looked pretty real to me," Molly said.

"Well, it's not. It's just a…temporary arrangement to protect me and the baby. Keefe has been incredibly generous, and he's—"

"Don't make the boy out to be a saint," Molly said, in an acid-toned echo of Rachel Walker's words. "I've known him a good bit longer than you have. He's one of the best but he's not ready for a halo and wings. Truth is, he's as pigheaded as they come. Once he's made up his mind to do something, it's like arguing with a mud fence to try and get him to change course." From the irritated tone of her voice, Tessa assumed that Molly was speaking from experience. "Still, he's a good man. Your sister was a fool to let him go, but you were always a great deal brighter than she was. If you've got half as much sense as I think you have, you'll hang on to him."

"Hang on to him?" Tessa gaped at the older woman. "I can't do that! He's not mine."

"Nonsense!" Molly said briskly. "You're married to him, aren't you? Possession is nine-tenths of the law."

Before Tessa could think of an appropriate response to that astonishing statement, Keefe came up to them.

"How are you holding up?" He set one hand against the small of her back, a light touch that offered both comfort and reassurance.

"Just fine." Tessa had to resist the urge to lean her head against his shoulder, to let his strength support her completely. If she wasn't careful, she was going to lose what little backbone she had, she thought ruefully. If only Keefe didn't make it so easy for her to lean on him.

"Of course she's fine," Molly said impatiently. "She's having a baby, not coming down with the plague."

"Thanks for pointing that out." Keefe's smile was wryly affectionate. "Glad you could make it, Molly."

"I wouldn't have missed it for the world." Molly gave him a speculative look, her sharp blue eyes smiling wickedly. "I was just telling Tessa that I hope she's smarter than her sister and has the good sense to hang on to you."

"Aunt Molly!" Tessa's horrified exclamation was nearly drowned out by Keefe's chuckle.

"You must have made your husband's life a living nightmare, Molly," he said, apparently not in the least disconcerted by her outrageous remark.

"He was lucky to have me," she said briskly. "And I made sure he knew it."

"I bet you did."

"I think everything went very well." Tessa rushed into speech, afraid of what Molly might say next.

"It went just fine." He smiled down at her, his eyes full of amused understanding.

"Your family has been so welcoming," she said wonderingly.

"Why shouldn't they be?" Molly demanded, before Keefe could respond. "He's lucky to get you, and they know it."

"You're right," Keefe agreed promptly.

"Aunt Molly!" Tessa had always admired her aunt's plainspokenness—until today.

"Well, he is," Molly said, ignoring both Keefe's amusement and Tessa's embarrassment. "There's good blood in your veins. Of course, you have to skip a generation to find any evidence of it. Your mother doesn't have the sense God gave a turnip, and your father is the biggest nitwit I've ever known. But the Walkers aren't the sort to hold that against you."

Keefe's laughter was so genuine that Tessa found herself smiling, albeit reluctantly. She supposed she should be offended on behalf of her parents. Unfortunately, there was more truth than otherwise in Molly's words.

"Lunch is about ready," Rachel Walker announced, and Tessa turned, grateful for the interruption. Heaven only knew what outrageous comments Molly might have ready to spring on them next.

He really was going to have to quit smoking completely, Keefe thought as he stepped onto the back porch and let the kitchen door close behind him. He was getting too old to be sneaking around like this. He slid the cigarettes out of his pocket and tapped one free of the pack.

"I've heard rumors that those are bad for you."

The voice, coming from somewhere off to his left, made him start guiltily. Turning, he saw Nikki sitting in one corner of the porch swing. She smiled when she saw his guilty expression. "Caught you."

"I've heard that same rumor," Keefe said, relaxing. He put the cigarette in his mouth. "But I figure it's a filthy lie."

"Like the rumor that fudge ripple ice cream is fattening?" she asked.

"Probably started by the same guy." He lit a match and held the flame to the tip of his cigarette. "I figure there's a government agency somewhere, whose only purpose is to tell the people that everything they like is bad for them."

"Paid for by our tax dollars." Nikki shook her head at the waste of it all.

"Exactly." Keefe shook out the match. "It doesn't matter, though, because I'm quitting."

She arched her brows. "So I see."

Keefe grinned at her through a thin veil of smoke. "I don't believe in rushing into things."

She nodded. "Very wise."

The silence that fell between them was comfortable. Keefe smoked his cigarette and looked out over his mother's casually landscaped backyard. Her huge dog, an enormous animal of uncertain parentage, lolled on his side in the middle of lawn.

"Looks like Mary and Danny wore Hippo out," Nikki commented. Cole's daughter and Gage and Kelsey's son had spent most of the morning playing with the dog.

"Maybe. Then again, Hippo doesn't seem to believe in expending any unnecessary energy."

"He's pretty energetic around half-cooked turkeys," Nikki said.

The first Thanksgiving after she and Sam were married, Hippo had stolen the turkey from the counter, leaving the rest of the family to dine on roast chicken and grilled hamburgers.

"He does show some speed around food," Keefe conceded, smiling at the memory.

There was another little silence, and then Nikki spoke again.

"Tessa seems very nice."

"She is." Sensing there was more to come, he waited.

"I didn't want to like her." The words seemed to come against her will.

Keefe's hand froze in midair, the cigarette halfway to his mouth. His brows rose in surprise. "Why not?"

"Because of the baby. Sam says she may give it

up.'' Nikki's hands lay on her thighs, her fingers clenched in the fabric of her jade-colored silk skirt. ''I wanted to hate her for that.''

Keefe took his time responding. He remembered his brother telling him that Nikki was going in for tests to find out why she wasn't pregnant yet. Sam hadn't mentioned it since, but Keefe had the feeling that he was treading on some dangerous emotional ground.

''Tessa has her reasons,'' he said finally.

''I know she does.'' Nikki exhaled a shuddering breath. ''I know she does.'' She repeated the words, her voice hardly above a whisper. ''It just seemed so unfair that...'' She stopped and looked up at him, her expression bleak. ''We found out last week that I can't have children.''

Keefe read the depth of the pain in her eyes and, for one cowardly moment, wished he hadn't given in to the urge to have a cigarette. He pushed it aside and groped for something to say, but there really wasn't much that could be said, beyond the obvious.

''I'm sorry. I know the two of you wanted children. Is there any hope that things might change?'' He crushed his cigarette out against the porch railing, concentrating on the movement as a way to avoid seeing the pain in her face.

''No.'' She shook her head. ''There's no hope at all. No question that it's my fault.''

''Fault?'' He looked at her, his brows raised questioningly. ''You didn't choose to have this happen, Nikki. It just did.''

''Semantics.'' She rejected his attempt at reason

with a sharp movement of her hand. "Because there's something wrong with me, Sam won't be able to have children."

Feeling as if he were tiptoeing through a mine field, Keefe reached for his cigarettes, but let his hand drop before it got to his pocket. Some situations were beyond the power of nicotine. The swing rocked gently, chains creaking, as he sat down next to his sister-in-law.

"If you're afraid that Sam is going to blame you, you can forget it."

"No, he'd never blame me." The knowledge didn't seem to give her any comfort. "But if it wasn't for me—"

He interrupted her firmly. "If it wasn't for you, Sam would be miserable. Listen to me. My brother is crazy about you. I don't know how much Sam wants kids, but I do know how much he loves you."

"But—"

"No buts," he said firmly. "I've never seen Sam as happy as he has been since he met you."

"What about years from now?" Nikki whispered.

"What about it?"

"What if he starts to think about what he missed out on?"

Keefe set his hand under her chin and lifted her face to his. Steeling himself against the tears swimming in her green eyes, he gave her a hard look.

"If you think there could ever come a time when Sam would resent you for something like this, then you don't know him at all."

She flushed and lowered her eyes. "I suppose you're right."

"I know I'm right," he said flatly. He released his hold on her, letting his hand drop. "Don't sell him short, Nikki."

"I won't." She sighed, and when she looked up at him, her expression was less bleak than it had been. "Thanks for listening, and thanks for pointing out what an idiot I'm being."

"I didn't say you were an idiot," he protested.

"Well, you could have, and I would have deserved it." She shook her head. "I don't think I've been rowing with both oars in the water the last few weeks. When Sam told me why you were getting married, I made up my mind to hate Tessa."

"Why?" he asked blankly, caught off guard by the blunt declaration.

"Because of the baby. Because she has something I can't ever have and she doesn't even want it."

Keefe was caught between a desperate craving for a cigarette and the equally desperate wish that he'd never heard of the damned things. If he hadn't slipped out here to have a smoke, he could have avoided a conversation for which he felt woefully inadequate.

Perhaps Nikki read something of his near panic, because her mouth curved in a half smile and a touch of humor lit her eyes. "Poor Keefe. I bet you're wishing you'd quit smoking completely. Don't worry. I'm not going to dump any more emotional baggage in your lap. I just wanted to tell you that I really think Tessa is very sweet and I think you're very sweet to be doing this for her. And I've got a feeling that everything is going to work out really well for both of you.''

"Thanks.''

"You're welcome.'' She smiled again, and the shadows seemed to recede a little farther. "Now, maybe you should go in and rescue her. You may not realize it, but the Walker family can be just a little overwhelming to the uninitiated.''

"Are you coming in?''

"In a minute. I'm all right,'' she added, seeing his concern.

Keefe hesitated a moment longer before he rose from the swing. She spoke again as he was reaching for the screen door.

"Keefe?''

"Yeah?'' He turned to look at her, his brows raised questioningly.

"Thanks,'' she said softly. "Thanks for listening.''

"That's what family's for.''

Chapter 9

It was long after dark when Keefe pulled the truck up in front of the ranch house. When he shut off the engine, the abrupt silence was startling. Tessa thought that she had never seen anything more lovely than the golden glow of the porch light.

"I have never understood why riding in a car is more tiring than running a marathon," Jace said as he reached for the door handle. The two of them had traded off driving duties, and the last leg of the journey had been Keefe's.

"One of the great mysteries of life." Keefe opened his own door and slid out from behind the wheel, sighing with pleasure as his feet hit solid ground.

"What we need is a transporter, like they have on the *Enterprise*." Jace got out and then turned to offer Tessa a helping hand down out of the truck. *"That's* where our tax dollars should be going. Talk about an improvement in the country's infrastructure.''

"You should write your congressman about it," Keefe suggested. He leaned over the side of the pickup and lifted their luggage out. "I'm sure the government just hasn't thought of it. A letter from you, pointing out the error of their ways, is bound to get them moving in the right direction."

"Wasn't there an episode where the signal got scrambled and somebody ended up trading personalities with a dog?" Tessa asked sleepily.

"They didn't trade personalities with the dog," Jace said. "The transporter split the dog into two dogs—only it wasn't really a dog. It had a horn. It died. But then it turned out that the transporter had split Kirk into two people, one good and one evil."

"You're a Trekkie," Tessa said, amazed.

"I believe the politically correct term is Trekker," Jace corrected her with exaggerated dignity.

"He's a 'Star Trek' nut," Keefe said dryly. "He's got every episode on tape, but he doesn't need to watch them, because he can recite the dialogue by heart."

"'Star Trek' is a genuine classic of American literature," Jace reminded him.

"Yeah, it's right up there with Steinbeck and Hemingway."

"Actually, I never much cared for Hemingway," Tessa said. "But I do like 'Star Trek.'"

"You have genuine class," Jace said. She caught the gleam of his teeth in the darkness as he grinned at her. "You can borrow my tapes anytime."

"I'm impressed," Keefe said as he handed Jace his overnight case. "He wouldn't loan those tapes to just anyone."

"Well, I certainly wouldn't loan them to someone who thinks 'Bonanza' is the epitome of American television art."

"You don't get much better than Ben and the boys," Keefe said, with an exaggerated western drawl.

Tessa's chuckle ended abruptly on a yawn. "Sorry."

"You're beat," Jace said. "We can discuss the relative merits of old television shows some other time. I'll see you guys in the morning." He lifted one hand in salute and turned toward the foreman's house.

Watching him walk away, Tessa was abruptly aware that his departure left her alone with Keefe. And Keefe was no longer just Keefe—he was also her husband.

"You know, I've always wondered why Jace doesn't stay up at the house," she said, anxious to fill the silence. "I mean, he didn't, even before I took over the guest room."

"We both like our privacy," Keefe said as he picked up their bags and started toward the house. "Besides, not only does he have lousy taste in television, he has lousy taste in music. There's a limit to the number of hours I can listen to Tchaikovsky."

"Jace likes classical music?" Tessa was momentarily distracted by this piece of information. "'Star Trek' and Tchaikovsky. He doesn't exactly fit the stereotype of the cowboy, does he?"

"Not exactly."

She hesitated at the bottom of the steps. It was silly to be nervous. It wasn't as if they were really married. Keefe set the bags down and reached into his pocket for the keys. Tessa's teeth worried her lower lip. *Husband.* The word had layers of meaning—companion, protector, lover. That was what the word should mean. But overlying those images was the reality of her marriage to Bobby. He'd used the word to control, to dominate, to assert his will and make her feel less of a person. *Husband.* There was power in the word. The thought made her uneasy.

"Tessa?" Keefe turned to look at her, his brows raised questioningly. "Something wrong?"

"No." *Nothing but the fact that I think I've lost my mind.* "I was just thinking of how many stars there are here," she said, blurting out the first thing that popped into her head. "I don't remember ever seeing skies like this before."

Keefe let the screen door close and crossed the porch toward her. Tessa tilted back her head to look at the sky as he walked down the steps, the click of his boot heels against the wood loud in the late-night stillness.

"I'd never realized you could actually see the Milky Way," she said, vividly aware of his size as he stopped in front of her. He was so big, bigger even than Bobby. She wouldn't be able to stop him if he— *Stop it. This is Keefe. He would never hurt me.* But you couldn't stop him if he did, a sly voice whispered. He's your husband now.

"It's because there isn't a lot of ambient light

messing up the view,'' Keefe said, responding to her comment. He glanced up at the sky—black velvet scattered with countless glittering jewels. "One advantage of living so far away from the city."

"It's hard to imagine why anyone would live in the city if it meant missing out on a view like this," Tessa said, trying to look as if she had nothing more than the view on her mind.

"But if everyone left the city and moved to the country, they'd spoil the view with their cars and their porch lights."

"I suppose." Her neck was starting to ache. She lowered her head and focused on the crisp rectangle of light that marked a window in the foreman's house. "Jace made it home," she said inanely.

"Looks like." There was a brief silence, and then he spoke again, his voice gentle. "Tessa, I'm not going to turn into a monster just because we signed a piece of paper that says we're married."

"I know that." She sighed, relieved to have her fears out in the open, embarrassed that he'd read her so easily. "I'm sorry to be such a fool."

"You're not a fool. You've got reason to be leery."

"No, I don't. Not with you." She kept her gaze focused on the light in Jace's window, speaking slowly, thinking out what she wanted to say. "I'd like to be able to say that Bobby changed after we got married, but if I'm honest with myself, I've got to admit that the signs were there all along. I just didn't want to see them. I thought he'd change after we were married." She sighed. "I guess that was pretty stupid."

"Not stupid. Just human." Keefe slid his arm around her shoulders and pulled her against his side. "When you love someone, it's natural to blind yourself to their faults."

Something in his tone made her wonder if he spoke from experience. Was he thinking of Dana?

"You don't have to worry about anything," he said, giving her shoulders a quick, affectionate squeeze. "I'm not going to change because we signed a piece of paper that says we're married. Nothing's going to change between us."

Tessa allowed him to shepherd her into the house. He'd made her see how foolish her fears had been. It had been silly to think, even for a moment, that she had anything to worry about. Keefe wasn't going to change.

Nothing's going to change between us.

Strange, but she found the reassurance oddly depressing.

It took Keefe a few days to realize just how wrong he'd been. No matter how much he told himself—and Tessa—that a marriage license was nothing but a piece of paper, holding only as much meaning as they chose to give it, he soon realized that that wasn't particularly accurate. Their marriage was like a move in a high-stakes poker game, with the Mallorys as their opponents. They were betting that fear of bad publicity would prevent the good senator and his wife from calling their bluff.

But whatever the reasons behind it, they *were* married and, when Keefe looked at Tessa now, he saw her in a different light. She wasn't the quiet little girl he'd known years ago. She was a woman who had survived an abusive marriage, a woman struggling to put her life back in order. She was his wife.

Keefe reached in his pocket and pulled out his cigarettes. One hand holding the reins, he worked a cigarette free and slid the pack back into his shirt pocket. Pulling out a book of matches, he sighed at the difficulty of lighting up with only one hand.

"I am quitting," he muttered as he drew his horse up. The bay flicked one ear back. Keefe struck the match and cupped his hands around the cigarette to light it. Drawing smoke into his lungs, he shook out the match. "This is my first cigarette today."

The bay's ears twitched, and Keefe frowned. "You don't have to sneer about it. I've practically quit. A few cigarettes a day hardly even counts."

The big gelding snorted his opinion of that rationalization.

"Easy for you to say," Keefe muttered as he nudged the horse into a walk. He narrowed his eyes against the smoke as he drew on the cigarette. He was supposed to be checking on the stock tanks, making sure the cattle had plenty of water. It was an undemanding task, giving him time to think—more than he wanted, really.

His eyes shadowed by the brim of his hat, he looked at the land around him. His land. His ranch. It was the fulfillment of a childhood dream. He'd been born and raised in the Los Angeles basin, in a small suburban house with a small suburban backyard—not a horse or a corral in sight. His father had been a police officer and, as far as he knew, there wasn't a single cowboy in the family tree. Yet he couldn't remember a time when he hadn't wanted to be a cowboy.

He'd been ten the first time he rode a horse. His parents had given in to his pleas and purchased riding lessons from a stable located in nearby Tujunga Canyon. From the moment he sat in the saddle, he'd known what he wanted to be when he grew up.

And here he was, riding across his own land. In the years since he won the Flying Ace in a poker game, he'd worked his butt off to turn it into a paying proposition. And it was happening. Very slowly, and not exactly surely, but it was happening. It was the fulfillment of a lifelong dream. A few weeks ago, he'd have said he had pretty much everything he'd ever wanted.

That had been before Tessa came back into his life. When he told her she was welcome to stay as long as she liked, he hadn't been thinking any farther than giving her the shelter she needed. It hadn't occurred to him that Tessa's presence would change his own life in any significant way.

Keefe's mouth twisted in a self-mocking smile. He doubted there was a crystal ball on the planet that could have foreseen how his invitation to Tessa to stay on the ranch would lead to marriage and potential fatherhood, not to mention facing down a United States senator. But what bothered him more than all of that was that Tessa's presence had made him aware that something was lacking in his life.

He drew deeply on the cigarette, narrowing his eyes against the smoke. It had taken him a while to get past the divorce. He'd done a lot of drinking and spent a few months trying to break his neck on the back of a bucking horse. But winning the Flying Ace in a poker game had given his life a new focus, and he'd pulled himself together. The past couple of years had been pretty good, and if anyone asked, he'd have said that he had his life pretty well in order.

Then Tessa had shown up, with her soft voice and sweet feminine scent. She'd thrown open the windows, swept the dust from the house, done her innocent best to starve him to death. And, in the process, she'd made him see just how damned empty his life had been before she arrived.

Keefe swung down out of the saddle at the first stock tank. Dropping the end of his cigarette, he ground it into the dirt with the toe of his boot. If Tessa hadn't come back into his life, he might have gone on for years without realizing how lonely he was. Now he was acutely aware of the gap she was going to leave in his life when she left. It was ironic that it had taken a pretend marriage to make him realize how much he missed having a real one.

Tessa caught the end of her tongue between her teeth as she looped the yarn over the right hand knitting needle, slid the tip of the needle under the stitch on the left-hand needle and attempted to transfer it from left to right. When the stitch was successfully completed, she allowed herself to breathe again. *Knitting is a relaxing hobby.* She remembered the woman in the yarn store telling her that, describing all the hours of pleasure that lay ahead of her, soothed by the rhythmic click of her knitting needles.

It had sounded like a good idea at the time, but six months after she'd bought the yarn to make a baby sweater, she had yet to find anything relaxing about knitting. She had a few inches of scruffy-looking blue fabric marked by tiny holes where she'd dropped half a dozen stitches. A sane woman would have thrown the whole mess in the trash and moved on to a simpler hobby—designing nuclear power plants maybe—but she continued to struggle.

She'd started the sweater when Bobby was still alive. She'd kept working on it after his death, though she'd already begun to think of giving the baby up for adoption. She wasn't sure why. Heaven knew, no new parent—adoptive or otherwise—was going to dress a child in a sweater that looked as if it had been knitted for an alien species. She sighed faintly as she tackled the next stitch.

"Problems?" Keefe asked, looking up from the magazine he was reading.

"Not really." She looked up from the wadded mass in her hands and smiled ruefully. "I'm starting to think that, to be really good at knitting, you need to be double-jointed."

"Don't they mention that in the instructions?"

"No. Do you suppose that constitutes false advertising? Maybe I could sue someone for misleading me."

"Emotional cruelty?"

"I think I could make a case for it." She held up her needles. "It's *supposed* to be a baby sweater."

Keefe looked at the lumpy, uneven swatch. His brows climbed a notch. "What kind of baby?" he asked finally.

"That was very cruel," Tessa said, her dignified tone at odds with the laughter in her eyes.

"I'm sure it's going to look just fine when you get it done," he said reassuringly.

"Well, I guess it can't get any worse than it is." Her tone was philosophical.

"It will be fine," Keefe said as he returned his attention to the magazine.

Tessa began working the needles again, struggling to transfer each stitch neatly. It occurred to her that, if anyone happened to look in through a window, she and Keefe must look like a stereotypical married couple. The two of them sitting together, her with her knitting and him with his magazine. All they needed was a fire in the fireplace and a shaggy dog sleeping on the hearth and they could have stepped right out of an advertisement for domestic bliss. Of course, it was July, which made a fire a little impractical, and Keefe didn't happen to own a dog, but even without those finishing touches, they presented a picture-perfect image.

Talk about false advertising. There was an edge of pain to her half smile. The problem was that she found herself wishing that this was real. The more time she spent with Keefe, the more she'd come to see all the things she'd missed in her first marriage.

There had been no companionship, no affection. Looking back, she found it difficult to remember why she'd married Bobby. She'd been so dazzled by his looks and by the idea of showing her parents that someone eligible—a senator's son, no less—would want to marry her that she hadn't stopped to consider what she really felt for him. She'd certainly paid a high price for her foolishness, she thought. She touched the heavy swell of her stomach. She was still paying it, in a way.

The baby kicked unexpectedly, and Tessa sucked in a quick, startled breath.

Keefe's head came up immediately, his dark eyes concerned. "What's wrong?"

"Nothing. The baby moved, that's all."

His gaze dropped to her stomach, his expression shifting from concern to curiosity. "Does it hurt?"

"Not really. It's more of a kind of quick pressure." She lifted her shoulders in a light shrug. "It's hard to describe."

"Does he kick often?"

"Often enough for an entire football team. Or maybe a chorus line, if it's a girl." It felt odd to be discussing the baby so casually with him. As if they were a normal married couple, anticipating the birth of their child. "Would you like to feel it?" she asked impulsively.

She immediately wanted to recall the words. She'd spent almost eight months trying not to think about this baby any more than she had to, afraid to let it become real to her. Inviting Keefe to feel the baby kick was stepping beyond the barriers she'd set for herself. But he was already sitting down next to her, the sofa cushion dipping beneath his weight.

"Are you sure?" he asked, as if sensing her hesitation.

"Of course," she said lightly. "Give me your hand."

She pressed his fingers against the side of her belly, feeling the warmth of his hand through the layers of her clothing.

"Once he gets started, he usually keeps it up for a while," she said. As if on cue, the baby kicked vigorously. She felt Keefe jerk in surprise.

"A placekicker," he said positively. The baby kicked again, and his smile widened into a grin. Tessa saw the wonder in his eyes and felt her heart twist. Her feelings about the child she carried were so ambivalent. She would have given almost anything to be able to share Keefe's uncomplicated pleasure in the moment.

"Feels like a healthy little guy—or girl," he said, still smiling.

"So the doctor tells me." Keefe had driven her into town the week before to see the doctor, and he had pronounced her and the baby to be in perfect health.

"Think he's through for now?" Keefe asked.

"Could be." Tessa was suddenly aware of the intimacy of the moment. Keefe's large hand was spread against her stomach. He was close enough that she could see the gold flecks that lightened the deep brown of his eyes. A thick lock of dark hair had fallen onto his forehead. She curled her fingers against the foolish urge to push it back into place, and she looked away, afraid of what her expression might reveal.

"Tessa?"

The husky sound of his voice sent a small shiver of awareness down her spine.

"Y-yes?" She had to clear her throat before she could get the word out.

"What would you say if I told you I wanted to kiss you?"

"Me?" She looked at him, her eyes widened into startled blue pools.

"What would you say?" he asked, leaning closer.

"O-okay," she whispered, a heartbeat before his mouth touched hers.

His lips were warm and firm, asking her response rather than demanding it. Tessa felt herself melting against him. His tongue skimmed her lower lip, and she opened her mouth, inviting him inside.

She'd forgotten what a kiss could be, she thought dazedly as his tongue fenced gently with hers. No, she hadn't forgotten. She'd never *known* a kiss could be like this—warm and tender and sensuous all at the same time. Her hand came up, settling against his chest, feeling the steady beat of his heart beneath her palm.

Keefe felt her surrender and lifted one hand, sliding his fingers beneath the silky dark gold weight of her hair, cupping the back of her neck. He tilted her head back and deepened the kiss. Somewhere in the back of his mind, he knew he shouldn't be doing this, had known even before it began. He was supposed to be taking care of Tessa, not kissing her. But she tasted so good, felt so right.

One kiss, he thought. *What harm could there be in one kiss?* Only he didn't want to stop at one kiss. He felt as if he could go on kissing her and holding her forever. But forever hadn't ever been part of their bargain.

Chapter 10

The shrill ring of the telephone shattered the moment as thoroughly as a hammer smashing through a pane of glass. Tessa's breath escaped her in a soft exhalation of regret as Keefe ended the kiss. Her eyelids felt weighted as she forced them open. Looking up into Keefe's eyes, she thought she saw a reflection of her own startled wonder. But the expression was gone in an instant, leaving her to wonder if it had been there at all.

"Tessa, I—" The phone rang again, cutting off whatever he'd started to say. He cast an irritated glance over his shoulder and then looked back at her.

"You'd better get that," she said, her eyes focused somewhere near his collarbone.

"Let it ring."

"It might be important." The phone rang again, a harsh jangle that held overtones of impatience. "Go on,'' she urged, her calm tone revealing none of the turmoil she felt inside. She even managed to curve her mouth into something resembling a smile.

Keefe did not find the expression particularly reassuring, but the phone rang a fourth time, the sound scraping across his nerves like fingernails on a chalkboard. With a muttered curse, he pushed up from the sofa and strode to answer it.

It was a brief call, questions from a neighboring rancher who was interested in boarding a mare on the Flying Ace, in hopes that Jace could soothe her fractious temper. A date for the animal's arrival was agreed upon, as was a price for Jace's work. Keefe hung up the phone, and the conversation vanished instantly from his mind.

He couldn't believe what he'd done. Kissing Tessa, for God's sake! Had he lost his mind? It had seemed so right at the time—inevitable, as if it were meant to happen. But no matter how it had felt, the reality was that he'd promised to take care of her, to protect her. Kissing her had never been a part of their bargain.

She responded, a sly voice whispered. Keefe slapped aside the attempt at justification. Considering all she'd gone through, she might have been afraid of what he'd do if she *didn't* respond. The idea that her gentle yielding might have been prompted by fear made his stomach knot. He spun away from the table, determined to make her understand that what happened had been a momentary madness.

But the room was empty behind him. She'd slipped away while he was on the phone. Whatever he wanted to say would have to wait. He was ashamed to admit that his primary feeling was one of relief. Given a little time, maybe he could come up with an explanation for what had happened tonight—one that would satisfy Tessa, if not himself.

Tessa spent most of a restless night telling herself not to read too much into what had happened. It had only been a kiss, after all. Just because it had sent shock waves through her, that didn't mean that Keefe had felt the same way. Apart from her disastrous marriage, she didn't have much experience with men. She was hardly qualified to judge whether his kiss had held any emotion deeper than comfort.

If it hadn't meant anything to him, she didn't want to know about it. And if it had? Tessa wasn't sure she was ready to know that, either. If her life was tangled, then her emotions were snarled beyond all hope of understanding. The idea that Keefe might feel something more than friendship toward her was enough to terrify, even as it delighted. She needed time to sort out her own feelings before she could even begin to think about Keefe's.

In the end, all her speculation and confusion boiled down to one simple question: How was she supposed to act when she saw him again?

Tessa closed her bedroom door and turned to find a broad expanse of naked male chest only inches from her nose.

"Oh!" Startled, she took a quick step back.

"Sorry. I didn't mean to sneak up on you," Keefe said.

"That's okay." With an effort, she dragged her eyes from the muscled width of his chest and met his gaze. "I thought you were taking a shower."

She'd counted on it actually. They hadn't been alone together since the kiss they'd shared the night before. Since it was now dinnertime, she'd had hopes of being able to avoid him until time for bed. Maybe by tomorrow, she'd have figured out what to say to him.

"Just finished," he said, sliding the fingers of one hand through his damp hair.

The movement drew her eyes back to his chest. His shirt hung open, revealing a solidly muscled expanse covered by a heavy dusting of almost black curls, tapering to a thin line that sliced across the flat plane of his stomach to disappear beneath the waistband of his jeans. She jerked her eyes back up, aware that her cheeks felt warm and hoping the light was too poor for him to notice.

"Have you got a minute?" he asked. There was nothing ominous in his tone, but Tessa felt her heartbeat suddenly accelerate.

"I need to set the table and put out salads and...things," she said hastily.

"This will only take a minute."

"All right." There was no sense in trying to put it off. She might as well hear whatever it was he wanted to say and get it over with.

Now that he had her acceptance, Keefe seemed hesitant about where to start. As if stalling for time, he drew the edges of his shirt together and began to button it. Tessa suppressed a sigh of mixed relief and regret.

"What happened last night..." Keefe began finally. "I don't want you to think..." He stopped, hesitated, and then spoke bluntly. "You don't have to be afraid that it will happen again."

"Afraid?" Tessa was startled into lifting her eyes to his face. "What do you mean?"

"That wasn't part of our bargain. You don't have to feel as if you're...obligated to me in any way."

It took her a moment to realize what he meant. "You think I kissed you because I *owe* you?"

"I don't know." His eyes were bleak.

Tessa felt as if she was out of her depth and floundering badly. None of her fevered imaginings had conjured up this scenario. "I didn't kiss you because I thought I had to. I...I wanted you to kiss me." Her face felt as if it were on fire, but she couldn't let him think that he'd coerced her into anything. "And I enjoyed it very much," she added, with an uncharacteristic touch of bravado.

Keefe stared at her in silence for a moment, as if weighing her sincerity. Apparently he was satisfied, because his mouth curved in a slow smile, his eyes warming in a way that made Tessa's heart thump against her breastbone.

"Actually, I liked it quite a bit myself."

"Well. Then there's nothing to worry about, is there?" she said briskly. He looked as if he might say something else, but Tessa's courage abruptly ran out. "I've got to check on dinner."

She was aware of Keefe's eyes on her as she walked down the hall. She would have given a great deal to know what he was thinking.

Tessa picked her way carefully across the rough surface of the ranch yard. She carried a flashlight, but she'd turned it off a few yards from the house, finding the sharp patches of darkness beyond the flashlight's beam more deceptive than the softer, less angular shadows created by the light of the full moon that floated just over the mountains to the east.

"Why didn't I just write him a note?" she muttered as she detoured around a fist-size rock. That would certainly have been the easiest thing to do, but when the phone call came in for Keefe, it had seemed to make perfect sense to deliver the message in person. So here she was, traipsing across the yard in the moonlight and wondering if pregnancy might have affected her sanity.

She sighed with relief as she climbed the two steps to the narrow concrete porch that stretched across the front of the foreman's house. Now that she thought about it, it seemed odd that, in all the weeks she'd been here, this was the first time she'd been here. She'd come to think of Jace as a good friend, yet she'd never seen where he lived.

It was a warm night, and Jace had left his front door open. Tessa tapped on the screen door and waited. Somewhere in the back of the house, she could hear the rumble of masculine voices, the sound too low for her to make out words. She heard Keefe say something. Jace's answering laughter was cut off by a metallic rattle, like the sound of a pan dropped carelessly into a sink.

Obviously, they hadn't heard her knock. She lifted her hand to knock again. Her nose twitched. What was that smell? She inhaled, trying to identify the scent that wafted through the screen door. Onions? And...frying hamburger? Ridiculous. Why would Jace and Keefe be cooking hamburgers and onions? Not more than an hour ago, she'd sat in the kitchen at the big house and watched them polish off bowls of vegetable soup and crisp croissants. They couldn't possibly be eating again. Could they?

Tessa let her hand drop to her side. Her teeth worrying her lower lip, she wrestled with her conscience. The right thing to do was to simply knock on the door—loudly and firmly. When Keefe or Jace responded, she could pass on the message about the horse that was arriving tomorrow morning and then go back to the house. It was not only the right thing to do, it was the *only* thing to do. She certainly couldn't just open the screen door and walk into Jace's home uninvited.

The door opened without so much as a squeak of protest. Feeling both guilty and consumed by curiosity, Tessa stepped inside. The house had been built for use by the ranch foreman in the days when the Flying Ace boasted a full complement of hands. Outside, the house was plain as a cardboard box, unadorned by any attempt at embellishment. The interior followed the same pattern. The front door opened directly into the living room, which was square and plainly furnished with items that appeared to have been chosen for comfort rather than style.

Glancing at the sofa, Tessa decided that it might have originally been upholstered in a crisp black-and-tan plaid. Time had faded the colors to a blur of undecided grays. Sitting at right angles to it was a big overstuffed chair covered in a fabric that defied description. Across from both sofa and chair was an aluminum stand with crooked legs that held a television and VCR. A boxy wooden coffee table sat in front of the sofa, and sitting on top of it was a laptop computer, a kaleidoscopic pattern drifting across the opened screen. Its sleek high-tech lines were at odds with the Spartan simplicity of its surroundings. Tessa stared at it curiously for a moment, but there were other things tugging for her attention.

The kitchen wasn't hard to find. Even had the house been large, she would have had only to follow her nose and the unmistakable scent of frying onions. Like the rest of the house, the room was small. The two men seemed to fill all the available free space as they worked companionably. Jace stood at the stove, watching over a pair of skillets, while Keefe stood in front of a narrow slice of counter, his back to her, blocking her view of his task.

"I think we should—" Jace broke off in midword as he looked up and saw her standing in the doorway. "Tessa!"

His partner's startled exclamation made Keefe turn abruptly. He stared at his bride in disbelief, his fingers tightening over the thin-bladed knife he'd been using to cut thick slices of tomato.

"Tessa! What are you doing here?"

"There was a phone call," she answered automatically. "Pete Rutherford wanted you to know that the new mare is arriving tomorrow morning. It sounded important, so I thought I'd let you know."

"It wasn't *that* important." Keefe set the knife on the counter.

"You didn't have to come all the way over here," Jace added.

"I knocked," Tessa said, as if it were significant. "You didn't answer, and I thought I smelled something cooking...." Her voice trailed off as she looked around the kitchen.

"We...ah...thought we'd have a little snack," Jace said weakly.

"You just ate dinner," she said, staring in disbelief at the thick hamburgers sizzling on the stove. "You said you liked my soup."

"It was great soup," Keefe said instantly. "The chicken broth and all those vegetables and...and stuff." He stumbled over the description, aware that there hadn't been much in the way of "stuff" in the bowls.

"And those were just about the best rolls I've ever eaten," Jace added, coming to his partner's aid.

"Croissants," Tessa said absently as she looked around the tiny kitchen. A bag of hamburger buns lay open on the counter, puffy rounds of cheap white bread.

"Croissants. That's what I meant to say. They were great croissants." Jace rolled panicked eyes in Keefe's direction.

"And the salad was real good," Keefe said, rising to the occasion. "I bet you could make a fortune with that dressing. It was...real good."

His voice trailed off as Tessa finished inventorying the kitchen and looked at him. The bewilderment in those big blue eyes made him feel as guilty as a kid caught shoplifting candy bars at the local market.

"If you liked everything so much, why are you here, less than half an hour later, making hamburgers?"

"I..." He looked at Jace, but Jace only shrugged. He was all out of clever explanations. "We were sort of still hungry," Keefe admitted finally.

"There was more soup," Tessa said.

"Yeah, and it was great soup," Jace said earnestly. "But there wasn't much stuff in it."

"Stuff? What kind of stuff?"

"Meat," Keefe said.

"Macaroni, maybe," Jace added helpfully.

"It was a vegetable soup. You don't put meat and macaroni in a vegetable soup."

It was best to make a clean breast of it, Keefe decided. He drew a deep breath and then let it out slowly. "The thing is, Tessa, vegetables just don't seem to keep you filled up when you're chasing down a balky cow or digging a posthole."

Tessa looked around the kitchen while she digested his words. She thought about all the times Keefe had left the house after supper, saying he wanted to check something in the barn or needed to talk to Jace about something.

"Have you been doing this all along? Eating at the house and then coming over here to eat more?"

Their guilty expressions answered the question without words.

"I haven't been cooking enough all along?"

"You cook plenty," Keefe assured her, throwing logic to the winds. "It's just that, working outside the way we do, we burn a lot of calories."

Of course they did, she thought, staring at the enormous hamburgers still sizzling on the stove. They spent their days doing hard physical labor. It was natural that they'd need more calories than someone who sat at a desk all day. She should have thought of that. *Why didn't you think of that? Are you stupid, Tessa? Stupid, stupid, stupid.* She seemed to hear the mocking echo of Bobby's voice, telling her she was worthless, belittling her, making her feel as stupid as he said she was.

"Why didn't you say something?" she asked.

There was a moment of silence, and then Keefe sighed. "We were afraid of you."

"Afraid?" It was the last answer she'd have expected. She gaped at him in disbelief, missing the startled look Jace shot in his direction. "Of me?"

"It was the knife," he admitted.

"Knife? What knife?"

"That butcher knife. I've seen what you can do to a carrot with that thing." He shook his head. "I wasn't about to cross you."

"Cross me?" Tessa felt as if she'd just stumbled into a scene in a movie and her script was different from everyone else's.

"Any woman who can handle a knife like that is someone to walk lightly around," Jace said solemnly, following Keefe's lead. "And the scissors." He shuddered. "I saw you lop one of those little chickens in half without even flinching."

"Little chickens?" Tessa stared at him, scrambling to keep up with the conversation. "The game hens?"

"Yeah. One minute, they were whole. The next, you had 'em hacked in two. It made my blood run cold."

"A woman who can do that to a chicken demands a certain amount of respect from a man," Keefe added. "It takes a braver man than I am to risk provoking someone like that."

"That's ridiculous!"

"Easy for you to say," Jace said indignantly "You were holding the scissors. It's easy to be brave when you're armed."

"Armed? With poultry shears?" Tessa gaped at him.

"I've heard that there are states where you have to register to buy a pair," Keefe said darkly.

She looked from Keefe to Jace and back again. They couldn't be serious. "*Register* poultry shears?"

"In Nebraska, you have to a have a license to carry them," Jace said, deadpan. "And if you're caught dueling with them, you go straight to the big house."

"Dueling with poultry shears?" Tessa felt laughter bubble up in her throat.

"Sure." Keefe's expression remained solemn, but his eyes gave him away. "Many a promising young life has ended in tragedy."

"Snipped in the bud?" Tessa asked.

"That's awful." Jace's pained expression was the final straw.

"Sorry." But she spoiled the apology by giggling. Laughter drowned out the last echoes of Bobby's ugly words. The knowledge that, for weeks, Keefe and Jace had been cooking behind her back, like a pair of children sneaking cookies from a forbidden jar, all to avoid the risk of hurting her feelings, left no room for old hurts and insecurities. Looking at Keefe and Jace, she felt a warm rush of affection. And if her feelings for Keefe ran much deeper, that secret was hers alone.

Chapter 11

In a more merciful world, no woman would have to endure the heat of summer while eight and a half months pregnant. Tessa contemplated the injustice of it as she walked across the ranch yard underneath a blazing July sun. Of course, she could save herself a considerable amount of discomfort by staying in the house, sitting in the path of the cooling breeze created by the fan Keefe had set up for her. But reading or watching TV or working on her mauled attempt at knitting provided too much time for thinking. Considering the tangled state of her life, thinking was the last thing she wanted to have time for.

So, here she was, aching back, swollen feet and all, risking heat prostration in the hope of finding something to distract her from the confused circle of her own thoughts. Keefe had ridden out right after lunch to check a section of fencing, but she'd seen Jace enter the barn a few minutes ago. Though no one had said anything, she knew that the two men were careful to arrange things so that she was never left alone. When she realized what they were doing, she'd considered telling them it wasn't necessary, but she'd been too grateful for their consideration to let pride get in the way.

Tessa sighed with relief as she stepped out of the sunlight and into the shadowy interior of the barn. It probably wasn't much cooler inside than it was outside, but the dim light lent the illusion of a lower temperature, and illusion was better than nothing. Her mouth twisted in a sudden, rueful half smile. At the moment, her whole life was a tissue of illusions.

Moving to the far end of the barn, Tessa paused on the threshold of the large, dusty room that served as storage room and workshop. Her nose twitched at the mingled scents of leather, axle grease and sawdust. Jace stood next to a scarred workbench, studying a length of wood he held. He glanced up as Tessa stepped into the room.

"I brought you a snack," she said by way of greeting.

Jace's smile faded into a grimace of mock pain. "I couldn't eat another bite. I'm still full from lunch."

"I just want to be sure you don't go hungry," she said, all wide-eyed innocence. Meals lately had been distinguished by quantity, as well as quality. There was no chance of anyone getting up from the table hungry.

"I'm going to get fat as a house," Jace complained. But when she set down a plate of cookies, he reached for one anyway.

"I thought it was supposed to be cool in the mountains," Tessa said, reaching up to brush damp tendrils of hair off the back of her neck.

"Not in July." Jace finished the cookie and dusted his fingers against the sides of his jeans. He glanced at her, blue eyes full of understanding, as if he recognized her need for distraction. "If you're not in the midst of something else, why don't you hang around for a while? Too much time in my own company and I start talking to myself."

"If you don't mind." Tessa hoped she didn't look too pathetically grateful for the invitation. She didn't believe for an instant that Jace needed her company. Like Keefe, he was a man who was content to be alone. She shifted restlessly, pushing her thoughts in another direction. She spent more time than was wise thinking about Keefe.

"What are you working on?" she asked, looking for distraction.

"Replacing some slats in a gate. During a portion of my misspent youth, I worked as a carpenter in Spokane," he said as he used a soft brush to clean sawdust off the surface he'd just sanded.

"Was that before or after you terrorized Dubuque's dark underbelly?" Tessa perched herself on the stool that sat in front of the workbench and watched him work.

Jace frowned as if it trying to remember the correct order. "After Dubuque, before Houston."

"What did you do in Houston?"

"I worked in the oil fields for a few months. It was the filthiest job I ever had, but the money was good. And it was better than being a short-order cook, which is what I did immediately after Dubuque."

"From crime fighter to cook? That was a bit of a comedown, wasn't it?"

"A bit. But my car died halfway across Kansas, in a little town in the middle of a cornfield. I was flat broke and the demand for martial arts instructors was pretty low, so I took what was available."

"How long did you spend behind the grill?" She picked up a sanding block and tested the roughness of its surface with her fingertips.

"The three longest months of my life," Jace said with a shudder of remembered horror. "Trust me, compared to grilling burgers and frying eggs, working in the oil fields was a walk in the park."

"So you went to Spokane when you left Houston?"

"No." Jace shook his head. He set the brush aside and picked up a tack cloth. "After Houston, I moved to Hollywood."

"California?" Tessa gave him a surprised look as she set the sanding block down.

"The one and only."

"Were you trying to break into the movies?"

"Nope." Jace shot her an amused look. "I'll bet you've never been to Hollywood. You probably have this idea that there are movie stars sauntering down Hollywood Boulevard and casting agents lurking behind every tree."

"I'm not quite that naive," Tessa protested.

"Good, because Hollywood ain't what it used to be." He stroked the tack cloth over the board, lifting the last traces of sawdust from the oak. "I worked as a mechanic at a service station not far from the Cinerama Dome, practically in the heart of Hollywood, but the closest I ever got to the glamorous world of the silver screen was when I changed a tire for a guy who knew someone who worked as a stuntman on a Stallone film."

Tessa giggled. "A real brush with stardom."

"Yeah. It had my heart doing double time," he said dryly. He set the tack cloth aside and ran his palm over the cleaned surface.

"So you've taught self-defense, flipped hamburgers, worked on oil rigs, been a mechanic and a carpenter, and now you're half owner of a ranch." Tessa ticked the occupations off on her fingers. "Is there anything you haven't done?"

Jace appeared to give the suggestion serious consideration. "Well, I've never hunted giant squid with a blowgun," he said after a moment.

"I don't think you hunt giant squid with blowguns," Tessa said, laughing.

He shrugged. "Must be why I've never done it."

"You've moved around a lot, lived in a lot of different places."

"A few." He set the sanded board aside. Picking up another, shorter piece of wood, he reached for the sanding block Tessa had looked at earlier. Laying the board on the workbench, he began sanding it. "The thing about moving on is that it can become a kind of goal in itself. You don't think much about where you're going, only that you're going somewhere.''

"The call of the road?" Tessa asked, watching him work.

"Yeah. It's almost an addiction, always wanting to find out what's over the next hill.''

"Where did you meet Keefe?" she asked idly.

"At a rodeo in Santa Fe about eight years ago.''

"Eight years ago? Then you knew him when he and my sister were married." Tessa hadn't even considered that possibility.

"I did.''

"You knew Dana?''

"I knew her.'' Jace kept his attention on the sanding block, concentrating on the back-and-forth motion, sanding along the grain of the wood.

Tessa waited, but he didn't add anything to the flat statement. "I didn't see much of them the last couple of years they were married.''

Jace stopped working and looked at her. "If you're wondering what happened between them, you'll have to ask Keefe.''

Tessa flushed, embarrassed that she'd been so obvious. "I wasn't hinting.'' He arched one brow, and her flush deepened. "All right, maybe I *was* asking— kind of—but I shouldn't have been. Their marriage is none of my business.''

"Well, I don't know that I'd go so far as to say it's *none* of your business, but it certainly isn't any of my business to tell you what happened. Besides, the only people who really know what happens in a marriage are the two involved in it.''

"I'll bet you have a pretty good idea of what made them get a divorce," Tessa said.

Jace shrugged, his blue eyes shuttered. "I know some of it."

"Did Keefe... Do you think he loved her a great deal?" she asked.

Jace winced at her wistful tone, but he answered her honestly. "I don't think he'd have married her if he hadn't been crazy about her."

"No, he wouldn't have." She focused her attention on arranging a handful of stray nails into a precise row on the workbench. "When I was growing up, I would have sold my soul to be half as beautiful as Dana."

"At the risk of sounding like someone's maiden aunt—beauty is only skin-deep."

"Yeah, but that's as deep as men look, at least at first," Tessa pointed out without rancor. "And when a woman is as beautiful as my sister, a lot of them never look any farther."

Jace straightened away from the workbench and looked directly at her. "If you're worried that Keefe is still in love with Dana, forget it."

"I don't have any right to be worried." But the unsteadiness of her fingers as she continued tidying the nails belied her dismissive tone.

"I don't know that feelings and rights have much to do with one another."

"Maybe not." She sighed and lifted her gaze to his. "I remember the way Keefe used to look at Dana, as if she lit up a room just by entering it. He's not the kind of man who loves casually. Feelings like that aren't just going to be there one day and then gone the next.''

No, but, given enough reason, they could die a slow, painful death. Jace didn't voice the thought out loud. Keefe wouldn't thank him for that kind of interference.

"Keefe and Dana have been divorced for a long time" was all he said.

Tessa forced herself to nod, as if the statement meant something. Divorce severed the legal ties, but divorce papers didn't mean an end to the emotional ties any more than a marriage license made a real marriage.

"It's none of my business," she said. "It's not like Keefe and I are really married. *Then,* I might have a right to wonder if he still loved her. But we aren't and I don't. I only wondered because I consider Keefe a good friend and I'd hate to think of him unhappy. About Dana, I mean.''

She eased down from the stool, settling one hand against the swollen mound of her stomach when her feet were on solid ground again. She gave a Jace a bright smile. "Thanks for the company.''

Tessa seemed unaware of the unshed tears that shimmered in her eyes, but Jace couldn't pretend not to see them. Damn Keefe for a fool, he thought as he set down the board he'd been sanding and went to her.

"Hey, what's this? I know I'm a little rough around the edges, but I don't usually drive pretty women to tears.''

His chiding tone drew a watery chuckle, even as a

single tear slid down the curve of her cheek. Tessa leaned her forehead against his shoulder, allowing herself a moment to grab for her rapidly dissolving self-control. Jace's gentle teasing reminded her of the way Keefe had treated her when they first met. To a lonely little girl, accustomed to being ignored, Keefe's freely given attention and ready laughter had been a revelation. She'd blossomed under his easy smile and given her heart to him with the abandon of a child.

It was a pity it had taken her so long to realize that she'd forgotten to get it back.

"Am I interrupting something?" Keefe spoke from the doorway behind Tessa, his voice coolly polite.

"Not a thing," Jace said. If Tessa was oblivious to the threat behind Keefe's cordial tone, Jace was not so unaware, but he released her in a leisurely fashion, ignoring the muscle that flexed in his partner's jaw.

"I was just being silly," Tessa said, wiping her eyes self-consciously. "Hormones, I guess. I'm sorry I sniveled on your shoulder, Jace."

"Mi shoulder *es su* shoulder." His words drew a watery giggle from Tessa, but Keefe's eyes remained cool.

"I should go start dinner," Tessa said, moving toward the door.

"If you don't feel like cooking, we can manage with potluck," Keefe said, the chill in his eyes replaced by concern.

"I feel fine," she said. With a quick smile, she brushed past Keefe and out the door.

He waited until the sound of her footsteps had faded away before speaking. "You want to tell me what was going on?"

Jace appeared to consider for a moment and then shook his head. "I don't think so."

A muscle twitched in Keefe's jaw and his eyes darkened with temper. "This is the second time I've found you holding Tessa."

Jace raised one eyebrow. "You keeping score?"

"I don't want to see her get hurt."

"And you think I do?"

"No, but it could happen without you meaning for it to."

Jace shook his head in disgust and reached for the board he'd been working on. "I couldn't break Tessa's heart if I wanted to."

"Meaning?"

"You figure it out."

Keefe gritted his teeth. "She's been through a lot."

One hand wrapped around the board, Jace looked across the crowded workroom at his partner. Keefe stood with his feet braced lightly apart, his hands held loosely at his sides. He looked like a man ready for a fight. Caught between amusement and irritation, Jace shook his head.

"I don't know what the hell you think is going on here. If I was planning a seduction, I'm not likely to try it with a woman who's damn near nine months pregnant. And even without that, I don't screw around with a friend's wife. You ought to remember that."

The tension eased from Keefe's shoulders as he met Jace's steady look. He *did* remember. It wasn't something he was likely to forget. He reached for his cigarettes and swallowed a curse when he remembered that he'd left them on the bureau in his room—the latest step in his attempt to give the damned things up.

"I was out of line," he said, offering the apology that was due.

"Yeah, you were," Jace agreed, without anger. He tucked a box of nails in his shirt pocket, slid a hammer into the back pocket of his jeans and lifted the boards he'd cut and sanded. "I'm going to finish up repairs on the gate. See you at supper."

Keefe nodded. He knew that, as far as Jace was concerned, the subject was closed, the brief moment of tension forgotten as if it had never occurred. It was easy enough for Jace to forget—he wasn't the one who'd made a fool of himself.

He jammed his hat on as he left the workroom and stalked the length of the barn. *Jace making a play for Tessa.* How could he have been so double-damned stupid as to think it might happen? If he'd stopped to think, even for a minute, he'd have known better. But he hadn't stopped to think. He'd seen Jace holding her and he'd bridled like a bull moose defending his harem. His first thought had been that Jace had no business putting his arms around *his* wife.

And even now, when he knew the embrace—if you could even call it that—had been perfectly innocent, there was a part of him that still resented it. He recognized the emotion roiling in the pit of his stomach for what it was—jealousy, plain and simple. Only there was nothing *simple* about it. Keefe narrowed his eyes against the glare of the late-afternoon sun as he stepped out of the barn. Where Tessa was concerned, he had no right to be jealous. No right at all.

He scowled. Damn. He'd give his right arm for a cigarette.

Keefe was lying on his back under the kitchen sink when the phone rang. Tessa had mentioned that there was a leak in the pipes under there over a week ago. He was willing to admit to himself that it was sheer guilt that was driving him to look at it tonight. He'd been way out of line this afternoon and the fact that she hadn't noticed didn't alleviate his guilt. Since he'd rather wrestle a porcupine with his bare hands than work on plumbing, he figured it was good a way as any to soothe his guilty conscience.

But that didn't keep him from feeling a definite surge of relief when the phone rang. Even talking to someone who wanted to sell him magazine subscriptions was better than confronting the mysteries of forty-year-old plumbing.

"Do you want me to get that?" Tessa asked as he scooted out from under the sink.

"You stay put. I'll get it." Gripping the edge of the counter, he levered himself to his feet. He glanced at Tessa as the phone rang a second time. She was sitting at the kitchen table, working on a grocery list. Over dinner, Jace had offered to make the drive into town the next day and pick up supplies.

"Walker," Keefe said into the receiver.

"How's life in the great outdoors?"

At the sound of his older brother's voice, Keefe's

mouth curved in a smile. "Better than a poke in the eye with a sharp stick," he drawled. "How's life among the criminal element?"

"Tolerable."

Sam caught Keefe up on family news: Cole's little girl was going to camp for a week, giving Cole and Addie a chance for a delayed honeymoon; Gage and Kelsey were planning on putting up another greenhouse in the fall and hiring full-time help for Kelsey's small-scale farming enterprise; the baby was growing like a weed; and their six-year-old son had decided that he definitely wanted to be professional hang glider when he grew up.

"I didn't know there were *professional* hang gliders," Keefe said, grinning.

"Danny may be the first." Sam's laughter died away, and silence hummed along the phone lines for a moment. Keefe waited. Out the corner of his eye, he saw Tessa press her hand against the small of her back, a faint move of discomfort flickering across her face. He frowned. It wasn't the first time tonight that he'd seen her do that.

"Nikki says she told you that she can't have children."

"She told me."

"We haven't said anything to anyone else in the family."

"No one's going to blame her," Keefe said.

"Nikki knows that. She *says* she knows it." There was a short silence, and when Sam spoke again, frustration put an edge in his voice. "She just needs some time, I guess."

Keefe's fingers tightened over the receiver. He wondered if Sam had considered how *he* felt about not having children, but he knew his older brother well enough to know that he'd probably focused himself completely on what Nikki was going through. Sam's instinct was to protect those he loved. It would be hell for him to find himself virtually helpless to alleviate his wife's pain.

"If there's anything I can do..." he said, knowing there wasn't a damned thing anyone could do. This was something Sam and Nikki were going to have to work out together.

"Thanks." Sam changed the topic abruptly. "Have you heard anything lately from Tessa's in-laws?"

"*Former* in-laws," Keefe corrected, his tone sharp enough to catch Tessa's attention. She looked at him, her eyes questioning. He shook his head and wished he'd thought to take this call in his office. If the Mallorys were up to something, he didn't want Tessa to worry about it.

"Former in-laws," Sam agreed. "Have you heard from them?"

"No." Keefe half turned away from Tessa, but unless he wanted to whisper into the phone, there was no way to keep her from hearing his end of the conversation. "I wrote and told them about our marriage. I figured that might head any trouble off at the pass."

"Did they contact you?" Sam asked, sounding more like a cop than a brother.

"No. But I didn't exactly expect them to send a card wishing her luck. What's this about?"

"Remember me telling you that someone was making inquiries about the family, poking into old records?''

"I remember."

"When you told me what was going on with Tessa, it seemed pretty obvious that it was the senator trying to track her down. But there's still somebody digging into old files, asking questions."

"The Mallorys know where she is." Keefe frowned at a hairline crack in the wall in front of him, courtesy of one of California's many fault lines. Behind him, he could feel Tessa's anxious gaze, but he didn't have any reassurances to offer her. "Why would they be asking about her?"

"The inquiries don't seem to have anything to do with Tessa. I only thought of her because of the problems she's had with the senator and his wife."

"Then who are they about?" Worry put an edge on the question.

"It's weird," Sam said slowly. "Whoever it is, they're digging up old records on Shannon."

"Shannon?" Shock made Keefe's voice louder than he'd intended. Out the corner of his eye, he saw Tessa start, but he was too distracted to offer her reassurance. "Why would anyone be making inquiries about Shannon?"

"I don't know."

"Hell, it's been more than twenty years since—" Keefe broke off, his throat suddenly tight. After all these years, it still hurt to think about it. "Why? After all these years?"

"I don't know," Sam said again.

Neither of them spoke as they considered the implications.

"Do you think it could be Shannon herself?" Keefe said, the words all but dragged from him.

"She was just a baby. She wouldn't remember enough." Sam spoke roughly, to conceal how much he wanted to believe.

"She was four. That's old enough to remember."

Sam didn't argue, but he didn't agree, either. Silence hummed between them.

"Have you said anything to Mom?" Keefe asked finally.

"I haven't said anything to anyone but you. There's no point in opening up old wounds without reason."

Especially when those wounds had never really healed. But Keefe didn't say that out loud. Sam knew as well as he did what this could mean—if it meant anything at all.

"Keep me posted," Keefe said, aware that there was nothing more to say. Whatever was happening, there was nothing to do but wait and see how it all unfolded. He hung up the phone and turned around. The cupboard doors beneath the sink still gaped open, and tools were still spread out on the floor. It had been only a few minutes since he abandoned the leaky sink, but it seemed much longer than that.

"Is something wrong?" Tessa asked, when he didn't say anything. "Are the Mallorys causing problems for your family?"

"No." He was glad he could reassure her on that. "I think you've heard the last of them."

She looked doubtful but didn't contradict him. He looked at the mess under the sink again, but he wasn't really seeing it. His mind had gone back two decades, memories flooding past barriers that had been in place so long that he rarely noticed their existence.

"Who's Shannon?"

"What?" Startled by the question, he jerked his eyes in her direction, pinning her where she sat.

"I'm sorry." Tessa flinched at his sharp tone. "I didn't mean to pry. It's none of my business." She struggled to rise, a simple task that had grown ridiculously difficult in recent weeks.

"I didn't mean to snap." Two quick strides brought him to her chair. He set one hand on her shoulder, pressing her down. "I'm sorry, Tessa."

"I shouldn't have asked—" she began, still disconcerted by his readiness to apologize when he found himself in the wrong.

"It's not a secret," he said. He leaned his hips back against the edge of the counter and slid his hands into his pockets. "Shannon was—is—my little sister."

"Your sister?" she repeated, staring at him. "I didn't know you had a sister. Where is she?"

"She was kidnapped when she was four years old. We haven't seen her in over twenty years." He made it a dry recitation of fact, as if it meant nothing to him, but Tessa saw the look in his eyes and knew the pain was still sharp and hard.

"Kidnapped?" Unconsciously she spread one hand across the heavy bulge of her stomach, as if to protect the child she carried. "Why would someone kidnap her?"

Keefe told the story in that same clipped tone, speaking rapidly, as if he needed to get through it quickly, without giving himself time to think about it.

"About a year after my father was killed, Mom remarried. I'll spare you the gory details, but the guy was a royal bastard. He resented the hell out of the four of us, and we felt the same way about him. The marriage didn't last very long, but Mom was pregnant by then. I was thirteen and I remember resenting the baby she was carrying. I figured the kid would be a reminder of Harlan, a reminder none of us needed. But then Mom brought Shannon home from the hospital and she was...she was the most incredible thing I'd ever seen."

His smile was soft with memory, and Tessa found herself thinking about the child she carried, about what a good father Keefe would be to that child, if she decided to give it up.

"We all fell in love with her. She could wind any of us around her little finger and she knew it. We spoiled her rotten. It's a miracle she didn't turn into a brat, but she had the sweetest temperament."

"She was lucky to have all of you," Tessa said, thinking of her lonely childhood.

"We were lucky to have her. The only real fly in the ointment was that Harlan—her father—had visitation rights. He took sporadic advantage of them. He used spending time with Shannon as an excuse to see Mom. He kept trying to persuade her to let him come back but she wanted nothing to do with him. I guess he must have finally believed her. Shannon was four when he showed up unexpectedly to take her for the weekend. Gage was the only one of us home. He let Harlan take her. Hell, Harlan had the legal right to take her, and even if he hadn't, Gage was just a kid, only fifteen years old. Harlan never brought her back.''

In the silence that followed, Tessa heard the soft *plink* of water dripping into the pan set to catch the drips from the leaky pipe under the sink. Somewhere outside, an owl hooted, a note of lonely inquiry in the sound.

"Didn't you... Wasn't there anything the police could do?"

"They did what they could." He lifted one shoulder in a half shrug. "It's just not that hard for a man to disappear with a child. Harlan was a bastard but he wasn't stupid. And he was a cop. He knew exactly how to go about disappearing."

"I can't imagine how hard it must have been on your mother—on all of you," Tessa said, her hand still cradling the child she had not yet made up her mind to accept into her heart.

"It was about as rough as it gets," Keefe admitted. "For a long time, our lives revolved around finding Shannon. But time goes by and life continues and you learn to put all the questions and fear in a compartment somewhere in your head and lock them away there. Otherwise, you go crazy."

"Yes, I imagine you would," she murmured, thinking of how terrible it would be not to know if your child was safe—or even still alive. Her fingers shifted against her stomach as it occurred to her that, if she gave up this baby, she'd be putting herself in exactly that position. She wondered, yet again, if she could do it.

Keefe's sleep that night was restless, punctuated by tangled dreams of Tessa, Shannon, and an endlessly dripping pipe that couldn't be fixed, no matter what he did. He woke abruptly, a headache pounding at his temples and his heart beating much too quickly. For an instant, he didn't know what had awakened him, but then the sound came again.

"Keefe?" It was Tessa's voice, high and thin.

He sat up in bed. She was standing in the doorway, and for a moment he wondered if he was still asleep and this was part of some new dream.

"What's wrong?" His voice was raspy with sleep.

"I'm sorry to wake you," Tessa said apologetically. "But I think it's time."

"Time?" He blinked at her. "Time for what?"

"For the baby to be born."

"It can't be," he protested blankly. "It's not due for two weeks."

"Tell that to the baby. My water just broke."

"Oh, my God." The words were more prayer than exclamation.

Chapter 12

"It's going to be all right," Keefe said, taking his eyes off the road long enough to give Tessa a reassuring smile. "You're going to be fine."

It was, by conservative estimate, the tenth time he'd told her that in the twenty minutes since she told him the baby was on the way. His initial reaction had been denial. Once convinced that the baby not only *could* be on the way but actually *was* on the way, he'd immediately told her not to worry, she was going to be fine. And he'd kept telling her that as he dragged on his clothes, grabbed the overnight case she'd packed a few days before and herded her out to the truck. He'd all but lifted her into the cab and then asked if she'd be okay while he let Jace know what was happening. He hadn't even cracked a smile when Tessa told him that she didn't think she was likely to give birth in the next two or three minutes.

She'd never seen Keefe thrown so completely off balance. At another time, she might have enjoyed seeing such a classic example of male panic. As it was, she had other things on her mind. Tessa dug her fingernails into the unyielding plastic of the truck's armrest and breathed her way through a contraction.

"We're almost there," he said as the contraction eased and she drew a deep breath.

In fact, they were still quite a ways from the hospital, but she decided it would be unkind to point that out. He was trying so hard to reassure her. The funny thing was, she didn't really need to be reassured. Now that the moment was here, she felt remarkably calm. The same could not be said of Keefe.

"It's going to be all right," he said again. Keefe knew he was repeating himself. His hand tightened over the steering wheel and he resisted the urge to push the gas pedal down even farther. He was already driving as fast as was safe. He glanced at the illuminated dial of the clock on the dashboard.

"How far apart are the contractions?"

"There's plenty of time," Tessa said, sounding ridiculously cool. "I'm not going to have the baby in your truck."

"God, no!" The exclamation popped out, his tone horrified.

Tessa's chuckle was a little ragged around the edges, but the fact that she could laugh at all astonished him so much that he hardly noticed. "Not in the mood to deliver a baby tonight?"

"Don't even joke about it," he pleaded, but his

hands relaxed their death grip on the steering wheel. He shot her a quick look. "How are you, really?"

"I'm fine. Really," she added, when he looked doubtful. "I'm just anxious to get this over with." She stared out the windshield at the night-dark road, frowning a little as she tried to sort out what she was feeling. "In a way, my life has been on hold for the last few months. I haven't been able to make any plans or decisions until the baby was born."

"What kind of plans and decisions?" Talking might help to distract her, he thought. And he wouldn't mind if it did the same for him.

"I don't know." She shot him a quick, self-conscious smile. "I guess I should have some idea of what I want to do, but I don't, really."

"You don't have to decide anything right away."

Tessa knew he was referring to the agreement they'd made when he asked her to marry him—that he would take the baby if she decided to give it up. When they made that bargain, she'd been more than half-sure that she knew what her decision would be. No child could hope for a better father than Keefe, so her conscience would be clear. She could walk away, finally put her marriage to Bobby behind her and pick up the pieces of her life.

Funny, that idea didn't hold as much appeal as it once had.

From the moment she realized that she was pregnant, Tessa had done her best to avoid thinking about how she might feel when the baby was born. She'd considered, in a detached sort of way, whether or not she should give the child up for adoption, she'd even allowed herself to wonder whether or not she'd be *able* to give it up, but she hadn't allowed herself to really *think* about how she was going to feel about the child she'd carried under her heart for nine months.

But no amount of thinking could have prepared her for the moment when she held her child for the first time. Looking down at him, she was awed by his tiny perfection, frightened by his fragility, terrified of his dependence on her. Everything he would be, all he would become—it all began this minute. And the decisions she made in the next few weeks would impact the rest of his life.

The weight of responsibility settled on her like a band around her chest, slowly tightening, threatening to cut off her air. She actually felt light-headed. She wasn't ready for this. She would never be ready for this. After the mess she'd made of her own life, it was a terrible, frightening joke that she should find herself responsible for this new, perfect life.

Tessa lifted her head and stared around the sterile hospital room with eyes that saw nothing but the yawning emptiness that had opened up in front of her. She couldn't do this. It was mistake, a huge mistake. Someone had to do something, had to—

"Tessa?"

Keefe's deep voice sliced through the choking layers of panic. Her head jerked toward him, her heart thumping against her breastbone, sheer terror in her eyes.

"Keefe." His name came out on a gasp. The hand she extended to him was unsteady. In her panic, she'd forgotten that she wasn't alone.

"Hey." His fingers closed, warm and strong, over hers. "It's okay."

Tessa wanted to tell him that it wasn't okay, that she didn't think it would ever be okay again. She opened her mouth to say as much—or maybe just to whimper in terror—and then her eyes met his. His gaze was calm and steady, offering a quiet reassurance that dampened her rising panic.

"It's okay," he said again.

It occurred to her that he might have used the same tone to soothe a fractious mare. The idea struck her as funny, and the fear receded another notch. Leaning back against the pillows, she closed her eyes for a moment, still shaky but starting to regain her balance. When she looked at him again, she was able to smile a little.

"I'm all right," she said, and hoped she wasn't lying.

"A little overwhelming, isn't he?" Keefe said. Tessa followed his gaze and looked down at the baby. A wave of fear surged through her, but the steady feel of Keefe's hand on hers made it easier to control. He stroked the baby's cheek with the tip of one finger. Next to the baby's head, his hand seemed massive.

"He's so helpless," she whispered. It was as close as she could come to articulating her fear. "What if I do something wrong?"

"You won't."

She didn't know whether to be flattered or appalled by his easy confidence. She only wished she could share it.

If Keefe had ever believed in love at first sight, his first marriage had served to drum that foolishness out of him. Love—real love—was something that grew from familiarity.

And then he held Tessa's child for the first time.

A sleepy, frowning, red-faced infant with a few wisps of pale hair perched on top of a head misshapen from the birthing process, the newborn had all the beauty of a wizened old man. Keefe looked down at the boy, felt the fragility of a life that fit in his two hands, and the world shifted around him. Unfocused, vague blue eyes peered up at him, and one hand escaped the soft yellow blanket to wave aimlessly in the air.

"Hey, how you doin'?" He spoke softly, his voice husky with unexpected emotion. The baby immediately stopped squirming and stared up at him, his gaze intent. "So, what do you think of the world so far?"

He continued to talk, carrying on a nonsensical one-sided conversation that would have made him feel faintly embarrassed if he overheard it from someone else, but the baby stared up at him as if fascinated by every word, and Keefe's heart dropped right into his fingers.

They named the baby David Tyler. David for Keefe's father and Tyler because Tessa liked the sound of it. She was startled when Keefe suggested his father's name—startled and a little uneasy.

"I'm not trying to push you into any decisions," Keefe said, reading her hesitation. "I just kind of liked the idea. But if you'd rather not, that's okay."

"No, I think David is a good name." It was a straightforward name, a solid name, reflecting the kind of person she hoped he'd become. She gave Keefe an uncertain look. "What if... I mean, you might have a son of your own someday."

Something flickered in his eyes, an emotion there and gone too quickly for her to identify. Hurt? Anger? Whatever it was, it was gone in less than a heartbeat, leaving his expression unreadable.

"Whatever happens, whatever you decide, I'd like him to have my father's name."

What have I done? Tessa wondered. The bargain they'd made a few weeks ago suddenly seemed full of pitfalls. If she decided to keep the baby, Keefe was going to get the short end of the stick. And if she decided to give him up? Her fingers curled into the soft blanket that swaddled him. She wasn't ready to think about that. One thing at a time.

She smiled at Keefe and hoped her eyes didn't reveal the turmoil she felt. "I'd like to name him David, if you're sure."

"I'm sure."

So, the name David Tyler Walker was put on the birth certificate. Keefe was listed as his father, and the lie he'd told the Mallorys became legal.

The truck rattled across the cattle guard, the wheels kicking up a cloud of dust on the dirt road beyond. Tessa leaned forward, anxious for the first glimpse of the ranch house. It seemed like weeks since Keefe had driven her to the hospital.

"Not much has changed in the last couple of days," Keefe said, smiling at her eagerness.

She laughed and sat back against the seat. "I didn't think it would have. I'm just anxious to get home."

Home. Tessa was surprised at how easily the word came to her. Looking out at the land and the mountains that rose up on every side, she realized that, though she'd lived on the Flying Ace for just a few weeks, it already felt more like home than the house she'd shared with Bobby for four years. For that matter, it felt more like home than the pseudo-southern Gothic mansion in which she'd been raised.

The realization was a little frightening. This wasn't her home, she reminded herself. She was likely to get hurt if she let herself forget that.

But the sobering reminder was not enough to dampen the pleasure she felt when the house came into sight. There was nothing elegant or refined about it, but its almost stark simplicity was more than half its charm, as far as she was concerned. There was something reassuring about the plain lines of it.

"Home at last," Keefe said as he stopped the truck in front of the house.

"Home at last," Tessa echoed, her heart in the words.

You've got to make a choice soon, she told herself as she saw Jace loping toward them. She had no claim on this place, on these two men. Forever had never been part of the bargain, and the longer she dragged things out, the harder it was going to be on all of them.

And then Jace was pulling open the door of the truck and smiling at her. "Welcome home."

Soon, she promised. *I'll make a decision soon.*

Chapter 13

Keefe paused in the doorway to Tessa's room. He was hot and dirty, but the crib was a more powerful lure than the prospect of a shower. He crossed the room quietly and peered over the rail of the crib. His face creased in a smile when he saw that David was awake.

"Hey, kid. How you doin'?" The baby's round face lit up, his blue eyes sparkling. Keefe reached in to take one little hand between his thumb and forefinger and shake it gently. "I guess your mom thinks you're asleep, huh?"

David babbled a response, his legs pumping. Clad only in a diaper, his whole body seemed to quiver with excitement. His mother might remain firm about not picking him up, but he knew Keefe couldn't resist temptation. At almost two months old, he had a pretty good handle on the people who formed his small world. His mother's hands were the softest, but she was more likely to insist on nap time being used for napping. The two men, on the other hand, could be counted on to pick him up.

"Figure me for a sucker, don't you?" Keefe murmured. His smile became a grin when David's legs pumped harder and his mouth widened in a damp, toothless smile. He gurgled with pleasure when Keefe's big hands slid under him. He waved his arms to show his approval as he was lifted from his crib and cradled against a broad chest.

Keefe held him with easy confidence. He'd always been fairly comfortable around babies. He and his brothers had helped take care of their infant sister, and when Cole's wife left him with a newborn daughter, the whole family had pitched in to help care for Mary. Those experiences had helped prepare him for the practical aspects of taking care of a baby. He could change a diaper, warm a bottle or manage a bath. None of that had prepared him for what it would be like to hold a child and think of him as your own. And whatever happened in the future, he considered this child his.

David gurgled happily, one hand waving as if to emphasize some point he was making.

"Hey, don't make too much noise," Keefe cautioned. "If your mom catches us, she'll have my head." David chuckled—a fat baby sound of contentment that made Keefe grin. He bounced the child gently in his arms. "I bet you think it would be funny to see your Mom come after me with a frying pan. You'd like that, wouldn't you?"

To Tessa, standing in the doorway, the two of them were a picture-perfect image of father and son. She'd been on her way in to check on David when she heard Keefe talking. She had tiptoed closer, smiling at Keefe's easy conversational tone. He never talked baby talk. Instead, he talked to David much the same way he would have talked to another adult. And David always seemed to watch and listen so carefully that there were times when Tessa half believed he understood every word.

Her smile slowly faded as she watched them together. Keefe held the baby so easily, his big hands cradling him with gentle care. He was a natural father. What was more, he was *David's* father, in every way that mattered. From the moment David was put in his arms, there had seemed to be a connection between them, a bond that had nothing to do with blood ties and everything to do with ties of the heart. She didn't pretend to understand it, but she knew it was real and true.

She backed away from the door, leaving the two of them their privacy.

Shaken by the sweet scene, Tessa went back to the kitchen. Seeing Keefe with the baby had forced her to face something she'd been trying to avoid. Since David's birth, she'd been letting time drift by, not thinking about the past or the future, just living from day to day. It had been so easy to do, so easy to think only of the moment. For the first few weeks, just taking care of David had absorbed all her time and energy. But that excuse only went so far. The truth was, she hadn't thought about the future because she didn't *want* to think about it.

Tessa opened the refrigerator and stared blankly at its contents. Keefe loved David, and David adored him. It shamed her to admit but Keefe had fallen in love with her child before she had. It had taken her a little while to work her way past old memories and old anger. Gradually she'd stopped thinking of Bobby when she looked at her baby and she'd begun to see him as a person in his own right. It seemed impossible that this perfect, happy baby had come out of the unhappiness of her marriage. And yet here he was, and she loved him.

Tessa shut the refrigerator without having taken anything from it. She turned and looked around the tidy kitchen without seeing it. Keefe loved David, too. How could she possibly separate them? But she couldn't give up her child. It seemed incredible that she'd ever thought she could.

She couldn't give him up, but she couldn't take him away from Keefe. She couldn't go, but she couldn't stay. That hadn't been a part of their bargain.

Hearing the shower come on, she knew Keefe must have put David back down. It was almost time for dinner. She lifted the lid off the slow cooker and poked a fork into a piece of beef, checking it for tenderness. It seemed incredible to her that, with the weather as hot as it was, Jace and Keefe could still want meat-and-potatoes meals, but they did. Her one venture into the world of pasta salads had been greeted with almost comical dismay. They'd eaten it, pronounced it delicious and then asked where the meat was.

Remembering that, Tessa smiled a little. At least they had been able to tell her the truth. She took that as a sign that she was a different person from the frightened woman who had arrived here all those months ago. Her smile faded as she set the lid back on the slow cooker and went to check the rolls she had warming in the oven. She was different. She had gained confidence, grown as a person. She had changed. Maybe it was time her bargain with Keefe changed, too.

Her teeth worried her lower lip as she considered the possibility. Though she'd hardly been aware of it, the idea had been floating around in the back of her head for the past couple of weeks. What if they changed the bargain, made a new one? Did she have the courage to suggest it?

Tessa sighed as she eased her hand through the mass of thorny canes and slid the blades of the pruning shears around the base of a dead cane. A quick snip and it was cut. She released her breath on a sigh of relief. One down and approximately a zillion to go, she thought as she started backing out of the shrub.

It didn't take a person with a green thumb to know that the roses hadn't been pruned since sometime before the Flood. The bushes were huge, unruly masses of thorns and flowers. Her knowledge of gardening was minimal, but it was enough to suggest that the dead canes should be removed before any attempt was made to tame the rest of the bush.

With that in mind, she'd put David in his carrier and settled him in a patch of shade, where he'd promptly gone to sleep, leaving her free to tackle the roses. Her attempts to cut the canes from above had been only marginally successful. She'd finally thrown dignity to the winds and crawled underneath the bush so that she could cut the dead canes out right at the base of the plant.

Tessa was halfway out from under the bush when she felt something catch at the back of her T-shirt. She twisted her body, trying to dislodge it, but it clung with a tenacity possible only in thorns and small children with sticky fingers. Lying on her belly, she tried to reach her hand around to get hold of the offending cane, but she couldn't get to it, no matter how she twisted and turned. It seemed as if, the more she tried to get loose, the tighter the cane gripped her shirt. She was just starting to think that she was going to become living mulch for the shrub when rescue arrived.

"I've heard of people getting caught up in their work, but I've never seen anyone put quite such a literal interpretation on it."

"Jace! Thank heavens. I'm stuck."

"No kidding."

She could tell by the tone of his voice that he was grinning at her predicament, but he was welcome to laugh all he wanted as long as he untangled her. He crouched down beside her, and she felt a tug against her shirt as he loosened the cane's hold.

"I think you can make a break for it now," he said after a moment.

"Thanks," Tessa said as she slid the rest of the way out from under the bush. "I was starting to think I was going to become a permanent part of the landscape."

"And a lovely addition you'd make," Jace said. He released the offending cane and rose to his feet, reaching down to give her a hand up.

"What are you doing home?" Tessa asked as she brushed herself off. "I thought you were supposed to be doing something with the cattle."

"Something with the cattle?" Jace grinned. "That leaves a lot of room for interpretation. Could you be more specific?"

"No," she admitted with a sheepish smile. "I wasn't really paying much attention when Keefe told me you were going to be gone most of the day."

"You're forgiven," he said generously. "We were going to be gone, but my horse pulled up lame, so I brought him home."

"Are you going back out?"

"Nope." He moved over to the baby's carrier and crouched down beside it. "By the time I got there, it would be time to start back. Keefe said he'd finish up what he could and then head in."

Tessa brushed a lock of hair back from her damp forehead and looked at the pile of prunings with satisfaction. There was still a lot of work that needed to be done, but she'd made a start. Maybe in the spring she could— She cut the thought short. *In the spring.* As if she'd still be here then.

"Hey, look who's waking up!" Jace said, and she turned, grateful for the distraction. David blinked sleepy blue eyes and gave Jace a friendly smile, acknowledging the presence of one of his favorite slaves.

"He sure is growing fast," Jace commented, grinning down at the him. "Pretty soon, he'll be ready for his own pony."

If we're here long enough, Tessa thought.

"You're very good with him," she said aloud, trying to distract herself from thinking too much about the future. "That doesn't exactly fit in with the bachelor image."

"I was married once." Jace poked David's stomach with one gentle finger and was rewarded by a gurgle of laughter. "We had a child."

"What?" Tessa stared at him, her eyes wide with shock. "You have a child?"

"Had," he corrected quietly. He brushed his finger against the baby's cheek and then stood up. He looked at Tessa, and she had the distinct impression that he wished his words had gone unsaid, but she couldn't simply pretend she hadn't heard him.

"Had?" Tessa repeated faintly.

"There was a car accident. A blowout, the car went out of control. It wasn't anybody's fault." He looked past her, his expression uncharacteristically grim. "She was two."

Tessa stared at him, at a loss for words. There didn't seem to be anything that could be said. "I'm sorry" seemed hopelessly banal but, in the end, it was all she had to offer.

"I'm sorry, Jace."

"Me, too," he whispered, speaking more to himself than to her. He shook his head, as if physically shaking off the memories. "It was a long time ago."

But Tessa saw the shadows behind his smile. "What about your wife? Was she—" She broke off, uncertain how to phrase the question. But Jace answered without forcing her to find the right words.

"Her injuries were minor—the physical ones, anyway. We were divorced a few months after the accident, and I haven't seen her since. Like I said, it was a long time ago." He glanced down at David, who was contentedly waving one hand in front of his face. "I haven't told anyone about that in a long time," he said, sounding surprised that he'd done so now.

"I don't know what I'd do if anything happened to him," Tessa said, looking at David. She shivered, suddenly cool, despite the late-afternoon warmth.

"At first you wish you'd died with them." Jace spoke slowly, almost as if talking to himself. "After a while, you figure out that a part of you *did* die. And then you start picking up the pieces and going on with your life." He looked at her and smiled, and Tessa thought the shadows had receded a little further. "There's not much point in doing anything else. You can't just stop loving people. You have to take chances. You might as well be dead if you don't."

Tessa thought about what he'd said long after he'd gone. She thought about it while she combed bits of leaves and pine needles out of her hair and changed into clean clothes. She thought about it while she gave David his bath and she considered it while she cooked dinner. *You can't just stop loving people.* Jace's words replayed themselves in her mind. *You have to take chances.*

She looked at Keefe as he came in for dinner, saw the strength in him, the gentleness. She thought of the way he'd opened his home to her, of the way he'd accepted David as his own. She thought of the way he'd held her when she cried, of the times he'd kissed her, of the way he'd helped her regain her confidence, her self-respect.

"Dinner smells good," Keefe said as he walked through the kitchen.

Tessa murmured some response and watched him disappear through the opposite door, on his way to take a shower.

You have to take chances.

Jace was right—but did she have the courage to take this particular chance?

"Could I talk to you?"

There was a tense edge in Tessa's voice that had Keefe's fingers tightening around the edges of the magazine he was reading. He didn't have to look at her to know that her eyes were anxious. He'd caught that look in her eyes often enough in the past few days. He knew what she wanted to talk about. She was going to tell him that their bargain was coming to an end. She was ready to take David and leave.

It took a conscious effort to loosen his grip on the magazine and look at her. He thought of all the reasons he could give her that she should stay, all the logical arguments about why it would be best for her and the baby, but he didn't say anything. He could probably persuade her to stay, but he wouldn't. He would stick to the bargain they'd made, and deal with the emptiness in his own life after she was gone.

"What's on your mind?" he asked, his easy tone revealing nothing of what he was thinking.

Tessa bit her lip and looked away. Why had she started this? There was no reason they couldn't go on just the way they had been. Everybody was happy with the arrangement, weren't they? But she knew it wasn't that simple.

"David is two months old now," she said, her carefully thought-out speech forgotten.

"He's growing like a weed," Keefe said, smiling a little. But his eyes were dark and watchful, and Tessa felt the knot in her stomach twist a little tighter.

"We... I don't think either of us planned to just let things go this long without coming to some sort of decision. About what to do about...David. I mean." Her voice trailed off. She was making a mess of it, she thought.

"I don't remember setting any schedules," Keefe said slowly.

"No, but you know we didn't plan this." She twisted her fingers together in front of her.

At another time, the familiar gesture might have made Keefe smile. Right now, all it did was make him think of how much he was going to miss her when she left—how much he was going to miss both of them.

"I didn't mean to let things go this long," she continued without looking at him. "I thought, when the baby was born, that I'd know right away...how I felt and what to do. But there seemed to be so much to do and so much to learn and time just drifted by and now it's been two months and you love David and he adores you. Any fool can see that. And I know I haven't been fair to you.''

Keefe stood up and crossed the living room with long, restless strides, stopping next to a window to look out into the darkness. He'd seen this coming, but damned if it wasn't hurting even more than he'd expected. How the hell was he supposed to let the two of them go?

''Let me worry about what's fair to me,'' he said, turning to look at her. ''If you're thinking you have to take David and leave to protect my feelings, you're wrong.''

''That's not it. Well, that *is* it. In a way. Kind of.'' Tessa caught herself and stopped. Another thirty seconds and she was going to be babbling like an idiot. She'd thought this out so carefully, but it wasn't going the way she'd planned. Drawing a deep breath, she started over. ''I thought that—this arrangement has been working pretty well so far, hasn't it?''

''Yes.'' Keefe left the window and moved toward her. The conversation wasn't going the way he'd expected. He sank down on the arm of the chair, putting himself at eye level with her, and waited for her to continue.

''You're good with David. It doesn't seem to make any difference to you that he's not...yours.''

''I think of him as mine.''

''You said that you didn't think it was likely that you'd marry again. Is that still true?''

"I guess so," he said slowly. *Where was she going with this?*

"I don't think I am, either—likely to marry again, that is."

"Okay." Keefe waited. Obviously, she had some reason for starting this discussion other than a desire to reconfirm their future marital prospects. But if she did, she didn't seem in any hurry to tell him what it was. She stood there, her fingers twisted together, her eyes fixed somewhere around his collarbone, and looked as if she wished she were somewhere else.

"Tessa?" He waited until she lifted her eyes reluctantly to his. "What are you getting at?"

She stared at him a moment, her blue eyes so big and scared that she made him think of a rabbit mesmerized by a rattlesnake. Just when he thought she was never going to speak again, she drew in a short, choppy breath and then released the words so rapidly that they nearly tumbled over each other.

"I thought, since *you* don't want to get married and *I* don't want to get married but we already are—married, that is—that maybe we could stay that way. Married, I mean."

Chapter 14

Keefe stared at her blankly while he tried to sort through what she'd said to come up with what she'd *meant*. Because she couldn't have meant what he thought she'd said. But no matter how he turned it over, it came down to the same thing.

"You're suggesting that we make our marriage permanent?"

Tessa nodded. Now that it was out in the open, she'd run out of words.

"For David's sake?" he asked.

"Yes. Well, mostly." She flushed and looked away. "For me, too, I guess. I...like it here. For the first time in my life, I feel at home. I suppose that sounds stupid, considering this isn't my home."

"No. This is your home for as long as you want it to be."

"Thank you." She reached up to smooth an invisible strand of hair back from her face and then let her hand drop to her side, wishing she'd had the foresight to wear something with pockets. Pockets would have provided her with a place to put her hands. As it was, they just seemed to hang at the end of her arms, with nothing to do. She linked her fingers together in front of her and drew a deep breath.

"It seems to me that we've all rubbed along pretty well together these last few months—you and me and Jace."

"Let's leave Jace out of it." He made a sharp gesture of dismissal. "This is between you and me."

"Okay." Tessa swallowed and reformulated her thoughts. She'd half thought of leaning on the idea that the four of them—Keefe and Jace and David and herself—formed a family of sorts. She began again.

"Well, it seems to me that we've done pretty well together. I don't know much about ranching, but I do know how to take care of a house. The cooking and cleaning and things." She waved one hand in a vague gesture to indicate what went into taking care of a house.

"We're not talking about me hiring you as a house-keeper," Keefe said gently.

"No, I know. But I'm just trying to point out some of the reasons we might consider... And there's David," she added, feeling on firm ground at last. "You love him."

"Very much," Keefe agreed. He shifted position, bracing his feet on the floor in front of the chair as he reached for her hands. "Come here."

Her movements stiff, Tessa let him draw her forward until she stood between his knees. She kept her eyes down, focusing on their joined hands. He had strong hands, she thought, with long fingers and broad palms, callused by hard work. They were the kind of hands that made a woman feel as if he could take care of her, keep her safe.

"Tessa?" He waited until she reluctantly lifted her eyes to his face. "Are you talking about a real marriage?"

"Real?" Her eyes widened, and her fingers jerked in his. "You mean, we would—"

"Share a room. Sleep together. Make love. Maybe even have another child someday." Keefe filled in the words she couldn't seem to get out. "Is that the kind of marriage you were talking about?"

Tessa stared at him, her expression blank with shock, her mind reeling at the images he'd created. Sharing a room with Keefe, making love with him, having his child.

Oh, my.

"You're thinking of this as being a permanent marriage, as in forever?" he prompted.

"Y-yes."

"Did you plan on both of us spending the rest of our lives celibate?" he asked gently.

"Of course not." The truth was, she hadn't given it any thought at all. She'd been so busy thinking of other things that she hadn't even thought about…that. She cleared her throat and tried to look casual. "I… Of course, I assumed it would be a real marriage."

"Did you?" His rueful smile called her a liar, and Tessa blushed.

"I didn't really think much about that part of it," she admitted.

"Well, think about it now. There's a lot more to a marriage than taking care of a house or even loving a child."

"I know that."

"Would it be so hard to think about sharing a bed with me?" he asked softly. His thumbs brushed across the backs of her hands, raising goose bumps all the way up her arms.

"It's not that. I just haven't thought about...*that*."

"*That?*" He repeated the word with her emphasis, and his gently mocking tone dragged a faint smile from her. But it faded as old anxieties washed over her.

"Actually, I'm not very good at...at it," she admitted in a rush.

"How do you know?"

"How do I know?" *What kind of question was that? How did he think she knew?* "I just know. That's all."

Keefe nodded, his expression thoughtful. "I don't suppose your late husband might have anything to do with you knowing that you're not good at 'it'?" Her guilty start gave him the answer. He nodded. "And, of course, we've already established that he was never wrong about anything."

"It's not just what he said," Tessa protested, goaded by his dry tone of voice. "It's not something that you need someone else to tell you. I'm just not very good at...at sex. All right?"

"All right." He nodded agreeably. "We can worry

about that later. Let's see what we have so far. I'd be a good father to David. You would take good care of the house. And we would share a bed, even though you're not very good at sex." He tightened his fingers over hers to prevent her convulsive attempt to pull away. "Am I forgetting something?"

Summed up like that, it seemed like a pretty flimsy basis for a marriage, and Tessa felt her heart sink.

"We could make it work," she said, a thread of desperation in her voice. "I know it doesn't sound like a lot, but I know we could make it work."

It was Keefe's turn to look down at their linked hands. "It sounds like quite a bit," he said slowly, but before she could feel hopeful, he shook his head. When he looked at her again, his expression was somber, the gentle humor gone, as if it never been. "I don't want to go through another divorce, Tessa, especially one where a child is involved. Have you even thought about the difference in our ages? You're only twenty-three."

"I'll be twenty-four in November," she offered.

Keefe's mouth quirked in a half smile. "And I'll be thirty-eight in January. Fourteen years is quite an age gap."

"It's not that much."

"When you're my age, I'll be fifty-two. That's not ancient, but it's not exactly a spring chicken, either."

"It doesn't matter. No, listen to me," she said, when he started to interrupt. "Fourteen years isn't that much. And the older we get, the less of a gap it will seem. When I'm seventy, you'll only be eighty-four. That doesn't sound so bad."

Keefe laughed reluctantly and shook his head. "I just don't want you to have any regrets later."

"I won't. Not about that. I didn't just come up with this idea, Keefe. I've been thinking about it for a while now, and I'm not just thinking about David."

"No?" He shifted his hold on her hands so that his fingers rested against the fragile skin of her inner wrists. Tessa knew he must be able to feel the erratic beat of her pulse.

"I want this for myself, too." Her cheeks felt as if they were on fire, but she kept her eyes steady. "I'm not an...independent kind of woman. I know it's not politically correct to admit that, but it's the truth. I don't want to strike out on my own and cut a swath through the world. I don't have any career plans. What I want is to make a home—for David and me. For you. I'm good at that." She swallowed and continued more slowly. "And I trust you. I know you'd never do anything to hurt either of us."

"Tessa, I—" Keefe broke off and stared at her helplessly. He knew her trust wasn't given lightly, and she was offering it to him without reservation.

He didn't know what to say to her. He knew what he *wanted* to say, but he had to think of what was best—not just for him, but for all of them. A few minutes ago, he'd thought she was going to take the baby and leave. He'd braced himself to deal with that. Now, she was suggesting that they take their pretend family and turn it into the real thing. It was something he hadn't dared to suggest himself, for fear she might agree out of some misplaced sense of gratitude. But the idea had been hers. Did she have any idea how much he wanted to accept what she was offering?

"Tessa, there's more to marriage than trust."

"I know." Her eyes were more gray than blue as she looked at him intently. "I...care for you. And I think you care for me. That's a start, and we can build the rest of it, can't we?"

"I don't know."

He wanted to tell her that they could. He didn't want to lose her or David. He'd been content enough before they came into his life, but that had been because he didn't realize how empty his life was, how lonely he was. If they left now, he didn't know how he'd ever manage to fill the void that would open up inside him.

He wanted to jump at her suggestion that they make their marriage permanent. *Care* for her? The bland word didn't begin to describe what he felt. But he couldn't—or wouldn't—put another word to it. Not now. Not yet. He wanted the baby. And he wanted Tessa, more than he'd have believed possible a few months ago. But wanting her didn't make it right for him to take what she was offering.

Tessa read refusal in his lengthy silence, and her heart thumped in sudden fear. He couldn't say no. This was right. She *knew* it was right. She just had to make him see it, too. She twisted her hands free from his and, stepping forward, slid her arms around his neck. Surprised, Keefe let his hands settle on her waist.

"We can make this work, Keefe. I'm sure of it."

She was close enough to see the flecks of gold scattered through the chocolate brown of his eyes.

"Are you?" His fingers shifted lightly against her waist, and Tessa's pulse jumped in response.

"I could learn to be good at...at things," she said, hardly aware that her voice had dropped to a whisper.

"Tessa, I'm not worried about our sex life." His laugh was pained. "No matter what you think, good old Bobby was not the voice of authority. Trust me on this one—sex is the least of our worries."

"It is?" Intrigued, she edged closer. "How do you know?"

"I just do." Keefe's hands tightened on her waist, and she thought he might push her away. But then she saw the look in his eyes and realized that he couldn't. Her experience with men might be limited, but even she recognized the way he was looking at her.

He wants me. The idea was both startling and novel—that Keefe Walker should find her desirable! Of course, he had kissed her before and had even said that he enjoyed it. Tessa considered the possibility that she'd been going about this whole thing the wrong way. She'd been trying to appeal to his practical, reasonable side, but maybe there was a better way. She found herself wondering what her sister would do in this situation. Certainly, Dana would never waste her time with reason if there was a more direct method.

She shifted a little closer, her hips brushing against the inside of his knees. Keefe reaction was almost infinitesimal, but she felt him shift, saw the awareness flare in his eyes. Her eyes dropped to his mouth. It was one thing to recognize that he desired her. It was something else to know what to do with that desire. Then again, maybe that was obvious. True, she wasn't particularly good at sex and, no matter what he said, she didn't expect much from it, but at least with him she wouldn't *mind* it, either.

Gathering her courage in both hands, she leaned forward and set her mouth to his.

For an instant, surprise kept Keefe frozen. Feeling his stillness and mistaking the cause, Tessa nearly panicked. She had to convince him, had to make him see that she was right about this. She pressed her mouth harder to his, as if she could force him to respond. Keefe's fingers were suddenly twined in her hair, pulling her head back so that her mouth left his. Reluctantly she lifted her lashes, half-afraid of what she might see in his expression. There was an oddly gentle laughter in his eyes, but there was something else there, too—a spark of something warm and masculine, something…hungry.

"Sexy is soft," he whispered. And then proceeded to demonstrate.

He'd kissed her before, but it hadn't been like this. No one had *ever* kissed her like this. His mouth touched hers lightly. Once, twice, and then again— quick butterfly kisses that offered a tantalizing hint of something more. He kissed first one corner of her mouth and then the other. Her lips softened in anticipation of a real kiss, but it didn't come. His fingers tugged gently at her hair, tilting her head back so that he could feather a line of light kisses along the edge of her jaw, first one side and then the other.

Tessa had read books in which the author said that someone's bones were melting, but she'd never experienced the phenomenon herself—until this moment. Tessa's fingers curled into the fabric of his shirt as his teeth worried gently at her earlobe. His tongue traced the delicate whorls of her ear, and her breath escaped her on a sigh that teetered on the brink of a whimper.

Keefe continued his leisurely exploration, brushing kisses along the arch of each brow, the curve of her cheek, building the tension within her until, by the time he made his way back to her mouth, Tessa nearly moaned with relief. His teeth closed over her lower lip, nibbling and tasting as if her mouth were an exotic delicacy for him to savor.

She tried to deepen the kiss, but he wouldn't let her, pulling his mouth from hers and beginning his exploration of her face all over again. By the time he reached her mouth for the second time, Tessa was almost frantic. He'd said that sexy was soft, but there was nothing soft about the aching need that was building inside her. She'd never felt anything like it, never realized she could *want* so much.

His teeth closed gently over her lower lip, and her nails dug into his shoulders in sharp, unconscious demand. She felt Keefe's lips curve against hers—a smile of purely masculine satisfaction—and then he was crushing her mouth under his. Tessa arched into him, opening to him. His tongue took possession of her mouth, demanding a response she was only too eager to give.

Tessa had no idea how long the kiss lasted. It felt like forever and it seemed less than a heartbeat. It drained her, yet she felt more alive than she could ever remember feeling in her life. If it continued another second, she would surely die, yet when he lifted his head, she felt bereft.

"Are you trying to seduce me?" he asked huskily.

"I don't know." Her eyelids felt strangely heavy, and it was an effort to look at him. Was *she* seducing *him?* It seemed to her as if the shoe were on the other foot, but she wasn't going to argue. "Am I succeeding?"

"I think so." Keefe's laugh was ragged around the edges, and she felt a surge of satisfaction that she hadn't been the only one affected by that kiss.

She let her hands slide from his shoulders to his chest, and her fingers began working the buttons on the front of his shirt. Keefe watched her, his dark eyes hooded and unreadable. If she thought about it, Tessa knew, she would be shocked by her own actions. She wasn't the kind of woman who unbuttoned a man's shirt. In the early days of their marriage, Bobby had complained bitterly that she was too passive in bed, that she never initiated anything.

It hit her suddenly that she'd never *wanted* to initiate anything with her husband because she'd never really wanted him, not the way she wanted Keefe. Not the way it seemed she'd always wanted him.

Her teeth worried her lower lip as her fingers combed through a mat of crisp dark curls, her palm flattening over his heart. It thudded against her hand, the beat holding a ragged edge that sparked an unfamiliar feeling of feminine triumph in her.

"Do you mind being seduced?" she whispered.

"I should." He cupped his hands around her face, forcing her to look at him. "Tessa, are you sure this is what you want?"

She knew he was asking about much more than this moment. He was asking if she was sure about the future, about wanting to make their marriage real. Her answer came without hesitation.

"I'm sure. This is what I want."

It was a risk to believe her, Keefe thought. And even if he did believe her, they shouldn't jump into anything too quickly. They should take things slow and easy, build up to this moment. There was no reason to hurry this. No reason except the fact that he would probably go crazy if he didn't have her now. He ached with wanting her, hungered for the taste of her, the feel of her in his arms, in his bed.

His hand slid down her back, urging her closer, until she was pressed against him, his thighs braced on either side of her. He saw her eyes widen as she felt the rock-hard length of his erection pressed against her through the layers of their clothing. He waited, half expecting her to pull away, frightened by his blatant arousal. She was still for a moment, as if startled by the feel of him, and Keefe braced himself to let her go. But then her eyes seemed to darken, going from soft blue to smoky gray, and she leaned into him, pressing closer.

The movement dissolved the last remnants of his

control. If there were regrets in the future, so be it. This was worth the risk. *Tessa* was worth the risk.

He stood abruptly and bent to scoop her into his arms. Surprised, Tessa gasped and brought her arms up to circle his neck, clinging to him as he carried her from the living room, holding her as if she weighed next to nothing. He walked past her bedroom, where the baby lay asleep and pushed open the door to his room. Keefe set her on her feet beside the bed, tantalizing them both with the feel of her sliding down his body.

"Welcome to our wedding night," he said softly.

If asked, Tessa would have said that she knew all she cared to know about sex. After the first few months of her marriage to Bobby, she'd realized that, whatever problems they had in bed, they were as much his fault as hers, but that hadn't stopped her believing that she wasn't a particularly sexual person. No doubt there were those who enjoyed the sort of grappling encounters she endured, she'd thought, and she hadn't doubted that, with the right man, sex would certainly be more pleasant than it had been with Bobby. But she'd felt that, if she never had sex again, it wouldn't be any great loss.

It didn't take Keefe long to show her just how wrong she'd been.

He kissed her and touched her as if they had all the time in the world. There was nothing impatient or hurried about it. He undressed her as gently as if this were her first time, which, in a sense, it was. Certainly it was the first time she'd ever felt what she was feeling. As the last of her clothes whispered to the floor, she was suddenly aware that she hadn't lost all the weight she'd put on while carrying the baby.

"You're beautiful," Keefe murmured, interrupting her incoherent apology. He caught her hands and drew them gently away from her body. "Beautiful." He drifted a line of kisses along her collarbone.

"Exquisite." His tongue explored the ragged pulse that beat at the base of her throat.

"Lovely." His mouth trailed downward, and Tessa sucked in a startled breath as his tongue painted delicate patterns across her breast.

"Delicious," he whispered, and she forgot how to breathe when he drew her nipple into his mouth.

Sensation jolted through her, and her knees buckled. His arm like a steel band across her lower back, he supported her easily, taking his time with her breasts, feasting on her until Tessa thought she would surely die.

When he finally lifted his head, her breath was coming in shallow pants and her eyes held a shocked, dazed look that tore at the already ragged edges of Keefe's control. For the first time, he thought he understood why some men found virginity so appealing. There was something undeniably erotic about knowing that he was the first one to show Tessa the potential of her own body, that he was the first one to make her tremble with pleasure.

"Keefe?" She made his name a question, a plea.

"Ssshhh..." He eased her down on the bed and reached for his belt, tearing at it with impatient fingers. In less than a minute, his clothes were lying in a heap on the floor and he was lying over her, easing his legs between hers.

Tessa felt his arousal press against her and stiffened a little. No matter how much surprise she'd felt earlier, she knew what would happen now. *This* wasn't going to change, and she couldn't stop a quick rush of disappointment that all those wonderful sensations should end here.

But she soon realized that she'd been wrong again. Keefe sheathed himself in her body with one long, gliding thrust, filling her completely. Her eyes widened and she stared up at him, stunned by the sensation.

"Okay?" he whispered, his voice strained.

"Y-yes." Her answer was hesitant. *Okay* didn't seem to be the word to describe what she was feeling, but she was in no condition to argue semantics. Fortunately, he didn't seem to need any other response.

Bracing his weight on his elbows, he began to move within her, and Tessa's mind went blank as she realized that she didn't know anything about sex. She had never known it could be like this, had never realized the potential for pleasure locked within her own body. If she'd had a moment to think about it, it might have frightened her, but she couldn't think. All she could do was feel.

Keefe felt her surrender herself completely to the pleasure and ground his teeth together against the need pounding in his veins. She was so sweetly responsive. There was no holding back. She gave herself without reservation. No coy games. No pretending. Just Tessa—all innocence and need.

He saw the startled wonder in her eyes as her climax took her, and then the feel of her body tightening around his dragged him headlong into the spinning whirlpool. Groaning, he gave himself over to the pleasure.

It was a long time before either of them spoke. Keefe used the last ounce of his energy to ease himself from Tessa's body and collapse on the bed next to her. Her murmur of protest ended when he slid one arm under her shoulders and dragged her against his body. They lay without speaking, listening to the ragged sound of each other's breathing slowly steadying.

"I guess I was wrong," Tessa said at last, her voice faint.

"About what?" Keefe turned his face into her hair, the crisp scent of her shampoo mingling with the earthy, musky smell of sex.

"About *this*." One hand flapped limply in the air over their lax bodies. "Maybe I could learn to be good at it."

Keefe's big body shook with laughter. His arm tightened around her shoulders in a quick hug. "If you get any better at it, I'll be in a wheelchair before I'm forty."

She smiled against his chest. "I guess this means our marriage is real now."

"I guess it does," Keefe said, and waited for the doubts to surface. But all he felt was a deep sense of contentment.

"I'm glad," Tessa said simply, and he could only agree.

*   *   *

Tessa hummed to herself as she slid two loaf pans from the oven. The bread looked perfect. She turned one loaf out and rapped on the bottom with her knuckles, nodding with satisfaction at the slightly hollow sound. It sounded perfect, too. As she set the loaves on a wooden rack, her mouth curved in a secret smile. Actually, now that she thought about it, *life* seemed pretty close to perfect right now.

She stretched out one hand to look at the plain gold wedding band on her left hand. Keefe had placed it on her hand months ago, but until last night, its only purpose had been to support the lie they'd told Bobby's parents. Viewed in the light of a new day and a new future, it seemed to gleam a little brighter than it had before.

She thought suddenly of the expensive rings she'd left behind in the house she'd shared with Bobby, and her smile faded. Over the years, she'd come to view those rings as symbolic of everything that was wrong in her life. Rubbing her thumb across the simple gold band, Tessa promised herself that *this* ring would stand for something very different. Not that she had to worry about her marriage to Keefe being anything like her marriage to Bobby, she thought, remembering his tenderness the night before.

Keefe might not be in love with her, but he cared for her and, given time and the right kind of nurturing, that could grow into love. And she did want him to love her, she admitted to herself. Tessa sighed, her expression growing wistful. After last night, she couldn't pretend anymore. She loved him. Heart and soul, for better or worse, she loved him.

Once she'd admitted it, it seemed as if she'd felt that way forever. She thought back to that first summer after he and Dana were married. She'd loved him then with all the passion of a young girl. During the years since then, she'd thought about him often and smiled a little at that childish infatuation. But in retrospect, it was as if her feelings now had grown out of what she'd felt then. Once acknowledged, it seemed the most natural thing in the world, as if it simply had to be.

She would have given a great deal to know how Keefe felt about her, but she wasn't going to dwell on it. Not today, not when she was feeling good about life. Love was something that could grow with time. For now, what she had was enough. It was so much more than she'd imagined possible. A home, a healthy, happy baby—and Keefe. Life was too good for her to waste a minute of it worrying.

As if thinking about him had conjured him up, she heard the front door open and then Keefe's voice calling her name.

"Tessa?"

Her mouth widened in a smile. She hadn't expected to see him again until dinnertime, three hours from now. He was back early, and her heart took a quick leap upward at the thought that maybe he hadn't wanted to wait until evening to see her again.

"I'm in here," she called, wondering why he'd come in the front door rather than the kitchen door.

She heard the thud of his boots against the wooden

floor and started forward to greet him. But his grim expression stopped her before she'd taken more than a step.

"We've got company," he said flatly, stepping aside to allow someone to walk past him.

Tessa stared blankly at the woman who entered her kitchen. Tall, slender, her light blond hair cut in a perfect—and very expensive—chin-length bob, with blue eyes that seemed to measure Tessa for a moment before her beautiful mouth curved in a smile that revealed a perfect set of sparkling teeth.

"Tessa! It's been ages."

Tessa felt the ground start to crumble beneath her feet.

"Dana?"

Chapter 15

"I know this is a surprise, but I hope it's not an entirely unwelcome one." Dana laughed softly, making a joke of the words, as if there could never be any question of her welcome anywhere.

"No, of course not."

When she was a girl, Tessa had been thrown from a horse, hitting the ground flat on her back, so hard that all the air was driven from her lungs. She remembered lying there, staring up at the sky and feeling quite calm as she waited for an angel to step off a cloud and take her away, because she was surely dead. She felt something very similar now. But there was no angel—then or now.

There was just Dana, standing there, looking at her expectantly.

"Of course you're welcome." Tessa didn't look at Keefe as she said it. She *couldn't* look at him, for fear

of what she might see in his eyes. What was he thinking? Feeling? He and Dana had been married. He'd
obviously loved her. Did he feel regret when he
looked at her now? Was he thinking that he was married to the wrong sister? But if she couldn't bring
herself to look at him, Dana didn't share her hesitation. She looked directly at him, her blue eyes sparkling with amusement, as if inviting him to share
some private joke.

"I guess this is what Emily Post would probably
have called 'a delicate social situation.' Ex-wife and
ex-husband meeting for the first time since the divorce, and as in-laws, no less. I wonder what she
would have suggested?"

"I doubt if it came up often enough for her to
worry about it," Keefe said coolly. He didn't seem
to share her amusement.

"Well, I'd say that we could just be good friends,
but friendship never was our strong suit, was it?"
Dana said, her tone adding intimacy to the words.

"No, we weren't ever friends," Keefe agreed
flatly.

"Well, I'm sure, if we give it a little time, we'll
get the hang of being in-laws. Although that sounds
awfully stuffy and official, doesn't it?" Dana wrin-
kled her nose, and Tessa wondered despairingly how
it was possible for her to look exquisite even with her
nose scrunched up.

"Why are you here?" she heard herself asking, and
then wished the words unsaid. Not that she didn't
want an answer to the question, but she didn't want
to sound too anxious, as if it bothered her to have her

exquisitely beautiful, ridiculously slender, perfectly groomed older sister standing there looking at Keefe as if he were a menu item she was thinking about ordering.

Dana looked at her, her expression surprised, and perhaps just a little hurt. "I know I should have called first but, well, to tell the truth, I wasn't sure you'd let me come."

"Not let you—" Tessa broke off, staring at her in surprise. She tried to remember the last time she'd seen Dana. It had probably been close to a year. She didn't remember the exact occasion, but she knew they hadn't exchanged any harsh words. In fact, she wouldn't be surprised if they hadn't exchanged any words at all. They had never had much to say to one another—good, bad or indifferent. "Why would you think that I wouldn't let you come here?"

"Well, I haven't exactly been a model big sister," Dana admitted with a smile that was both rueful and apologetic. "I didn't even come home from Europe for Bobby's funeral. I know I should have, but I've never been very good at things like that." She waved one hand in a vague gesture of dismissal.

"It's all right." Tessa had been so dazed that she barely remembered the funeral. She couldn't imagine that having Dana there would have made any difference at all.

"No, it's not all right," Dana said, sounding determined to shoulder the blame for past misdeeds. "I should have been there. No matter how difficult it was for me, I should have been there."

"It's all right," Tessa said again, biting back an

unexpected jolt of amusement at the inadvertent implication that the funeral might have been harder on Dana than it had been on Bobby's widow. "There wasn't anything you could have done," she said truthfully.

"Maybe not, but I should have been there for you," Dana said.

Tessa tried to think of any time when Dana had been "there" for her. Nothing came to mind. But she seemed sincere in her regret.

"We're family," Dana was saying. "We may not always have been close, but family still means something. At least it should. I was hoping you wouldn't mind me hanging around for a little while—a few days, maybe. I think it would be nice if we took some time to, well, to get to know one another again."

Her smile was sweet and just a little self-deprecating. Despite past experience, Tessa felt herself softening. This was a side of Dana she'd never seen before. Of course, if they got to know one another, there wouldn't be any "again" about it, because they never *had* really known each other—a circumstance that had never seemed to bother her sister in the past. But people could change.

"How did you know where Tessa was?" Keefe asked abruptly.

"When I came home from Europe and found that Tessa had vanished without a trace, I called Aunt Molly," Dana said. "She told me all about your whirlwind courtship. I guess maybe *courtship* isn't exactly the right word to describe it, since she said you two already have a baby." She glanced across the kitchen to where David lay in his carrier, happily gumming a bright pink plastic ring. "This must be my nephew."

"That's David. My—our son," Tessa said, glancing at Keefe as she corrected herself. But he didn't seem to notice. He was watching Dana, his expression still unreadable.

"Isn't he adorable?" Dana said, and this time her smile was patently false, but Tessa didn't hold it against her. She couldn't imagine anyone less likely than her sister to be captivated by a baby. What was surprising was that she'd even made the effort to comment. The Dana she knew wouldn't have bothered— unless she wanted something. And, of course, she did want something—she wanted to stay with them for a few days. Coming from Dana, it seemed such a strange request that Tessa couldn't help but think that maybe her older sister really had been seized by a wave of family feeling. What other possible reason could she have for coming here?

She glanced at Keefe, trying to read something of his thoughts, but whatever he was thinking, his expression revealed nothing. If he had any objection to having Dana as a houseguest, she couldn't tell. And if he was anxious to have his ex-wife stay, she couldn't read that, either.

"We aren't really set up for entertaining," she said slowly.

"I don't expect you to entertain me," Dana said lightly. "I'm perfectly capable of entertaining myself."

Tessa was doubtful. The Dana she remembered had

not been particularly good at providing her own amusements. But then, that Dana wouldn't have expressed any interest in "family," either. People could change, she reminded herself again. The last thing she wanted was to have Keefe's ex-wife staying with them, especially now, when their relationship had just taken such an amazing new direction. But the fact that his ex-wife was also her sister complicated things. True, the relationship had never seemed to mean much to Dana before, but if she really *had* changed...

And why didn't Keefe give her some clue as to his preferences?

"If you're sure you want to stay," she said, letting the words trail off as she glanced at Keefe again. But his expression was closed, and his eyes were unreadable. Whatever he was thinking—or feeling—he was keeping it to himself.

"I knew I could count on you," Dana said with a dazzling smile.

Tessa smiled weakly in return and hoped she hadn't just made the worst mistake of her life.

"You want to run that by me again?" Jace asked. He'd been in the midst of unsaddling his horse, but he'd abandoned the task and turned to look at his partner, his expression one of disbelief.

"You heard me the first time." Keefe's tone bordered on surly, but he didn't try to soften it. For the first time in weeks, he wished he had a cigarette.

"Dana? Here?" Jace packed complete disbelief into the two words.

"She showed up midafternoon."

"What the hell for?" Jace's horse shifted restlessly, and he turned to lift the saddle from the gelding's back.

"Says she wants to spend time with Tessa, get to know the baby."

"Bull! The day she takes an interest in anybody but herself is the day I grow sideburns, put on a spangled jumpsuit and become an Elvis impersonator."

Keefe smiled, but it was perfunctory. "That's all she says she wants."

"And you believe her?" Jace asked disbelievingly.

"If that isn't what she wants, then why is she here?"

"I don't know, but you can bet the ranch that there's another reason." Jace opened the corral gate and slapped the gelding on the rump to send him through it. He tilted his hat back on his head and looked at Keefe, his blue eyes holding a warning. "She's poison. Pure poison. You know it and I know it."

Keefe couldn't argue. "I'll keep an eye on her."

"You'd be better off throwing her skinny butt out," Jace said bluntly. "I don't know why you agreed to let her stay in the first place."

"It wasn't my decision." He reached for the cigarettes he no longer carried and then let his hand drop with a muttered curse. "She's my ex-wife, but she also happens to be Tessa's sister. I can't tell Tessa that she can't have her family here."

Jace shook his head as the corral gate thudded home and he swung the latch into place. "Family means something to the Walkers. Don't make the mistake of thinking it means something to everyone else. Dana and Tessa may share blood, but that's all they share. Take my advice and get rid of her as soon as possible. Tell Tessa I'll be eating at my place tonight. I'm not in the mood to deal with your ex.''

Keefe's jaw was set tight with frustration as he watched the other man walk across the yard to the foreman's house. Jace was right about Dana. She was trouble. Four years of marriage had taught him just how *much* trouble. And he wasn't such a fool as to believe that all families shared the closeness that he and his family did. But that didn't change the facts. Dana was Tessa's sister, and Tessa had asked her to stay. As long as Tessa wanted her here, he couldn't ask her to leave. The only thing he could do was keep an eye on her and make sure that she didn't cause any trouble.

He just wished he knew what she was doing here. Still frowning, he took his hat off and ran his fingers through his hair. While he was at it, he might as well wish that, if she had to show up, she'd done it some other time. After last night... Keefe shook his head as he started up to the house. Hell, he still didn't know what to think about last night, but he knew he didn't want his sister-in-law around—especially not when she also happened to be his ex-wife.

''I hope it was okay to ask Dana to stay,'' Tessa said, her expression anxious.

''She's your sister,'' Keefe said.

He began unbuttoning his shirt, and she looked away. They were in his bedroom—her bedroom, now, she reminded herself. It was the first time they'd been alone together since Dana's arrival. She wasn't sure what bothered her more—talking about her sister, who happened to be his ex-wife, or watching him undress.

He shrugged out of his shirt and draped the garment over the back of a straight-backed chair. Tessa's heart bumped unevenly. His chest was solidly muscled, with the kind of long, ropy muscles that came from hard labor, rather than from hours in the gym. A mat of crisp black hair spread across the upper part of his chest, tapering down across his abdomen to disappear beneath the waist of his faded jeans. Just looking at him, she felt her breasts tighten and swell at the memory of those tight black curls rasping gently against her nipples.

His hands dropped to his belt buckle and she looked away, her mouth going dry. Despite what they'd shared last night, it seemed almost painfully intimate to watch him undress. Last night, everything had happened more or less on impulse and she'd let herself get swept along on the tide. Last night, she'd been so dazzled by the sensual response he stirred in her that she was hardly aware of him taking off his clothes. Events had simply flowed one into the other in a natural, inevitable progression.

Tonight, nothing seemed natural. Too much had happened, too quickly. Twenty-four hours ago, she hadn't known anything of what the future might hold. Then everything had seemed to fall into place with an ease that was little short of miraculous. For a few hours, she'd thought that maybe—just maybe—her life was finally on the right track.

And then Dana had shown up.

"Did David settle in all right?" Keefe asked, his belt buckle jangling faintly as he pulled his belt free of his jeans.

"He seemed to." Tessa glanced at the partially open door on one side of the room. The baby had been sleeping in Tessa's room, but now that everything had changed—Tessa's moving into Keefe's room, and Dana's unexpected arrival—David's things had been moved into the small room next to Keefe's bedroom. The few things that had been stored there had been either moved out or shoved to one side to make room for his crib.

"I wonder if that room was intended to be a nursery," Tessa said chattily, trying not to hear the rasp of a zipper being lowered.

"Could be." Keefe sat down on the edge of the bed and reached for the bootjack.

"You're sure you don't mind Dana staying here?" The subject was like a sore tooth—she just couldn't leave it alone.

"She's your sister," he said again. His boots thudded to the floor, first one and then the other. Tessa twisted her fingers together and wondered uneasily just how she should interpret that statement. Did he mean that Dana was only welcome because they were sisters? She wanted very much to believe that.

"I know it's awkward...." she began. Keefe hooked his thumbs in the waistband of his jeans and shoved them down over his hips. She kept her eyes resolutely turned away and hoped he wouldn't notice the odd little catch in her voice. "She's my sister, but she's also your ex-wife. I hadn't really given it much thought until now. I mean, I'd *thought* about it, but not really—about it being awkward, I mean. I guess, if we'd been closer—Dana and I—maybe I would have thought about it more, but we've never been particularly close, so it didn't seem…"

Keefe stood up. She knew he was moving toward her, because she could see his feet. She couldn't bring herself to raise her eyes any higher.

"…to matter," she continued, speaking a little more quickly. "I was surprised that she'd want— But I can't think of any reason why she'd lie about it, so I guess she must really want to…"

Keefe's hand slid beneath the thick fall of dark gold hair to cup the back of her neck, and Tessa's words broke off in midsentence. She closed her eyes as a shiver of awareness spread outward from where he touched her until her whole body seemed to tingle with it.

"Dana is my ex-wife, and that's the end of my interest in her," he said softly. "She's your sister, and that makes her welcome here for as long as you want her to stay."

Tessa might have tried to explain that *want* wasn't exactly the word she'd have chosen, but he was loosening the belt of her robe with his free hand and she suddenly seemed to be having a difficult time putting together a coherent sentence.

"I don't want to talk about her anymore tonight, okay?"

"O-okay," she whispered, her voice catching in her throat as her robe fell open and he set his hand against her hip, where it seemed to burn through the thin cotton of her nightgown.

"Now, I've got a question for you," he murmured, his fingers shifting against her.

"What?"

"Are you ever going to look at me again?"

Tessa wouldn't have believed it was possible to put both amusement and desire in the same question. There seemed to be no end to the things she didn't know, she thought dazedly.

"I'm not sure," she said, answering his question in a voice thinned by nerves.

"I promise not to bite," he whispered, and then proved himself a liar by catching her lower lip between his teeth and worrying it gently.

Tessa's hands came up to grab hold of his shoulders as her knees threatened to give out under her. His skin was smooth and hot beneath her fingers. He smelled of soap and coffee and a faint, pleasantly musky smell that she could only define as "man." He took her mouth in a slow, deep kiss that left her drugged with hunger and clinging to him.

She offered not a word of protest when he bent to catch her under knees and shoulders and carried her to the bed. Her doubts were forgotten. Dana disappeared. Nothing existed but the two of them.

"I suppose I'm the last one up," Dana said as she entered the kitchen the next morning. "I have this vague idea that ranchers start their day before the sun comes up.''

"More often than not," Tessa agreed. She glanced up from the cookbook she was looking through, her welcoming smile wilting a little when she saw the other woman.

It didn't seem fair that her sister could look so beautiful first thing in the morning. Dana wore a pair of slim black jeans and a skinny little hot-pink rib-knit top that clung to her slender body in all the right places. Tessa was immediately conscious of the extra ten pounds she still carried from her pregnancy and the fact that her hair looked dishwater-blond in comparison to Dana's exquisite pale gold bob.

But it would take more than a haircut and clothes to close the gap between them, she admitted silently. Nature had simply been in an exceptionally generous mood when her older sister was born. She wanted to attribute Dana's flawless complexion and sapphire-blue eyes to a good foundation and colored contact lenses. But the truth, disgusting as it was, was that Dana was ridiculously beautiful, without the slightest need for cosmetic aids.

"Would you like some breakfast?" she asked, pushing fruitless comparisons to the back of her mind.

"I wouldn't mind a cup of coffee." Dana pulled out a chair and sat down, secure in the knowledge that someone else would provide what she'd requested.

"Cream or sugar?" Tessa asked as she got up and took a mug from the cupboard.

"A little of both, please. I don't suppose you have cappuccino?"

"Not even the instant kind," Tessa admitted, and then bit back a smile at her sister's slightly martyred sigh. She set the coffee down in front of Dana and then got a carton of cream from the refrigerator.

"Right from the carton," Dana commented, her thin brows arching in a silent comment. "It reminds me of the days when *I* was married to Keefe. He doesn't much care about the elegancies of life, does he?"

"Pouring the cream into a pitcher just makes for more work. The house and the baby take plenty of time, without me adding extra dishes to the picture." Tessa kept her tone light with an effort. She didn't care what Dana thought of the way she did—or didn't—set a table but the reference to Dana's marriage to Keefe cut like a knife. If only she could be sure he didn't still feel something for his first wife.

He couldn't have made love to me the way he did last night if he still loved her, she told herself. *Or could he?*

"I wasn't criticizing. Just commenting. I didn't mean to imply that I left Keefe over cream pitchers."

Dana's soft laugh grated on Tessa's nerves but she forced a smile. She wanted, more than anything, to ask just what *had* ended the marriage. David stirred, waving one tiny hand and cooing a demand for attention. Tessa turned to lift him from his carrier, grateful for the interruption. She wanted to know what had happened to Keefe's first marriage so badly that she was afraid the words might spill out against her will.

"He seems...healthy," Dana said, looking at the baby as if he were a member of an alien species.

"He's very healthy." Tessa looked down at the

infant, her mouth softening in a smile. "And happy. Aren't you, sweetie?"

"Hmmm..." Dana took a sip of her coffee, her expression thoughtful. "From what I saw last night, Keefe seems very fond of him."

"I don't think *fond* is quite the right word," Tessa said, thinking of the light in Keefe's eyes when he held David.

Dana turned the coffee mug between her cupped hands. "I was surprised when Aunt Molly told me that you and Keefe were married." Her laugh was short and held little humor. "*Astonished* is a better description. I had no idea the two of you were so cozy."

"We always got along well." Tessa kept her gaze on David's face, afraid of what Dana might read in her expression.

Dana laughed again. "That must be something of an understatement! I didn't know you kept in touch after the divorce. I'm astonished that you did. Bobby Mallory struck me as the possessive sort."

Tessa barely controlled a flinch. *Possessive?* Yes, he'd certainly been that. She tugged David's T-shirt down over his tummy, aware that her hand was not completely steady. Time—and Keefe—had helped her to put most of the bad memories behind her, but there were moments when they swept back in through some little crack. This was one of them.

"Obviously, Bobby didn't know that Keefe and I were in touch," she said, pleased by the steadiness of her voice.

"'In touch,'" Dana repeated the phrase with an

ironic twist. "Now there's an interesting way of putting it."

Tessa glanced up in time to see her sister cast a pointed look at the baby in her arms. Of course. Dana thought that David was Keefe's child, conceived while Bobby was still alive. She felt the color creep up her throat and into her face.

"We—"

But Dana cut her off with a wave of one French-manicured hand. "I'm not passing judgment. It's none of my business. But I will admit that I was pretty surprised when I heard about it. I didn't think you had it in you. And Keefe, well, frankly, his strictly middle-class morality was one of his least attractive characteristics, as far as I was concerned. I certainly wouldn't have thought he'd mess around with a married woman. He must have changed quite a bit since the divorce."

Tessa sorted through several possible responses, abandoning each in turn. She finally settled for a vague murmur that her sister could interpret as agreement, embarrassment or indifference, whichever she pleased. Dana might be sincere in her desire for them to get to know each other better, but they were a long way away from being confidantes.

David's eyelids were starting to droop, and his mouth rounded in a perfect O as he yawned. Tessa rose and settled him gently back into his carrier, setting one hand on his stomach in a gentle rocking motion until he relaxed into drowsy contentment.

"Do you want anything to eat?" she asked, looking at her sister.

"Toast and orange juice, if you have it."

"It's not fresh-squeezed," Tessa warned as she slid two slices of bread into the toaster.

"I expected that," Dana said, sounding resigned. She didn't offer to help, and she didn't speak again until Tessa set the toast in front of her, along with butter, jelly and honey. "Thanks."

"Are you sure that's all you want?"

"This is more than I usually eat." Dana spread an infinitesimal layer of butter over one-quarter of a piece of toast. Tessa thought of the pancakes and bacon that she'd had for breakfast and sighed. She supposed she need look no farther for the reason she hadn't lost those last few pounds that stood between her and her prepregnancy weight. Looking at Dana's slender figure, she renewed her vow to watch what she ate.

Her mind suddenly flashed on a memory of Keefe saying she was beautiful as he undressed her, his hands on her body. She'd felt beautiful, she thought. The way he looked at her, the way he touched her— she'd *felt* beautiful.

Tessa looked across the table at her sister. *How many times had Keefe said those same words to Dana? And meant them?* The thought slipped in— unwanted and unwelcome. She'd been trying very hard not to think about Keefe's relationship with her sister, but there was no escaping the fact that they had been married, had loved, had made love. The image of Dana in Keefe's arms—in his bed—was painfully vivid. She wasn't sophisticated enough to ignore their past relationship. Her mouth twisted ruefully. No doubt another example of what Dana had so contemptuously referred to as "middle-class morality."

"I don't want you to feel uncomfortable about any of this," Dana said as she reached for a second piece of toast.

"Uncomfortable?" Tessa made an effort to focus on the conversation.

"About my being here." Dana gestured gracefully with the knife. "I know it's awkward—me being Keefe's ex-wife. But there's really nothing for you to worry about."

"I'm not worried," Tessa lied.

"Good. Because what was between Keefe and I is gone and forgotten. I mean, we certainly did have *something*. Something rather amazing, actually." Her mouth curved in a slight, reminiscent smile that made Tessa's stomach knot. "But it was a long time ago," Dana continued, more briskly. "I just didn't want you to worry about...anything."

"Thank you, but it wasn't really necessary to tell me that." Tessa forced her lips to curve in an unconcerned smile.

Had there ever been a less reassuring piece of reassurance? She wondered if it was possible that Dana's intention had been exactly the opposite of what it seemed—to plant doubts rather than to assuage them. But Dana's blue eyes were as clear and open as a child's, and Tessa pushed the suspicion aside.

But she couldn't push aside her words, or the doubts they'd planted.

Chapter 16

Wrist-deep in sudsy water, Tessa contemplated the Zen-like qualities of washing dishes. Like a domestic prayer wheel, it occupied the hands while leaving the mind free to contemplate the deeper meanings of life. Or to contemplate the not-so-deep questions of day-to-day living.

She liked this time of day, she thought as she rinsed a plate and set it in the drainer. Dinner was over, David was down for the night—or at least for a few hours. The darkness outside the window enfolded the house, cutting off the rest of the world as if it didn't exist. It was a peaceful, quiet time. A shrill burst of canned laughter from the television in the living room reminded her that it wasn't as quiet as it might have been. Frowning, she ran the dishcloth over a bowl.

Dana had been here nearly a week now, and Tessa was no closer to knowing why her sister was here than she had been the day she arrived. If it was because she wanted the two of them to get to know one another better, she had a peculiar way of going about it. It was true that they'd spent quite a bit of time together, but considering the ranch's relative isolation, there wasn't really any way for them to *avoid* each other. But spending time in the same house wasn't exactly getting to know one another, unless Dana thought it was all going to happen by osmosis.

Tessa fished a handful of flatware out of the water. She wiped each piece before dropping it into the rinse water. If she'd ever thought that blood was thicker than water, this past week had taught her differently. She and Dana had nothing in common beyond the fact that they'd been born to the same parents. There was no hidden bond of sisterly love just waiting to be uncovered, no dormant well of family feeling ready to spring free.

Closer acquaintance hadn't revealed any new and appealing aspects of her sister's personality. The fact was, Dana was astonishingly self-centered. As far as she was concerned, everything revolved around her. Not that she was entirely to blame for that attitude, Tessa thought. Considering the way she'd been raised, it would have been a miracle if she *didn't* think she was the center of the universe.

But understanding how she'd come to be the way she was didn't make her any better company. Tessa scooped the flatware out of the rinse water and dropped it into the basket hooked on the side of the drainer. She felt vaguely guilty for feeling the way she did. She couldn't shake the idea that she *should* love Dana, should feel some ties of blood and bone linking them together. But the feelings simply weren't there, and she wasn't going to pretend to herself that they were. With a sigh, she admitted to herself that she just didn't like her sister. And she didn't think Dana was any too fond of her, either. Which left the question of why Dana had made the effort to seek her out up in the air.

Or did it?

Tessa's fingers tightened around the edge of a plate, and she caught her lower lip between her teeth as she considered the probable answer to that question. Keefe. It was the only possible explanation. Dana hadn't come to see her, she'd come to see Keefe. The thought made Tessa's breath catch in her throat. She could never hope to compete with Dana. Not only was her older sister intimidatingly beautiful, but Keefe had once loved her. *Still* loved her? Tessa wondered, and felt her chest ache at the thought. She hadn't seen anything to suggest that Keefe was still in love with Dana, but that didn't necessarily mean anything. If he felt anything for his ex-wife, he wouldn't let it show.

If he still loved Dana, he wouldn't make love to you the way he does. The thought eased her fears, even if it didn't eliminate them. She knew better than to equate sex with love, but she couldn't believe that Keefe would make love to her so passionately if he was in love with another woman. Some men might be able to do that, but not Keefe. Still, it would have been nice to know just what he *did* feel—about her sister and about her.

Absorbed in her thoughts, her back to the door, Tessa didn't realize that she was no longer alone until she felt someone right behind her. She sucked in a quick, startled breath and then released it on a sigh as a pair of masculine arms slid around her waist.

"You startled me." But she was smiling when Keefe pulled her back against his chest.

"Sorry."

"You don't sound it." She tilted her head to one side as he bent to nuzzle the sensitive skin under her ear.

"No, really, I'm terribly sorry." Since he was busy placing a biting series of kisses down the side of her neck, his apology was somewhat muffled. Tessa decided not to question his sincerity any further. Her hands were limp in the cooling dishwater as she leaned her head back against his shoulder and gave herself up to the shivers of pleasure racing through her.

This was a side of herself she'd never known existed, this warm, sensual creature who responded so easily to his touch. She'd never even imagined this person existed.

"Are you about done with the dishes?" he asked.

"Yes." The counters could have been stacked to the ceiling with dirty plates and she would still have answered in the affirmative. One of his hands slid from her waist to boldly cup her breast, and she forgot how to breathe. His touch burned through the layers of shirt and bra.

"It's getting late," he whispered against her throat. "Are you about ready to go to bed?"

His mouth closed over hers before she could say anything, but her response was all the answer he needed. Her head tilted back against his shoulder, she met his kiss with all the passion in her—a passion he'd taught her. She could feel the hard strength of his big body against her back, feel the solid length of his arousal pressed against the soft fullness of her bottom. Her hands clenched around the edge of the sink as she felt the newly familiar sensation of bones and muscles dissolving.

He couldn't possibly love Dana and still kiss me like this, hold me like this. Even in her own mind, she didn't know whether the thought was statement or plea. Then Keefe's thumb brushed across her nipple and she stopped thinking at all.

"I don't know how you stand living out here. Even the TV reception is lousy." Dana's complaint preceded her entrance.

Her voice acted like a bucket of ice water on the couple by the sink. Keefe wrenched his mouth from Tessa's. For an instant—no more than a heartbeat— their eyes met, and she read pure frustration in his.

"What do people *do* for entertainment…?" Dana's voice trailed off as she walked into the kitchen and saw the two of them.

Keefe stepped away from Tessa. Picking up a dish towel, he took a plate from the drainer and began to dry it with more vigor than was strictly necessary. Still half turned from the sink, Tessa stared at her older sister blankly. There was a moment of dead silence, and she saw Dana look from her to Keefe. Her eyes narrowed into thin blue slits.

"Am I interrupting something?" she asked in a silky-soft tone.

"N-no." Tessa cleared her throat and managed a smile that probably looked as false as it felt. She shot a quick glance at Keefe, but he was drying a glass, focusing all his attention on the task. "We were just...ah...finishing up with the dishes."

"I don't remember you offering to help with the housework when we were married," Dana said, looking at Keefe. Her tone was light, but the look in her eyes was anything but.

"I don't remember you spending much time *doing* housework," he said without looking at her.

"I suppose not." She laughed, as if he'd just paid her a compliment. "I guess domesticity was never my strong suit."

"Not hardly." Keefe draped the towel across the top of the drainer and glanced at Tessa, his expression unreadable. "I've got something to talk over with Jace before I turn in."

"Okay."

She watched him walk out the door and then turned back to the sink, careful not to look at her sister. The water was cool. She pulled the plug and stood watching it drain out. She was acutely aware of Dana's eyes on her back.

"I don't know how you can stand having Jace Reno living here," Dana said.

"What?" The comment was so unexpected that Tessa turned to look at her.

"I couldn't stand him when Keefe and I were married," Dana said, coming farther into the room. "He was always such a sanctimonious bastard."

"Jace?" The description was so far from the man she knew that Tessa shook her head in disbelief. She knew Dana and Jace were not on good terms—the icy politeness with which they treated one another made that unmistakably clear—but still... "He's Keefe's best friend. And he's been a good friend to me since I came here."

"I didn't mean to offend you," Dana said, pulling her mouth down in a pretty grimace of apology. "It's just that...I've always thought Jace was at least partially to blame for the failure of my marriage to Keefe."

"Jace?" Tessa gaped at her in disbelief. "I can't imagine that."

"Perhaps you don't know him as well as you think," Dana said. She lifted one shoulder in a shrug.

"I think I know him well enough to know he'd never do anything to hurt a friend," Tessa said firmly. Whatever Dana was up to, she wasn't going to let her criticism of Jace go without comment. "What did he do?"

Dana shrugged again, looking uncomfortable. "Oh, it's a sordid little story, nothing you want to hear. Nothing I want to repeat, for that matter. Besides, it was a long time ago. No doubt he's changed a great deal since then. Just like the rest of us." She smiled faintly and wandered from the room.

Tessa watched her go and wished, not for the first time, that months ago she'd thought to ask her aunt Molly not to tell any of her family where she was.

Keefe scraped his knuckle on the edge of the manifold and muttered a curse. If there was one job he hated above all others, it was car repair of any kind. He avoided it when he could, but the fuel pump on his truck had breathed its last, leaving him no choice but to venture under the hood. But he didn't have to like it.

"How about something cold to drink?"

The voice came from the rear of the truck, soft and feminine. Keefe started to smile. Tessa.

"I'd just about kill for a cold beer," he said as he ducked out from under the hood and straightened. He set the wrench down on the fender and turned to face his visitor, his smile fading when he saw the woman who was approaching. "Dana."

"In the flesh," she said, apparently oblivious to the lack of welcome in his tone. She lifted one hand to display the amber-colored bottle that dangled between her fingers. "I come bringing gifts."

"Thanks." Keefe took the beer from her, though his enthusiasm for it wasn't what it had been a moment ago. He didn't like accepting any favors from his ex-wife, not even a beer from his own refrigerator.

"I saw you working out here and thought you might be thirsty."

"Thanks," he said again. He tilted his head back and took two deep swallows. The feel of her eyes on him made him uneasy. She was up to something. He didn't know what it was, but he was willing to bet that he wouldn't like it.

"It's awfully hot, isn't it?" Dana plucked at the thin fabric of her skinny little top in a move designed to draw attention to her body. She was braless, Keefe noticed, and the bright blue top clung to every curve. She was, what—thirty six now? But her body was still as tight and firm as it had been the day they met. Either she'd spent a lot of hours in a gym or she'd had a little surgical enhancement here and there. He wondered idly which it had been.

"I just took a shower, but I feel all sticky again." She laughed girlishly. "I feel like I might melt, just like a piece of candy left out in the sun."

"Or the Wicked Witch of the West standing under a sprinkler," Keefe said dryly.

Dana's smile seemed to freeze, and for just an instant he saw fury in her eyes, but it was gone instantly. She laughed again, a little ruefully. "You always did have an irritating sense of humor."

"Just one of my many charms." He took another swallow of beer and set the bottle on the workbench. He'd pulled the truck into the building that functioned as a sometime garage and full-time tool shed. It was a few degrees cooler than it would have been working in the full glare of the late-August sun. He waited, hoping Dana would leave, but she lingered.

"I hope it hasn't been too awkward—my being here, I mean." She widened her blue eyes in a way that he'd once thought revealed her vulnerability. "It's a strange situation, isn't it? Tessa being my sister, and now the two of you are married."

"Not all that strange." He shrugged. Dana's eyes dropped to his bare chest and he resisted the urge to reach for his shirt, which he'd tossed carelessly onto the truck's seat. He'd be damned if he was going to grab for his clothes like a terrified virgin in some Gothic novel!

"I was surprised to hear that you'd married Tessa," Dana said. She trailed one finger along the truck's battered fender. "And then, when I heard about the baby, it all made sense."

"Did it?" He watched her with the same caution he'd have felt toward a rattler. He knew from past experience that she could be just as dangerous.

"Of course." She laughed again, a soft sound of understanding. "I know your penchant for taking on lame dogs and birds with broken wings. When Tessa came to you, you would have felt you had to help her. She—"

"That's enough." Keefe spoke quietly, but there was a core of steel in the words. "My marriage is none of your business. You're here because Tessa asked you to stay, because you're her sister. You're a guest. Don't start thinking that the fact that we used to be married gives you any rights beyond that. Our marriage was over a long time ago."

Dana looked shaken by his flat tone, but she recovered quickly. "It may be over, but I don't think it's forgotten." She set one slim hand against his chest and lifted her eyes to his face. "Can you honestly say you've forgotten?"

"No, I can't. But then, I broke my leg when I was ten, and I haven't forgotten that, either."

Her fingers curled, exquisitely manicured nails digging into his skin. "That doesn't seem like a particularly apt comparison."

"It works for me."

He stepped back so that her hand dropped from him, but she followed, setting both hands on his chest and sliding her palms up to his shoulders, her fingers curving into the hard muscles there.

"You can't tell me you don't still feel something when you look at me," she murmured, crowding closer. "What we had between us was too strong to just die."

The tool bench pressed against his lower back, and Keefe chose not to slide away from Dana's grasping hands. They might as well have this out, here and now.

"Catching you in bed with another man didn't go a long way to making me feel good about our marriage," he pointed out.

"I made a terrible mistake!" she cried. Quick tears filled her eyes, and her mouth trembled. "It wouldn't ever have happened again. I told you I was sorry."

"Sorry didn't really cut it. Especially since it wasn't the first time."

"Who told you it wasn't the— Jace! I knew he was feeding you lies about me. Damn him!"

Keefe shook his head, cutting off her vicious tirade. "Jace didn't say anything. He didn't have to." His laugh was short and held little humor. "Man, you must have thought I was deaf, dumb and blind. Did you think I didn't know what you were doing? Hell, I saw you corner Jace and damn near rape him that last night we were in Santa Fe. The next day, when he said he'd decided to head for Houston instead of going on to Denver with us, I knew why he was doing it. Catching you with that two-bit bronc rider was just icing on the cake."

"That's not what happened," Dana said desperately. "Jace had been making passes at me. And you hadn't touched me in weeks."

"You were sleeping with half the damned country," he snapped. Despite his determination not to let her get to him, the memory still stung.

"I wasn't! And if I was, it was only because I knew I was losing you and I…I just couldn't bear that!"

Before he realized what she intended, she had her arms wound around his neck and had put her mouth to his. There had been a time when the feel of Dana's lips on his, her slender body in his arms, had been enough to bring him to rock-hard arousal. But that had been a long time ago, before he realized that her beauty was nothing but a shell, before he kissed Tessa, held Tessa.

He jerked his head back, breaking off the one-sided kiss, and lifted his hands to pull her arms from around his neck. The move was only half completed when a small sound made him lift his head. Someone stood next to the tailgate, silhouetted against the bright sunlight outside, staring into the shed. Tessa. In the instant he realized she was there, she turned and disappeared.

"Damn!" Keefe knew exactly how the scene must have looked to Tessa—him with his shirt off and Dana in his arms. As if he could read her mind, he knew what she'd be thinking. He wrenched Dana's arms loose, ignoring her faint gasp at his roughness.

"Keefe—"

"Shut up!" He sidestepped the hand she reached out to him. The need to see Tessa—to explain what had happened—beat in him with every breath he took, but he paused long enough to fix his ex-wife with a look of such burning contempt that she flinched back away from him. "You're not spending another night here. Pack your things and get out."

He turned and left the shed without waiting for a response, dismissing her from his thoughts the instant she was out of his sight. Dana was of no importance. Only Tessa mattered. He crossed the yard with long, ground-eating strides, barely restraining the urge to break into a sprint. His boots thudded against the porch floor, and then he was shoving open the screen door and stepping into the kitchen.

He paused just inside the doorway. After the bright sunshine outside, it took a moment for his eyes to adjust to the comparative dimness of the kitchen. But when they did, he saw that the room was empty, except for David, sound asleep in his carrier. Walking quietly, Keefe crossed the kitchen. He had to talk to Tessa.

She wasn't hard to find. She was standing in the middle of the living room, her hands held loosely at her sides, her expression almost blank. He had the sense that she wasn't quite sure what to do with herself, where to go. She seemed unaware of his approach.

"Tessa."

At the sound of his voice, she started and spun to face him. Keefe felt something twist painfully inside him at the look in her eyes. It was gone in an instant, but he knew he'd never forget the stark pain he'd seen there. He started to go to her, wanting to pull her into his arms and offer her comfort, but she shook her head and took a quick step back, one hand coming up, as if to keep him at a distance. And the ache in his chest grew tighter.

"I know what you saw." With an effort, he kept his voice low and calm. "But it wasn't what it looked like."

"Don't." She shook her head again, her eyes focusing somewhere near his collarbone, as if she couldn't bear to look at his face. "You don't have to explain anything to me."

"Tessa—"

"No, really. I'd rather you didn't." Her mouth twisted in a pathetic effort at a smile. "I know you haven't...that you wouldn't *sleep* with her. Not as long as we're married."

"I don't *want* to sleep with her!" But his forceful tone slid right past her.

"No one can control their feelings," she continued, as if he hadn't spoken. Her tone was quietly reminiscent. She might have been talking about something of little importance. Only the familiar way her fingers knotted together gave her away—that, and the hurt that left her eyes more gray than blue. "I knew, of course. I remembered the way you used to look at her. I used to think that I'd give anything in the world to have someone love me the way you loved Dana."

"It wasn't love," he said, realizing the full truth of that statement only now.

"I knew you didn't love me that way, and I thought that was okay," she said, ignoring his protest. "I thought it didn't really matter. You cared for me, and that would be enough. But, seeing you—the two of you—just now, I realized something."

"Tessa, it wasn't—" He took a step toward her, hands outstretched but she backed away, shaking her head with an abrupt movement that made her golden hair swing around her face.

"Don't!"

The sharp plea stopped him instantly. He let his hands drop to his sides, staring at her in helpless frus-

tration. How could he make her understand what had
happened, make her see that all he felt for Dana now
was contempt and dislike and that what he felt for her
years ago had been a tangled mix of lust, infatuation
and a ridiculous belief that she needed him to take
care of her?

"I won't be second-best," Tessa said slowly, as if
working her thoughts out as she spoke. "I thought it
wouldn't matter. I thought I loved you enough that it
wouldn't make a difference, that my love would be
enough for both of us. But I just realized that I can't
do it. I love you too much to be second-best in your
life."

Keefe felt as if all the air had been knocked from
him. He stared at her, his thoughts scattered in a hundred different directions. She loved him? *She loved
him?* The knowledge rolled over him in a slow, warm
wave. Tessa loved him. Of course she did. It was as
inevitable as...as him loving her. He didn't have to
think about it or question it. It just *was*. As if it had
always been and would always be.

He was distantly aware of hearing the squeak of
the screen door opening and thought vaguely that it
was probably Dana. He hoped she was on her way to
pack her clothes. He hoped even more that she'd have
the good sense to go straight to her room.

"Tessa, what you saw, it wasn't what it looked
like." Keefe was surprised by how steady his voice
was. Hell, considering the turmoil in his head, he was
surprised he could put together a coherent sentence at
all.

Her smile broke his heart. "I know. Your middle-
class morality," she said, laughing a little, as if at

some private joke. "You wouldn't have an affair, not even when our marriage isn't real."

"Our marriage *is* real," he said, raising his voice slightly, trying to get through to her.

"No, it isn't. You're in love with someone else."

"I am *not* in love with Dana." He didn't want to talk about his ex-wife, but maybe they had to get it out of the way before they could move on to other things. At the very least, he had to make Tessa see that his feelings for her sister were not an issue between them. He pushed his fingers through his hair as he sought the words to make her understand something he wasn't entirely sure he understood himself. "I don't think I was ever in love with her. I was in lust with her, maybe, but not in love."

"I saw the way you used to look at her," Tessa said, as if there were no arguing with that look. "You worshiped her."

"You were fourteen years old—too young to know the difference between love and lust." He shook his head, his mouth twisting in a rueful half smile. "Besides, I'd convinced myself I was in love with her. Maybe, at the start, that's almost the same thing."

She looked at him, her eyes searching, and Keefe dared to hope that he'd gotten through to her. He wanted to put his first marriage behind them, once and for all. But before she could say anything else, they were interrupted.

"Let go of me!" Dana's demand was punctuated by a sharp crack as the kitchen screen door was jerked open with force enough to hit the side of the house.

"Just as soon as you provide some explanations," Jace said grimly. Overlying the sound of their footsteps was a thin, angry wail that galvanized both Tessa and Keefe.

"David!" Tessa started forward, only to stop abruptly, her eyes widening in surprise.

Jace walked into the living room. The baby was tucked securely in the crook of his left arm and the fingers of his right hand were wrapped, just as securely, around Dana's upper arm. That she was with him unwillingly was obvious.

"I'll sue you for every miserable penny you've ever had." She spit the words at him, jerking futilely against his hold.

"She was getting into her car with the baby," he said, looking at Keefe and Tessa and ignoring Dana as if she didn't even exist.

"With David?" Tessa hurried forward and took the baby from him. The infant's fussy wails subsided into annoyed mutterings when he felt his mother's arms.

"Is he okay?" Keefe loomed over the two of them, his big hand dwarfing the baby's head as he brushed a gentle finger down his cheek.

"I think so," Tessa said. Their earlier discussion was forgotten, pushed aside, their attention all for their son.

"Oh, for God's sake, I didn't hurt him," Dana said impatiently. She yanked against Jace's hold again, stumbling as he abruptly released her. She regained her balance and glared at him. "Bastard!"

He lifted his brows and placed himself directly— and obviously—between her and the door.

Assured that the baby was unharmed, Keefe lifted his head and looked at his ex-wife. "Where were you taking him?"

"Nowhere." Dana rubbed her hand over the marks Jace's fingers had left on her arm. "You had no right to manhandle me like that."

"Nowhere?" Jace ignored her complaint. "You were just going to sit in the car and commune with him?"

"I was just going to take him for a little ride," she said. She caught their looks of disbelief and flushed. "That's not a crime."

"Why?" Her baby secure in her arms, Tessa looked at her sister. "You've barely looked at him since you've been here."

"I..." Dana glanced from Tessa to Keefe, her expression uneasy. "He was fussing, and I thought a car ride might soothe him. I read that somewhere."

"He wasn't fussing," Tessa contradicted her flatly. "I would have heard him."

"Maybe you were busy with...other things," Dana suggested, sliding a quick glance at Keefe and then looking away.

"I would have heard him," Tessa repeated, in a tone that left no room for argument.

"Where were you going?" Keefe asked.

"I already told you. I was taking him for a ride. Now, if you don't mind, I'd like to go." Chin in the air, she glanced at the doorway that Jace was blocking. He didn't move.

"Oh, for God's sake," she snapped, turning to glare at Keefe. "You told me to leave, didn't you? Well, I can't do it unless you let me out of this room."

"I want to know where you were going with my son."

"Only he's not your son, is he?" Dana snarled, anger stripping aside caution.

Taut silence followed her comment.

"Why would you say that?" Keefe's tone was softly threatening, and Tessa saw something that might have been fear flash across her sister's face. Dana's tongue came out to wet her lower lip, and she stared at him blankly for a moment.

"I... Molly told me," she said finally. Her voice took on new confidence as she continued. "She said I wasn't to mention it, and I wouldn't have, if you hadn't started this ridiculous inquisition."

"You're lying," Tessa said. "You haven't seen Aunt Molly in over a year."

"Of course I have. I saw her last week. Right before I came here. And I'm just now seeing what a mistake *that* was," Dana added, shaking her hair back from her face with a quick, easy movement. "I'm sorry if I brought up a painful subject, but really, you've all acted like a bunch of maniacs, so you really don't have anyone to blame but yourselves."

"Aunt Molly called a little while ago," Tessa said. She spoke slowly, working things out in her mind. With everything that had happened since, Molly Thorpe's call seemed as if it had been days ago. "She said she hadn't seen you in over a year. She was surprised when I told her you were here." She stopped and glanced at Keefe. It was the first time she'd looked at him since Jace dragged Dana into the room. "That's why I came looking for you. I thought it was so odd that Aunt Molly hadn't seen her, yet—"

"Yet she told us that Molly was the one who told her where you were," Keefe finished for her. He looked at his ex-wife. "So, if it wasn't Molly, just how did you know where Tessa was?" he asked softly. "There aren't that many people who know. My family and—"

"The good senator," Jace said grimly.

"Don't be ridiculous," Dana said, but she sounded more frightened than angry. "Of course it was Aunt Molly who told me. She probably just forgot. She's getting old, and—" Her eyes darted from one face to another, reading nothing but implacable determination to get at the truth. She must have realized that there was nothing she could say, no lie she could tell. Her hands clenched into fists at her sides, and her eyes blazed with a mixture of fury and fear.

"Damn you all," she shouted. "I wish I'd never come here." Sinking down on the sofa, she burst into tears.

"Now there's a sentiment I think we can all share," Jace said dryly.

Once Dana stopped crying, she was willing to tell them the whole story.

"It isn't like you're going to have me prosecuted," she pointed out, with a return of her customary confidence.

"There are places around here where a body would never be found," Jace pointed out gently.

From the look in Dana's eyes, she wasn't entirely sure he was kidding. Neither was Tessa. She'd seen occasional glimpses of something very dangerous beneath Jace's easygoing facade.

Dana was still sitting on the sofa. Jace stood in the doorway, though it was obvious that Dana wasn't go-

ing to try and escape. She was not only resigned to
telling her story, she seemed almost to be looking
forward to it, which made Tessa a little uneasy. She'd
put David down in his crib, lingering over him a moment, savoring the knowledge that he was safe,
though she still couldn't quite believe that they'd almost lost him. And now, she was back in the living
room, waiting to hear Dana's story.

It was really very simple. Dana had come back
from Europe. She'd called her sister—probably on a
slow day, Tessa thought cynically—and when she
found the phone disconnected, she'd called the Mallorys. Dana had always gotten along better with
Tessa's in-laws than Tessa had. The senator had been
away from home, but Anne Mallory had invited her
to lunch and, over three or four dry martinis, had told
Dana the whole story.

Tessa had a hard time picturing her reserved
mother-in-law sipping more than a glass of wine, let
alone drinking enough to loosen her tongue. But then,
Bobby's death had hit his mother hard, had changed
her even more than Tessa had realized.

Apparently Anne had been blunt about wanting her
grandson, at any price. Dana was vague about who
had come up with the idea that she could come to the
Flying Ace and find a way to take David from them.
Tessa wanted to believe that it had been Anne Mallory. The last faint ties of family feeling made her
reluctant to think that Dana had thought the plan up
on her own.

"But why would you agree to something like
that?" she asked when Dana paused.

"Why?" Dana laughed sharply. "Why do you

think? Money.'' She laughed again when she saw the shock Tessa couldn't hide. ''Your dear mother-in-law offered me a considerable sum to snatch her precious grandchild. My life-style is rather expensive to maintain. Besides, you never know when it might come in handy to have a senator—or a senator's wife—in your pocket.''

Jace made a sound low in his throat, a sound that could only have been described as a growl. Beside her Tessa felt the tension in Keefe's body. She was too stunned to share their anger.

''Didn't it bother you?'' she asked, bewildered by Dana's casual attitude.

''Didn't what bother me?''

''Taking David away from me—from us.'' Unconsciously she reached out, and Keefe's fingers wrapped around hers.

''Well, I wouldn't make baby-snatching a hobby,'' Dana said casually. ''But I figured this was something of an exception. From what Bobby's mother told me, you can't have been very fond of him, so it didn't seem likely that you'd be too broken up over his kid, and since it isn't Keefe's child, I didn't see why he would care all that much.'' She laughed again, carelessly. ''Not that I needed Anne Mallory to tell me it wasn't his baby.''

She looked at Keefe, her blue eyes sparkling, as if at some private joke that the two of them shared. ''I, of all people, know better than to believe you'd have an affair with another man's wife. Besides, even without that, I could never believe you'd sleep with Tessa.'' She glanced at Tessa, her eyes bright with malice. "No offense, little sister, but you're hardly his type. Not even in the running."

Tessa stared at her. She was too stunned to feel offended. Her sister didn't even seem to see anything really wrong with what she'd done—what she'd tried to do. She sought some response to Dana's words and found her mind had gone completely blank.

But, if she couldn't find any words, Keefe didn't have the same problem. "Tessa is twice the woman you could ever hope to be. If there's one thing in my life that I'm ashamed of, it's the fact that I was once so stupid that I actually thought I was in love with you. But I'm not sorry I did it. Because if I hadn't married you, I wouldn't have met Tessa, and having her is worth every minute of misery you put me through."

Tessa caught her breath at the stark sincerity in his voice. She turned her head to look up at him and felt a sense of wonder at what was in his eyes. Dana spoke before she could decide just what it was she'd seen.

"I guess that puts me in my place," she said, but her laugh couldn't conceal how shaken she was by his contemptuous dismissal of her.

"I want you to leave now," Tessa told her with quiet dignity.

"I'd like nothing better," Dana said. She stood up, but hesitated a moment, looking at Keefe and Tessa. She seemed almost confused. "You really love each other, don't you?"

"Yes." That was Keefe, and Tessa felt something melt inside her at the flat sureness of his response. "And David is my child. You can tell Anne Mallory that, and you can also tell her that, if she ever comes near us again, we'll go to the press with everything we know and a few things we'll invent. By the time the media frenzy dies out, he'll have about as much chance of getting into the White House as Saddam Hussein.''

Dana didn't say anything, but she nodded before turning and walking out of the room. Jace stepped out of the doorway to let her pass and then looked at Keefe.

"I think I'll just follow along and keep an eye on her, make sure she gets her things packed and gets off the property with no problems.''

"Thanks.''

Jace lingered a moment longer, his eyes going from Keefe to Tessa and then back again. His smile held wicked humor. ''You're a little slow on the uptake sometimes, but I'm glad you finally figured things out.''

He was gone before Keefe could respond.

He left behind a deep silence. Tessa was acutely aware of the feel of Keefe's hand on hers, of the hard strength of his body next to her. She wanted to look at him, but she couldn't seem to raise her eyes to his face. What if the love she'd heard in his voice wasn't in his eyes?

"Jace is right—I am a little slow on the uptake sometimes,'' he said quietly. ''But I figure things out eventually.''

"What did you figure out?'' she asked, finding the courage to lift her eyes to his face.

"That I love you.'' He said it quietly, without flowery words or fanfare. Tessa had never heard anything more beautiful in her life. "I thought that marrying you was the right thing to do. I kept telling myself that it was a practical arrangement, that we could make a good marriage because we suited each other."

He brought his hand up to cup her cheek, and Tessa thought she might just drown in the warmth of his eyes. "It took almost losing you for me to realize how much I love you."

"I don't care what it took." She set her hand on his chest, just over his heart.

"About what you saw, earlier, with Dana..." he began.

"No." She pressed her fingers over his mouth. "Not another word about Dana. As far as I'm concerned, once she leaves this house, she's out of our lives forever. I no longer even have a sister."

"If that hurts you—"

"It doesn't." She shook her head. "Blood ties aren't what makes a family. It takes ties of the heart to do that."

"Ties of the heart," he repeated. His mouth curved in a smile. "We have plenty of those."

"Yes, we do," she whispered, just as his lips touched hers.

And Then

Rachel Walker's living room had never really been intended to hold nine adults, two children and two infants. It was Labor Day weekend, and the family had gathered at her house for a barbecue. But, in direct defiance of all laws governing southern California weather, it was pouring rain, with no sign of stopping. The barbecue had been scrapped in favor of take-out pizza, which was to be delivered at any minute.

Having everyone in the same room made things a little cramped, but no one seemed to mind being crowded. Certainly, Tessa had no objection to having Keefe's large figure looming over her as he perched on the arm of her chair. She looked around at the rest of the family and felt her mouth curve in a helpless, foolish smile of contentment.

Family. This was her family now. They had accepted her as one of their own, without question, without hesitation.

"He's growing like a weed," Keefe said, leaning over to brush David's cheek with the tip of his finger.

"I still can't believe how close we came to losing him." Tessa's voice trembled. It had been two weeks since Dana left the ranch, but the memory of what she'd almost done still sent chills up her spine.

"But we didn't." Keefe set his hand on her shoulder and pulled her close. "And I don't think we have to worry about the Mallorys anymore. After talking to Molly, I don't think he's got a snowball's chance in hell of making it into the White House."

Gage overheard his comment and gave a sharp bark of laughter. "With Molly Thorpe on his tail, I suspect he'll be lucky if he manages to hang onto his senate seat."

"I hope he loses that, too," Nikki said. "The last thing this country needs is someone like that holding an important office."

"Don't kid yourself, they're all like him," her husband said cynically.

"No politics," Rachel Walker decreed as she rose from her chair. "There isn't enough room in here for a free-for-all. The pizza should be here any minute. I'm going to go see what we have to drink. I don't need any help," she added, as various members of the family moved to get up. She paused in the doorway, turning back to look at them. Her eyes touched on each of her sons in turn, then moved on to their wives and children. Her mouth curved in a soft smile. "It's good to have the whole family here."

The room was silent for a moment after she left, as each of them considered her comment. For the four brothers, family was something they'd always been able to take for granted. No matter what else happened, they'd always had each other. For their wives, it was more akin to a miracle that never quite lost its shine. But Rachel's words had given them all pause. It *was* good to have the whole family together.

The melodic chime of the doorbell interrupted the moment.

"That must be the pizza," Sam said. "I'll get it."

Before he could get to his feet, his mother's voice called out from the kitchen, "Come in."

"She left the door unlocked again," Gage muttered in exasperation. "I've told her again and again that it's not safe."

"Los Olivos isn't exactly a crime center," his wife said comfortably.

"Maybe not, but she still ought to lock her door."

"Yeah, but think how handy it is not to have to get up to let in the pizza guy," Cole said, looking on the practical side of things.

But the woman who stepped into the living room wasn't delivering a pizza. Tall and slender, she wore a calf-length floral-print dress in soft shades of peach and ivory. Her strawberry-blond hair was drawn back and held against her nape by a plain gold clip. The gentle severity of the style might have looked harsh on another woman, but it suited her, highlighting the elegant sweep of her cheekbones and the delicate line of her jaw. The deep, clear sapphire of her eyes was emphasized by long, dark lashes.

She was, quite simply, the most beautiful woman Tessa had ever seen. She stood in the doorway and looked around the crowded room, her lovely eyes resting on first one person and then another, lingering on Sam a moment before drifting to Keefe, Gage and Cole in turn. Conversations ended abruptly as each of them became aware of her. Gage had been sitting on the sofa, holding his infant daughter, but when he saw the newcomer, he handed the baby to his wife and rose, his expression blank with shock. Tessa glanced up at Keefe, seeking an explanation, but he was staring at the woman, also. She felt his arm tense around her, and then he withdrew it and stood up.

Barely a minute before, the room had been filled with voices, conversations layered one on another, childish chatter blended with deeper adult tones. Now, the silence was so thick, it was almost visible. Even Danny and Mary were quiet, their wide eyes moving from their parents to the woman in the doorway.

Finding herself the focus of nearly a dozen pairs of eyes, Tessa would have broken and run. But the stranger stood her ground, her expression calm. Only the color that tinted her cheeks suggested she might not be as unaffected as she seemed.

"What does everyone want to drink?" Rachel's voice preceded her as she left the kitchen. "Pizza always seems to call for beer, but it's a little early in the day for that. Oh, hello." She smiled at the newcomer. "You don't look like you're delivering pizzas."

"No, I'm not." The woman's voice was low and a little husky. She half turned to look at Rachel, and the color slowly ebbed from her face, leaving her skin ivory-pale. "I'm sorry to interrupt. It looks like you're having a party."

"Not exactly," Rachel answered, absently. Her

dark eyes were searching the woman's face. "We were just..." She let the words trail off. She lifted one hand and pressed her fingertips to her chest, as if to still the sudden acceleration of her heartbeat. When she spoke again, her voice was a whisper. "Who are you?"

"Mom." Sam took a step forward, his expression tight and hard. "Don't—"

"Who are you?" Rachel asked again, louder this time.

For a moment, it seemed as if the woman weren't going to answer. She looked away from Rachel, her glance skating over the tense figures of Sam, Keefe, Gage and Cole. She looked back at Rachel, who was looking at her with a mixture of hope and fear that was painful to see.

"I shouldn't have come," she whispered, almost to herself. "I didn't mean to—"

"Please." Rachel's hand came out, almost but not quite touching the woman's arm. "Please, tell me. Who are you?"

"I... My name is Shannon. I think I'm your daughter."

* * * * * *

Take 4 bestselling love stories FREE

Plus get a FREE surprise gift!

Special Limited-time Offer

Mail to Silhouette Reader Service™

3010 Walden Avenue
P.O. Box 1867
Buffalo, N.Y. 14240-1867

YES! Please send me 4 free Silhouette Intimate Moments® novels and my free surprise gift. Then send me 6 brand-new novels every month, which I will receive months before they appear in bookstores. Bill me at the low price of $3.34 each plus 25¢ delivery and applicable sales tax, if any.* That's the complete price and a savings of over 10% off the cover prices—quite a bargain! I understand that accepting the books and gift places me under no obligation ever to buy any books. I can always return a shipment and cancel at any time. Even if I never buy another book from Silhouette, the 4 free books and the surprise gift are mine to keep forever.

245 BPA A3UW

Name	(PLEASE PRINT)	
Address		Apt. No.
City	State	Zip

This offer is limited to one order per household and not valid to present Silhouette Intimate Moments® subscribers. *Terms and prices are subject to change without notice. Sales tax applicable in N.Y.

UMOM-696   ©1990 Harlequin Enterprises Limited

At last the wait is over...
In March
New York Times bestselling author

NORA ROBERTS

will bring us the latest from the Stanislaskis as
Natasha's now very grown-up stepdaughter,
Freddie, and Rachel's very sexy brother-in-law
Nick discover that love is worth waiting for in

WAITING FOR NICK

Silhouette Special Edition #1088

and in April
visit Natasha and Rachel again—or meet them
for the first time—in

The Stanislaski Sisters

containing TAMING NATASHA
and FALLING FOR RACHEL

Available wherever Silhouette books are sold.